Family Secrets

Family Secrets

Patricia Fawcett

ROBERT HALE · LONDON

ISBN 978-0-7090-8266-8

Robert Hale Limited
Clerkenwell House
Clerkenwell Green
London EC1R 0HT

2 4 6 8 10 9 7 5 3 1

Typeset in 11½/15pt Times New Roman
by Derek Doyle & Associates, Shaw Heath
Printed and bound in Great Britain
by Biddles Limited, King's Lynn

To Jo, in Argentina
with special thanks to Natasha and Emma for their help

CHAPTER ONE

Josie Bailey stuffed the bumper pack of cheap wrapping paper down the side of her supermarket trolley and headed determinedly for the checkout, closely avoiding running down a woman, who was dithering in the wine aisle. Honestly, she thought, as she smiled a brief apology, get your act together. Christmas Eve, with the shop closing shortly, was no time for dithering.

She had attacked this last minute shopping with the precision of a general working out a battle strategy. Providing the powers that be at the supermarket hadn't opted for a complete shift round of stock, which they were irritatingly apt to do from time to time, she was on target this evening for a relatively smooth shop. Not only had she come armed with a list, she had come with a list broken down into aisles. Super efficient, she reckoned, with not one single extra item added, although she had nearly succumbed to the temptation of a chocolate hazelnut gateau.

Impulse buys were off limits tonight.

Josie was working to a strict time schedule. She was allowing herself a further twenty minutes to get out of there and home, otherwise her carefully planned itinerary would be knocked for six. She was very aware that she was not of the natural-talent school of cooking and had to work hard at it to achieve something approaching edible, let alone delicious. She couldn't go wrong with the Christmas dinner this year, not if she followed the timing countdown in her woman's magazine. The only snag was she would have to wake up at seven o'clock in the morning if it was to work. Thirty minutes for this, five for that, and woe betide him if Ray cocked it up. Tonight, she still had the trifle to finish off – Ray was such a baby about a home-made sherry trifle – and there were a couple of presents left to wrap, plus some emergency ones, just in case a neighbour surprised her at the very last minute.

She scanned the checkouts, making a quick and probably foolish decision, weaving her trolley into position at the end of the smallest queue and letting out a huge relieved sigh. The woman in front, mistaking the reason for it, turned and gave her a sympathetic glance.

'Terrible, wasn't it? That thing in Scotland,' she said with an excited gleam in her eye and Josie knew instantly what she was talking about. 'It doesn't bear thinking about. Just before Christmas too. I can't get it out of my head, can you?'

Josie nodded, upset to be reminded of it.

'You don't get on a plane, do you, and expect it to be blown sky high? Nor do you expect a plane to explode right over your house.'

'No, you don't,' Josie said, seeing again the wreckage of that Pan-Am jumbo jet blown apart over Lockerbie. It was one of those news items, like the Kennedy assassination, that stop you dead in your tracks. She and Ray had visited Lockerbie once and she had loved it, wandering round the little streets, enjoying the peace and quiet, the pleasant Scottish accents, the welcoming smiles. Just imagine, there you are wrapping presents, decorating the tree, doing all sorts of normal family things and then an awful noise in the sky and wham. It had hit her hard, bringing tears to her eyes, which was daft seeing that she did not know any of the victims, not personally. It was seeing all those scattered suitcases, coats, Christmas presents and even the seats from the plane just lying there that had done it. People had set off with a purpose, such hopes, so excited to be going home for Christmas or just visiting a new place for the first time. She could see them on the plane, talking, laughing together. She hated things like this. Whenever there was a tragedy of these proportions, she could not disentangle herself from it. She always took it to heart, put herself in the position of the victims and she should know by now that it did no good. Ray had given her a swift cuddle, told her to buck up; that there was nothing they could do and that the victims both in the air and on the ground wouldn't have known what had hit them.

Maybe not.

Josie had just started to put it out of her mind or try to and this damned woman had raked it all up again.

'Mad, isn't it?' the woman carried on, Lockerbie gone from *her* mind. 'All this panic buying. They open again on Tuesday, wouldn't you know? There's no need to get paranoid, is there? Nobody's going to starve. Anybody would think we were in for a six month siege.'

As her trolley was also loaded to kingdom come, that seemed a bit rich but Josie nodded in agreement, in no mood for a chat as she checked her list for the very last time.

Above their heads, a new tune jingled from the loudspeakers and Josie frowned, feeling like killing whoever it was who was in charge of the medley of grotesque seasonal music that had been blaring out since sometime in late October. Corporate policy, she had been told when she complained, and the staff did not like it either but there was nothing they could do.

'I wouldn't mind if it was something religious,' Josie had told the girl who was standing in for the manager, who, it seemed, did not have the guts to face an irate customer. 'Carols or something.'

'We do have carols,' the girl had said, cold-eyed, the-customer-is-always-right philosophy obviously passing her by. "Winter Wonderland", "Little Donkey". You can't have been in then.'

'They are not carols.'

'They are.' She was a tough one, standing there with her arms crossed. 'Anyway, nobody else has complained,' she finished with a sniff.

Josie had given up at that point, worried for a second that she was turning into her own mother, who had over the years honed grumbling about anything and everything to a fine art.

Keeping busy by rearranging the items in her trolley, Josie supposed she could have made it easier on herself by taking up Ray's lukewarm offer of help, but she was not letting him anywhere near her list. She was totally focused when it came to lists and he meandered. He would end up buying kids' cereals and tins of baked beans and sausages, things she absolutely did not need or want.

It did not feel like Christmas Eve. She had been awake at seven as usual even though she had the day off and, strictly speaking, could have allowed herself an extra half-hour in bed. It was mystifying why she had to drag herself out any other day and today she had been raring to go as soon as she opened her eyes. She had always loved Christmas, even the lead up to it, if she was honest, and the excitement had been childishly getting to her. The office party had been got through without Kenny Balfour trapping her underneath the mistletoe, and at last she had felt she could allow herself to dream of the wonderful day itself.

After that initial euphoria, it had all gone downhill. Unwisely, she had allowed her hairdresser to coax her into trying both a new colour *and* a new cut. Ray would go spare when he saw it. It was very short, razored, and she had caught a glimpse of herself by the frozen foods counter. It had taken a moment to cotton on to the fact that the woman with the reddish unruly mop on her head was her.

Josie touched her hair self-consciously, willing it to calm itself down a fraction, peering ahead at the same time to check how things were progressing. Oh for heaven's sake, somebody was querying the bill and mutinous grumbles were creeping up the queue. There was no time for this, why didn't they just pay it and sort it out later? This checkout looked like a bad choice, the girl predictably the slowest on the line. Wearing a tinsel halo, with silver wings pinned on to her overall, looking about as angelic as a stripper, she yawned hugely a while later as, having got rid of the troublesome customer, she embarked on the next one. Her name tag declared her to be Charlene, which said it all really.

'Christmas does my head in,' said the woman ahead of her as she shuffled uncomfortably and managed a thin tired smile. Josie had her pegged in an instant. Poor soul. No clothes sense. She was kitted out in a lime-green shell suit in a crinkly material, which did absolutely nothing for her and was so loose that she could have been anything from a size ten to a sixteen. Maybe that was the idea. She had a friendly smile though. 'Have you got people coming?' she asked.

Goodness me, she was not easily put off. 'Just my son and his girlfriend and my sister,' Josie heard herself saying, confident that at least *she* looked her best in a pale blue swing coat.

Owing to yet another dispute at the till, she might be here some time and there was every chance of a lifelong friendship developing between her and the woman in front.

'Have you people coming?' she asked, throwing the question back at her and wondering if she had enough toilet rolls. She had forgotten to check. . . .

She listened politely as the woman rattled on, giving a potted family history and becoming so animated as a result that she had to be reminded when her turn came to stop the prattling and start offloading her trolley.

CHAPTER TWO

Josie lived in the Riverside district of Felston, one of the districts that the town council would prefer not to exist, as the moody residents there caused more trouble than any two of the other districts combined. She lived now in a street about three away from the house she was born in, the one she frequently visited still because her big sister Margaret lived there and, aside from double glazing and fitted kitchens, things had not changed so much in forty odd years.

The council acted as if Riverside really let the side down, although Josie thought they exaggerated the problems and that actually things were improving. However, she had to acknowledge that, if Felston had a Monopoly board then their street, Crook Terrace, would be the equivalent of Old Kent Road, rock-bottom value and the cheapest rents. The houses in their street were generally well looked after and they had got rid of the only bad family recently, a family who hadn't given a pig's snout about the house and garden: four snotty-nosed kids and a mangy dog, and it was good riddance when they'd upped tracks. Crook Terrace sat bang up against the football ground and Saturdays and opposing supporters were something else. When Felston Rovers scored, the house shook with the cheers.

One Sunday morning, Josie had drawn the curtains back and seen what looked like a body lying under the hedge in the front garden.

She had sent Ray down to investigate and it had turned out to be a lad from Manchester who had spent the night there, his pals having deserted him. It had been a warm night but, if the lad had had a bit more gumption, he could have been more comfortable in their garden shed, which they never bothered to lock for all it had in it was a lawnmower that had seen better days. They had a bigger than average corner plot but the state of their garden sometimes made her spit with annoyance and she would send Ray out with a spade and a wheelbarrow in the hope that he would suddenly develop an enthusiasm for it. Some hope. He would be out there all afternoon, supplied with endless cups of tea but he did the minimum, leaning on his spade chatting over the fence as often as not. As she was no great shakes in the gardening stakes either, it was no surprise that they struggled.

That Sunday morning, she had made that poor lad a cup of coffee and a bacon sandwich before sending him on his way with a ten pound note stuffed in his pocket because he didn't look as if he had two pennies to rub together and was barely streetwise, so she worried how he would get home. She had tried to slip him the note secretly, but Ray had spotted her and afterwards he had gone daft, telling her that the lad had her number, a soft touch if ever there was. Never mind. He'd had such beautiful blue eyes, had been about sixteen, somebody's son, and he had touched her heart, reminding her of Matthew when he was that age. Matthew, their boy, had remained a sweet innocent for almost too long but then he was like his dad, a bit lost where the opposite sex was concerned with absolutely no talent for sweet-talk.

Anyway, Riverside was definitely on the up with new people moving in, doing up the houses and moving on, and as soon as the council twigged that, they would be increasing the rates, so it was perhaps as well they were behind the times. Unbeknownst to Ray, she had got the particulars of one of the last remaining flats in an exclusive development by the old docks. If she got the job she was up for, then she was determined they would move, and one of those new flats with no garden to sigh about would be just up their street. They were beautiful and, for what they were, a bargain, but Ray would take some persuading. Her sister Margaret wouldn't mind at all, in fact Margaret would shoo her on her way, happy so long as she was within easy travelling distance, but Ray wouldn't think he was up to it, living in a place like that, not with the sort of people who had snapped them up, executives and all, people with brief-cases and posh cars. Ray had no confidence, that was his trouble and she was getting a bit sick of trying to boost it. She'd spent years trying to get him to take one more step up the ladder, but he was ground down in his belief that it was far better if you accepted who you were and didn't try to get too big for your boots.

Just like her mum.

What a load of twaddle. It was Felston Town Council who was getting too big for its boots these days. It was trying, heaven forbid, to be trendy. Moving on. The description 'northern industrial town' made the council shudder with all that it implied and they had appointed a PR man from down south who knew nothing about the town, found the means of giving him a huge salary, and briefed him to drag the town forward as the nineties approached, discarding unpalatable cargo, such as its long industrial heritage, along the way. It drove Josie mad that they tried to sweep all that had gone before under the brand new red carpet at the town hall. Working as she did in the treasurer's office up on the second floor, she knew precisely how much that carpet had cost and it wasn't some off-cut from Felston Carpets Centre either. She knew all about that outfit, too, as Ray had been on their books as a carpet fitter for years.

Miraculously, the magnificent nineteenth-century town hall with its awkward interior still remained, despite a plot to blow it up during the demolition crazy days of the sixties. In fact, to give the council credit, it had been done up recently, been given a face-lift, years of pigeon droppings removed and the stone cleaned. Notwithstanding the rejuvenation of the town hall, the council seemed to have more money than sense and she should know. The town centre had been modernized, paved, with sickly-looking saplings dotted here and there, the attempt at pedestrianization coming to naught, as people still carefully walked either side along what had once been the pavements.

A couple of controversial sculptures were now lodged in the market square, their commissioning and cost to the ratepayer still causing rumbles and grumbles in the letters page of the *Felston Gazette*. Josie had very nearly written a letter herself because, although she seemed in a minority, she liked the damned things. When it came to art, people round here were so provincial. She decided not to pen the letter because she thought her boss might object to her getting involved in a public slanging match and Ray said he didn't want her showing them up. Along with the bulk of Felstonians, he couldn't understand the concept anyway. What the hell were they supposed to be?

'They don't have to be anything,' she had told him, trying to curb her impatience. 'Art can get away with not being anything.'

'What are you talking about?' He had put on his puzzled daft look and, knowing it was hopeless, she had given up at that point. It was true the statues only vaguely resembled people but Ray thought that, if that was the case, then if you looked closely, it didn't look as if they were up to any good.

'It's art, for heaven's sake, Ray,' she had repeated, not knowing whether to laugh or cry at his indignation. 'Not pornography.'

Arriving at the trolley porch, Josie saw, without surprise, that it had started to rain. Well, that figured because it had been on the verge of it all day. It was sleet at that and, pulling up the hood of her coat, she hurried as best she could to the outer reaches of the car park where she had left the car. It was a big old Volvo estate, nice and roomy, and it ran well, but it was a right so-and-so to park. The rain had a cutting edge to it, the easterly wind catching it and swirling it, so that by the time she had dumped the shopping in the boot, she was soaked through.

Flinging the coat in the back seat, she sat there demisting herself

15

and the car before backing out. Traffic was surprisingly light as if everybody had given up, and she had a clear run. Now that the last of the shopping was bought in, she could begin to relax and she was so looking forward to having Matthew back home for a few days.

After he finished his technical theatre course, he had worked briefly as a props boy at the Theatre Royal in Felston and she had liked having him at home, although, a year on, she had had enough. He was no longer an endearingly sheepish sixth-former but a grown-up man and, because Ray wouldn't tell him, she did. She didn't actually throw him out but she did tell him it was high time he moved on and out of the family home. She was fed up with tidying up after him, picking up his laundry, ironing his shirts and so on. She knew she only had herself to blame but it was easier to do it than let it sit there. Anyway, it was time he did it himself. He'd had it too cosy here and, even though he would soon turn a place into a pigsty, it would be his own pigsty not hers. She got her wish with a vengeance, for not only did he move out but he landed on his feet, getting a job as an assistant stage manager at a little theatre up in the Lakes.

Perversely, she missed him and the house seemed empty now and altogether too tidy. The girlfriend he was bringing down for Christmas was called Alice and she was twenty-three, but other than that Josie knew nothing about her. Matthew had been a bit slow on the uptake where girls were concerned and, for a time, she had worried about it, not wanting to arrive at the obvious conclusion. She had never dared say anything to Ray about her concerns because, salt of the earth northerner as he was, he wouldn't have tolerated having a gay son but, in the end, it all turned out fine. Alice was not even Matthew's first girlfriend although, judging from his voice when he talked about her, she might very well be the one that mattered. He had known her since summer and it was about time they met her, otherwise they would start thinking something was wrong with her.

Even so, Josie had been surprised when her casual invitation to bring her along for a few days at Christmas had been accepted. It had never happened to her, this assessment by the potential in-laws, because she had lived in the same street as Ray all her life and known his family nearly as well as her own. Matthew was twenty-five and that seemed young to her to be getting into a serious relationship, although she had some room to talk. She and Ray had married young and, by and large, she supposed she would do it all again and Ray certainly would. Better the devil you know and all that. She had known Ray since they were school kids together and had been singularly unimpressed by him, although, as she seemed to recall, he had gazed at her even then with a rapt expression. Ray didn't say much, never had said much, embarrassed by what he called lovey-dovey stuff but she knew he would be in a pretty pickle without her. As she would, without him. Life was life and it didn't stay a bed of roses for ever.

It wouldn't really bother her too much if Matthew and Alice just moved in together but Ray would not like it. Ray was just a touch stuffy about things like that. You'd think he was the one with the staunch Baptist background.

Not knowing Alice, Josie had bought her a little gift – a hand cream and body lotion set from Boots, more a stocking present but she didn't want to embarrass her by going over the top. Ignoring Ray and his doubts, she had put the couple in the spare room together, making up the twin beds, after gently probing Matthew for what was expected. They could push the beds together if that's what they wanted and she was sorry she couldn't supply them with a nice double.

'Bloody hell, Josie, your mum would never have done that for us,' Ray had protested. 'Not before we were wed.'

Too true. But then her mum was of an abrasive and unforgiving nature and Josie did not care to be reminded of her. Hetty, nudging eighty-five, was in a nursing home now over in Upper Felston, getting on everybody's nerves. Josie had bought her a new night-dress from BHS for Christmas, which she knew would be sniffed at and tossed aside as every present she had ever bought her had been. She wouldn't care but she had gone to some trouble about it, choosing a colour she thought her mum would like, brushed cotton with long sleeves and a few frills round the neck. Margaret had gone to some trouble, too, buying her some new slippers. She and Margaret would pay mother a duty visit on Boxing Day, although she would not expect Matthew to come along and certainly not Alice. She wouldn't put the girl through that experience for anything for Hetty would very likely give her the third degree, jumping to all sorts of ridiculous conclusions.

Hetty was dangerously unpredictable at the best of times and these days she was likely to go swanning off at a tangent, talking about the past, mixing up past and present like nobody's business. It made visiting her unsettling to say the least, just in case she got on to *that* subject and, if she did take to rambling, then you could guarantee she would start making inappropriate remarks.

Sometimes, Josie felt like throttling her. If ever there was a woman who was adept at ruining the lives of those nearest and supposedly dearest to her, it was Hetty Pritchard. There was just something about her and, when she had been younger and fitter, nobody in their right mind would do anything to go against her wishes, certainly not Josie. It was just as well that Josie had learnt over the years to keep the lid firmly shut on all those feelings of old, of the what-might-have-beens if Hetty hadn't put her foot down.

She saw no reason to acquaint Ray with the facts for some things were best kept in the dark. She saw no reason to acquaint Matthew with the facts either, for it didn't seem fair to have him know that his dad, whom he thought the world of, had been very much her second choice. He came a close second, true, but he wasn't quite the man of her dreams.

CHAPTER THREE

Earlier that afternoon, Ray Bailey found himself standing outside one of the big stores in town, trying to pluck up the nerve to go in and buy his wife's Christmas present. Josie had the Volvo but he had the use of the big carpet van and, because, as he might have known, there was nowhere to park this afternoon, he had left it sitting there for all the world to see on a double yellow line, half on the pavement at that. It was Christmas Eve, the season of goodwill, and he hoped the spoof 'Carpet fitter on call' card he had left in the van window would raise a smile rather than a parking ticket.

Ray was a big, handsome, dark-haired man with dodgy knees, the result of spending so much of his working time on them. He knew that, sooner or later, he would have to admit to Josie that they were bothering him, the knees, but he didn't want to make a song and dance about them – not yet, not at his relatively young age. Dodgy knees ran in his family and, looking back, carpet fitting had been a bad choice of a job. He should have stuck to plumbing, but plumbing ran in the family as well and, just to be awkward, he had wanted something different.

He felt his right knee twinge but that could be nerves because they were always worse when he was anxious and he had put this off already too many times. It was Christmas Eve and it had reached the stage where it was now or never. It would only take a few minutes to nip in the shop and buy it. Whatever it was. The trouble was he felt out of his depth. Screws, nails, tins of paint, car stuff was no problem but a woman's present . . . bloody hell, Ray, just do it, it can't be that bad.

Squaring his solid shoulders, he walked in through the swing door and found himself ambushed in the perfume section right off. It offended his nostrils, ponging as it did to high heaven, a woman's heaven at that, and he hesitated a minute, fumbling in his pocket for the little bit of paper on which he had noted down the name of the scent on Josie's dressing table. Good thinking that. He had rummaged through her underwear drawer as well and written down sizes, although scent would be easier than knickers. He would die a thousand deaths in the knickers and bras section. He had seriously considered buying her a new electric kettle because the other one was playing up but Matthew had laughed out loud when he'd suggested that on the phone.

'She'll have your guts for garters, Dad,' he warned.

Pity. It would have been a whole lot easier. It was Matthew who had suggested perfume or underwear.

Hell. He had lost the scrap of paper and he couldn't for the life of him remember the name of the scent. Panicking, he stood at the nearest counter looking in amazement at the bottles on display. How many scents were there? There were any number of fancy shaped bottles that made the ladies' eyes light up.

'Can I help you, sir?'

He stared into the well made-up eyes of the girl behind the counter. She was a brunette like Josie but nowhere near as pretty, even though she was young enough to be her daughter. His Josie was some looker, always had been and he worried that, whilst she seemed to be holding her own in the age stakes, he was rapidly going downhill, although, thank God, he still had his hair, another thing that ran in the Bailey family, a nicer trait this time.

'Scent,' he muttered, knowing at once it was a pretty damned fool thing to say. 'For the wife. For Christmas,' he added, feeling daft and awkward as he caught her smile, which verged on patronizing.

'Did you have anything in particular in mind?'

'God, no.' He picked up the nearest one – a prettily shaped bottle that looked as if it contained a urine sample – wanting to get out of here asap. 'This will do.'

She gave him one of those withering female looks. Josie was good at them too. 'If I might make one or two suggestions. . . .'

'Go on then. But I'm on double yellow lines outside.'

'Right.' She quickened her pace. 'Vanderbilt is very popular. And Guerlain's Samsara is really lovely. That's new. Then there's Chanel, of course, if you want to push the boat out and Obsession. Does your wife like Obsession? Or Ysatis . . .' she was getting desperate he could tell, 'and Lou-Lou.'

'That's it.' He pounced on that happily as the name clicked. 'I'll have a big bottle of that.'

It wasn't so simple. There were mysterious choices within the range, which she rattled off in a bored fashion but, wisely, he settled on the most expensive, which turned out to be the smallest bottle. He also resisted the urge to say, '*How* much?' when she told him the price. Josie was worth it. Every penny. Although he could have got a top of the range kettle, one of those new fangled shapes for less than that and thrown in a set of kitchen knives.

The girl, hampered by her extremely long, red painted finger-nails, wrapped it for him better than he could ever have managed himself and then, pleased as punch, sticking the little parcel in his pocket he picked up the van, which had miraculously escaped a ticket and drove home. That was a first and it had been a doddle. He had done it. He had been in town, on his own, and bought Josie's Christmas present single-handed. He couldn't pretend it hadn't been a bit of an ordeal and, before he'd gone in the shop, he'd wished for a minute that he had taken up Lynn's offer to get it for him as she usually did. It was kind of her but he sometimes wondered about Lynn and her motives. The chiffon scarf she had bought on his behalf for Josie's birthday had been emerald green, the only colour that he knew Josie did not like. He had never seen it since, so she

21

must have taken it back to the shop and exchanged it. If he didn't know Lynn better, he thought she might have done it deliberately. He couldn't make her out, sometimes it was as if she was jealous of Josie and he couldn't think why. She was an old friend, an old mate, and she was Josie's friend, too, so he couldn't understand it. Lynn had done well for herself and was a chartered accountant now. By rights, it was Josie who should be jealous of her because she hadn't made it, giving up on the exams after a while and settling for a part qualification.

The little present for Josie was upstairs now, in the drawer beside the bed at his side and he would remember to give it to her first thing tomorrow. He couldn't wait to see her face. She was a little cracker, his Josie, his girl. He wouldn't do a Mick, trade her in for a younger model as Mick had done with Lynn, not in a million years.

Mission accomplished.

He sat down in his chair in the lounge, drinking his coffee, thinking with a smile of Josie, thinking, not for the first time, that he was so lucky to have her.

CHAPTER FOUR

Josie had popped in to see Margaret that afternoon, confirming the arrangements for tomorrow, so there was no need to stop off at Percy Street. Driving down Crook Lane, Josie could see the lights, the Blackpool illuminations as Ray called them, before she saw the house. Ray always went crackers with the decorations at Christmas and, whilst it had been nice when Matthew was little, it seemed daft now with just the two of them.

Kenny had laughed his head off when he saw it and, surprising herself, instead of leaping to its defence, she had felt suddenly ashamed of it, the twinkling on and off fairy lights, the 'Season's Greetings' banner, the blown-up Santa Claus and the reindeers – the whole caboodle. Worse, she had felt ashamed of Ray that he should be so boyishly proud of it all.

It had taken him all day to set it up, hanging on the ladder with her directing operations from below. It was an anxious time with all the stretching and twisting, twiddling and fiddling with the electrics, and the delight in his face when he finally switched on and they all sparkled into life was something to behold. Josie, scared to death about him either falling off the ladder or going up in a puff of smoke, had hugged him and, at the time, shared his joy. But then, standing there with Kenny, she had seen it for what it was. This sort of over the top display could only happen down here in Riverside and maybe, behind the façade of admiration, the rest of the street was hanging on to its sides with laughter. When did you see one of those detached houses in Greenfield – Kenny's neck of the woods – done up to the nines like this? Mind you, a lot of those folk were as tight as they come, some of them living on their wits at that, so cost could be a reason.

She knew she had been comparing the two men of late and she ought not to be doing that. That was dangerous. She was married to Ray – they'd celebrated their silver wedding anniversary last year – but she was spending more time these days with her colleague Kenny. Ray was hardly ever at home because, as well as the carpet fitting, he supplemented their income by doing odd jobs, assembling flat-pack furniture, putting up shelves, that sort of thing, so he was often out in the evenings and at weekends too. She didn't know what he did with that extra money because it never seemed to come her way, but she knew he didn't gamble it or spend it on himself. Knowing Ray, he would be shovelling it into a deposit account for a rainy day and there were enough of those in this part of the world.

Apart from gardening, he was handy with his fingers, a plumber by trade, and it was no great hardship for him to be doing these jobs, for sometimes it seemed he was only happy when he had a screwdriver in his hand, but it was beginning to irritate her more and more. They could manage without the extra money he coined in but Ray had a thing about it, needed to earn more than she did although, if she got the promotion, he would be hard pressed to manage that, even if he took on three extra jobs. The promotion, if it happened, would shoot her up not one but two grades and it would make an enormous difference.

Josie rarely saw Kenny out of the office but he had been round here last week on some lame-dog of an excuse, bringing round a sponsor form for some deluded soul in the office who was up for a charity parachute jump. She ended up giving a fiver, adding Ray's name, too, and putting him down for the same because she could never in a month of Sundays jump out of an aircraft, charity or no charity.

'Thanks, Josie.' Kenny slipped the sponsor form back in the pocket of his black leather jacket, clicked his pen and popped that away, looking odd in informal get-up because she only ever saw him in his office suit.

With Ray out, she was taking the opportunity to pamper herself, do her nails and have a leisurely bath and so on. She had just washed her hair – longer and darker last week – and had a towel wrapped round her head when she answered the door. She saw him glance at it, at her make-up free face and her generally tousled appearance, and the look that had passed between them had seemed too intimate somehow and had flustered her, so she hadn't invited him in, just stood there on the step, whilst he jeered at Ray's handiwork with the illuminations.

Shutting the door on him eventually, pleading it was cold which it was, she knew she would have to put a stop to the silly flirting before it got completely out of hand. People, colleagues, were beginning to cast sidelong glances their way and it might get back to Ray. Mind you, she couldn't imagine it having much of an effect on him. He was too knackered with all the work he did and didn't have enough passion these days to get wildly jealous if another man looked at her. The days were long gone when he might have fought a duel on her behalf. He once had, years ago, well not exactly a duel but he had told Jack Sazzoni in no uncertain terms to leave her alone. Jack had seen the look in his eyes and known he meant business. She had rushed over to separate them, fearing the worst, worried that they were actually going to come to blows, but thankfully they had stopped short. Just as well because Ray was considerably bigger and heavier, and Jack would have surely come off worse. Ray had been blazing mad, the first and only time she had ever seen him very nearly out of control and that had upset her, making her wonder what she was letting herself in for. Had her mother ever seen her dad like that before they got married? Had she wondered if he would ever turn that anger on her? And had she dismissed that idea as daft, as she did then? Up close, she had heard

Ray spitting out the words inches only from Jack's face.

'She's my girl, Sazzo, and don't you forget it.'

Jack, showing admirable control, holding out his hands in surrender, had stepped back, looking at her all the while.

'Are you, Josie?' he'd asked quietly. 'Are you his girl?'

It could have gone either way at that moment. If she had followed her heart, she would have told him no. But, mindful of the family, her mum, her dad, Margaret, she made the decision that would shape her life for the next twenty-odd years.

'Yes I am,' she'd said.

CHAPTER FIVE

Ray was sitting dozing in his favourite chair, paper spread out at the sports page, gas fire full on, his slippered feet on the sheepskin rug that was gathering bits of glitter that would be a devil to shift. In the corner opposite the television, twinkling lights were draped over the artificial tree. It was covered in baubles and little bits and bobs that Matthew had made when he was little, things she knew she ought to throw away, things she could not bear to throw away. They used to have a proper Christmas tree but, last year, when she was still hoovering bits of it up in July from the deep pile 80/20 carpet that Ray had got at a heavy discount, she said never again.

On the mantelpiece, she had moved the small carriage clock and her collection of little brasses and put holly and other bits of greenery from the garden in their place. The cards were pegged on to silver ribbon but she had put Matthew's special one in pride of place on top of the sideboard. He always remembered, even when there was no girl in his life to prompt him. He remembered her birthday and their wedding anniversary and, sometimes, he remembered to remind his dad. Ray hadn't sent her a card this year but then he seldom did. She had sent him one: 'To my darling husband at Christmas', and it sat there, large as life, accusingly awaiting its partner. Fat chance of that. Ray was blissfully unaware that it bothered her. He had asked what she wanted for Christmas and she had said a surprise would be nice.

'A surprise?' he had echoed in dismay. 'You know me, Josie, I'm no good with surprises.'

Quite. But then she had known when she married him, that there would be precious few surprises. What you saw with Ray was what you got. There were no hidden depths. It hadn't mattered then, for there had been something terribly attractive about him, a rough-hewn look that she liked, a no-nonsense, salt of the earth persona that delighted her, a rough passion that, after Jack's gentle romancing had been exhilarating. Rough but kind-hearted, that was Ray, the sort of man who would not knowingly hurt a fly and would never dream of hurting her and, after her dad and his uncontrollable rages, that mattered a lot.

Now she longed for somebody with a touch of style, the sort of man who was at ease with his feminine side, who wouldn't consider it soft to shed a tear at a poignant moment or present her with a bunch of flowers for no reason. Somebody like Kenny. Kenny dressed well and had clean fingernails but then he wasn't on his hands and knees all day, tugging on carpet and hammering it into place. Kenny was a lazy so-and-so and didn't do a lot round the office but had a clever way of always *seeming* busy. He had breezed in two years earlier taking up the post of chief office clerk, smarter dressed by far and driving a superior car to Mr Walsh, but it was quickly rumoured that he had a wealthy wife, ten years his senior. Enough said.

As to her Christmas present, Ray would do what he always did. Ask their friend Lynn to get her something. Lynn would wrap it as well, beautifully and neatly, although she would get him to sign the little card attached. No wonder he always looked as surprised as she did when she opened it. She hoped Lynn would steer clear of chiffon scarves this time. She knew she didn't like green, especially the emerald variety, and it had ruined her birthday that. She would give her the benefit of the doubt. Ever since her husband had gone off, she and Ray had tried their best to offer her some friendly support. Josie had the feeling that Lynn was trying, not always subtly, to tone her down. On a recent shopping trip together, searching for an evening frock for the work do, Lynn had pursed her lips as Josie slipped into a fantastic silvery dress with puffed sleeves and a low-necked bodice. For a moment, looking at herself in the mirror in the changing room she had felt like Princess Di and then Lynn had burst the balloon by saying in that voice of hers. 'Do you really think, Josie, at your age you should be showing so much bare skin?'

She had seen red at that. Lynn could take a running jump. Sometimes it was no surprise that Mick had left her and taken up with a younger woman. Goodness knows how she had tried to fix her up with somebody else but it had been hard enough first time round.

Lynn might think the pair of them were on their last legs at knocking on forty-six, but she didn't. She wasn't going under yet, not for a long while. She had ended up buying the dress just to spite Lynn but, when she got it home, she wasn't sure she liked it anyway and it had never been off the hanger since. She had shrugged and put it down to yet another of her 'shooting herself in the foot' moments.

'That Kenny bloke's been on the phone,' Ray, roused from slumber, called out from the lounge as she set about unloading the shopping. She had peeped in but he hadn't looked up so, thank heavens, he hadn't noticed her hair yet.

'What did *he* want?' she asked, feeling her heart give a little jump. 'I hope it's not a panic about work.'

'What else would it be about?'

What indeed?

The nervous relationship she had with Kenny could be termed sexual harassment, she supposed, but in an odd way she enjoyed the feeling of power she had over him. She could drop him in it any time she chose and she suspected he knew it but it didn't seem to worry him unduly because he didn't think she had it in her to make a fuss.

Maybe he was right However, she was keeping an eye on what was going on elsewhere. The newspapers were full of it, this so-called sexual harassment, and women like her were getting *thou-*

sands. The problem was it was her word against his and she hesitated because mud stuck and, unable to shake off some aspects of her stern upbringing, she minded about her reputation and minded also about what Ray and their son would think. But it was what it would do to Margaret that really mattered the most. She could not risk upsetting her sister. It would make the headlines in the local paper and there would be a picture of the two of them, Kenny looking handsome and innocent and swearing blind he had never touched her.

Could she, a policeman's daughter, put her hand on the Bible, the book she still regarded with reverence, and swear that she hadn't led him on, just the teeniest bit? She'd always been able to catch a man's eye and perhaps it was all getting a bit desperate now as she grew older. She needed to know, as she and Ray dipped ever more into the old married couple mode, that she was still capable of causing a man to catch his breath. But she really didn't feel she could cope with the publicity, so who was she kidding? Kenny could rest easy in his bed next to Dorothy, whom she had met a couple of times. It was a shock meeting Dorothy for she had imagined a dull, older woman, maybe with greying hair, because that was how Kenny talked about her. Dorothy was older, yes, but she was an eye-catching woman. She had perfect make-up, smooth skin and – surprise, surprise – long straight blonde hair caught up into an elegant plaited ponytail. Classy clothes too.

Josie bit her lip, smoothing down her jeans that were tucked into knee-high, tan leather boots. Maybe the jeans were a touch tight round the bum and maybe the neckline of her sweater was a bit low and maybe Lynn, whose dresses would offend nobody, was right. Perhaps it was time she sobered up her image a little before she started looking like mutton dressed as lamb. The trouble was when you were as curvy as she was, you either showed it off or hid it and she had no intention of covering herself up completely. She had not won the 'fantastic knockers' competition that the boys at school had run for nothing. The girls were not supposed to know about that but by heavens they did.

She had no intention either of returning Kenny's call. Whatever it was, it could wait until after Christmas. Nothing could be that urgent and she was fed up with carrying that lot in the office. If the general public knew about the workings or non-workings of that department, they would go to town on it. That was another thing she could blow the lid on if she had a mind to. She did the lot in that department, worked her socks off, and nobody would thank her for it. In any case, just now, she and Kenny were rivals for the deputy job and she felt she had to be on her guard. They were the only internal candidates for the promotion and because the external ones had been a useless bunch, she suspected that it was going to go to Kenny. She hadn't had a good interview and one of the councillors on the panel, keen to flaunt his authority, had asked some awkward questions and got her in a bit of a frazzle. It was annoying because, taking Lynn's advice for once, she had toned herself down for that interview, wearing the navy suit with the padded shoulders and a cream ruffle-necked blouse. She'd gone easy on the make-up and even calmed her hair down. As for jewellery, she had discarded the bracelets she was so fond of and just worn her plain wedding band and her engagement ring.

She hadn't recognized herself when she'd looked in the mirror – Ms Po-Face – and maybe that had something to do with it. It had succeeded in inhibiting her. It was wrong to pretend to be someone you were not. She should have gone for her usual glitz, and stuff what they thought.

She would, she decided, be gracious in defeat, even though it would scupper any ideas of moving house. She suspected that Kenny would get the promotion simply because he was a man. Discrimination of this sort would be hotly denied but it was a fact of life in the town hall and the treasurer, Mr Walsh, was so old-fashioned he might as well come to work dressed in Victorian clothes. He treated the women in the office as if they were about to expire any minute, whereupon he would very likely produce a bottle of smelling salts. The worst scenario would be Kenny getting the

31

deputy job now and then getting the chief job a year on. He would make her life a misery then.

How dare he ring her on Christmas Eve at home? And how dare he buy her a bottle of the perfume she liked best just now – Giorgio Beverly Hills – when they had all agreed to spend no more than a pound on a daft little gift? The perfume had to be a bribe for keeping quiet if ever there was. She grew hot as she thought of the little flirty moments in the staff rest room when the easiest thing was to just laugh it off and push him away. She ought not to have accepted the perfume, that was for sure, but she hadn't been prepared and couldn't come up with a satisfactory reason to hand it back.

An hour later, with the vegetables prepared and the trifle somehow squashed into the overflowing fridge, she relaxed at last opposite Ray. He had finally noticed her hair, raising his eyebrows before saying that it was very nice, looking as convincing as a serial crook up before the court. Ray knew nothing about current fashion, so it didn't worry her too much. To be honest, it was growing on her, the new look, made her look quite perky and she had no intention of following in the footsteps of her mum, who had looked ancient by the time she was in her mid-forties.

Matthew and Alice would be here around nine o'clock depending on the traffic. It had been touch and go for a while whether they would manage it at all because Matthew was in the middle of the Christmas pantomime season and he had to pull a lot of strings to get a couple of days off. Honestly, the way they worked him! It was like the slave trade. She consoled herself because she knew he loved the job and it was nice to be doing a job you loved. She didn't love her job, sometimes didn't even like it, but it brought in the money. You couldn't blame Ray for not exactly getting over-excited over the carpet fitting either for that could hardly be called a vocation.

She wondered what this girl would be like. It wouldn't matter. If Matthew liked her, loved her even, then that was fine with her. If she took an instant dislike to her, as she was apt to do with some people, then it wouldn't matter. She would put her personal feelings aside and act up for all she was worth. And so would Ray. She would make very sure of that.

She wasn't being the cause of any family friction. No way was she going to be another Hetty.

CHAPTER SIX

Clutching the jar of luxury mincemeat, Valerie Sazzoni headed for the baskets-only till, surprised and irritated to find there was even a queue there. It was extremely annoying having to do this last-minute shopping when she thought she had everything organized. She hadn't even known about the baskets-only till, until somebody had pointed it out. Quite clearly, the notice stated one hand basket only but, unlike some supermarkets apparently, there was no limit on the actual number of items in that basket and she picked up a few grumbles about that. Glancing ahead, it looked as if everybody else had a basket heaped with things, stretching credibility to the limit. It reminded Valerie of those awful carvery restaurants where you helped yourself from a buffet, which some people took as meaning that they could pile their plates with as much food as would sensibly remain on the plate. Sheer greed such as that appalled her.

For a moment, she contemplated going to the front of this queue, smiling sweetly and saying that, as she only had one item and had cash, the exact change in fact, could she possibly skip them all?

No. She thought better of that idea. Everybody looked as harassed as only last-minute Christmas Eve shoppers could look, and about as likely to be flexible with the rules as sheets of steel, so she decided she would simply have to wait her turn. It had taken a surprisingly long time to locate the jar of mincemeat, as she rarely came into supermarkets, which she considered to be perfectly ghastly places. She had no need to visit them anyway, not when she could get such fine foods sent over from the delicatessen. The bulk of her day-to-day shopping for what she considered the boring yet essential stuff was done by her housekeeper, Mrs Parkinson. She was a genteel lady who really ought not to be working for a living but there had been a problem with her late husband's pension and she was really rather hard up and was so grateful to have the little self-contained flat in the annexe. She was a touch above the sort of woman you might expect to be employed as a housekeeper and Valerie thoroughly approved of that.

It worked admirably for both of them. Valerie had come to rely on her more and more and would really miss her over the holidays, but the poor woman was due some time off and she wouldn't exactly be enjoying herself on her visit to the States to see her dying sister. Jack had insisted on paying her fare but then that was Jack. Generous to a fault. His charitable giving verged on the insane. Valerie restricted her personal contributions to charity to two causes and all the begging letters went straight into the bin.

Despite her doubts about the wisdom of paying for Mrs Parkinson's air fare themselves, she would much prefer to be married to a generous man. She had a loose rein with her personal expenditure and he liked her to look good, insisted on it in fact. This Christmas, for the first time in a very long time, there would be just the two of them here at home because Alice was going down to Lancashire to visit her boyfriend's parents for Christmas Day and Boxing Day. They would be back up here for New Year. Even though Alice lived only a short drive away over in the South Lakes, they did not see her as often as Valerie would have wished but then she could hardly expect her to spend her precious leisure time visiting them, and Jack was not in favour of popping over on the off-chance. Dropping in unannounced wasn't fair on Alice, he said, and they had to respect her privacy.

Alice had always been of a private nature, close to secretive, and Valerie found herself both worried and hopeful of the outcome of this new relationship. She knew Alice was still young and there was lots of time, but she wanted to see her settled. Alice had met this man in the summer, shortly after she moved to her cottage and, even though they had visited her there on a couple of occasions and she had been back here several times, they hadn't yet met him, which was worrying her. Other than being told that his name was Matthew Bailey and that he worked at the Little Gem Theatre, Alice was giving nothing away and Valerie knew from experience that the harder she pressed, the less fruitful the outcome. Alice was a slow starter when it came to boys and, for her age, a touch naïve. She had been too caught up in her dancing as a teenager and that absorption, amounting at one time to an obsession, meant she operated in her personal little capsule and everything else, including boyfriends, was put on hold. She was an unusual looking girl, her father's dark brown eyes a pretty and surprising contrast to the honey blonde hair she had inherited from Valerie.

She was putting them in adjacent bedrooms at New Year in the guest wing of the house, many walls away from her and Jack, so no sounds would travel. Nice and convenient all round. It was really up to them whether or not they made anything of that, for she did not feel able to ask Alice if she was having a sexual relationship with this man. Jack had merely laughed when, fretting about the sleeping arrangements, she commented on it.

'What's the problem?' he asked with a grin, the same infectious smile he had been shooting her way for the last twenty-odd years. 'It's not as if they're teenagers, darling. I would be worried if they *weren't* sleeping together. We were at their age, weren't we?'

'We were *married* at their age,' she told him tartly.

He was right to be unconcerned and she determined that she would adopt a modern attitude if it killed her and turn a blind eye to whatever happened in that direction.

With an impatient sigh, Valerie edged forwards in the queue, feeling out of place in her smart clothes. Why did women think they could abandon all attempts at style directly they entered shops such as these? At least the checkout lady seemed efficient in spite of the Santa Claus hat she was wearing on her brassy blonde, newly-permed hair. With a bit of luck, if she continued to proceed at this rate, she might be home before Jack arrived back. She had left a note in a prominent place but she doubted he would notice it. She could leave a suicide note and he would probably never find it.

There was no longer any danger of that. She had climbed out of the depression. There was a time, after she had lost the last of the babies, that she had thought about it, so bogged down as she was with sadness and despair. That depression had been slow to lift but lift it had, although she felt fragile still when she thought about it. Conceiving Alice had been so easy, the pregnancy and birth perfectly normal and she had just assumed, as had Jack, that it would continue in that vein, that they would have the large family they both craved. Not so. After Alice, after the other baby who lived for a day only, she never had any trouble becoming pregnant again but it was hanging on to the baby thereafter that had been the problem. After she suffered the last miscarriage, the third in as many years, Jack had taken her hand, stroked her hair and said simply 'enough'.

'I love *you*,' he told her as she wiped away her tears. 'And it doesn't matter. It really doesn't matter and I'm not putting you through all this again. We have Alice after all.'

Yes, they had Alice but he did not have his son and Lorenzo never had his grandson, the son and grandson they so wanted, the fine boy who would carry on the family business – Sazzoni & Son – and no matter how much Jack pretended not to mind, she knew that, with no son to succeed, he would sign the business over to his cousin and wife next year with a very heavy heart. Alice had no interest in the business and they could not force her into it.

The young woman ahead of her turned, frowned, and said something but Valerie pretended not to hear. She was not in the mood for conversation with anyone and particularly not with this Goth-like creature. She had a dead white pan-caked face, black-rimmed eyes and blood red lipstick. She wore black cobweb lace mittens, Valerie noticed with surprise, for they would be rather charming in any other context. She really didn't know how to react to somebody like this, whether to brazen it out and look her in the eye or simply ignore her. It was their parents' fault, she thought, knowing that she would have soon put a stop to it if Alice had shown any of these tendencies.

It was snowing as she came out of the supermarket, proper snow at that, fat frothy flakes, and she acknowledged that the weatherman had been right in saying that they would catch the bulk of the snow before it swept across the rest of the country. This supermarket had to be in one of the prettiest locations and the planning application had been rubber-stamped on the understanding that it was to blend in as far as was possible with the beautiful surroundings.

Valerie could feel the hills around her, if not see them, as she drove carefully out on to the narrow winding road that skirted the lake, the dark deep lake that was almost too beautiful in soft warm daylight but vaguely sinister now. The road surface was icy and she concentrated fiercely, worried that a single lapse of concentration could send her spinning into those gently moving inky depths with not a hope of getting out of them alive.

And all for a jar of mincemeat!

CHAPTER SEVEN

The occasional lights of the large houses fronting the lake were welcome and Valerie steered by them, the familiarity of the road losing itself as the snow flurried and dazzled against the windscreen. Bing Crosby might be dreaming of a white Christmas but she was less thrilled. She was a summer person and would really prefer to spend the whole of winter at their villa in the Italian lakes, close to the little village from where the Sazzoni family originated, but they couldn't contemplate doing that, not realistically, until Jack retired. With no money worries, he was intending to retire early at fifty, although she would believe that when it happened.

After so many years, this area in the northern lakes was home and now, when she occasionally visited the town where she was brought up, she felt almost like a stranger. Not quite a stranger for some of it was the same, but enough had changed to make it mostly unrecognizable. The Sazzoni brothers including Marco, Jack's grandfather, had emigrated in 1905 settling in Felston, armed with some capital and a lot of verve, starting first with an ice cream parlour and confectionery business. Valerie knew she ought to be grateful to Felston for providing those long ago opportunities for the family, but she had precious little affection for the place and had long since ceased to visit.

Having successfully demoted Felston to the back of her mind, it wasn't entirely a happy coincidence then that this boyfriend of Alice's originated from there. Unfortunately, after a little gentle probing, she learned that he was from Riverside, which, when she had known it, had been the closest Felston had to a no-go area. Worse, his parents still lived there.

Valerie's Felston address had been much more salubrious, living as she did on the leafy and wide-avenued outskirts, but then her father had been a consultant ophthalmic surgeon at Felston & District General Hospital. Valerie, an only child born late to her parents, had been educated privately at the Catholic school where her mother taught Classics but she had floated through that privileged education and come out of it with poor grades that had sorely disappointed her parents, especially her mother, who had high academic hopes for her.

'The sky's the limit for girls these days,' she told her. 'Look at Maggie Thatcher. Wonderful woman.'

'We can't all be like that,' Valerie said, privately not too upset to be compared unfavourably to her.

'If you'd just applied yourself a little more. . . .' The sigh was deep. 'I don't know what we're going to do with you, although I suppose with your looks you'll land a good man at least. But you should have something to fall back on.'

Oh that. To please them, Valerie had started a course in domestic science with a view to teaching eventually, but then she met Jack and she gave it up before she got the diploma, which succeeded in exasperating her mother all the more.

Shortly after she and Jack were married, his father, expanding the delicatessen side of the business, had entrusted his son with the running of a new enterprise in the Kendal area and she and Jack had quickly taken root there. With a bit of a leg up from both sets of parents, who had tried to outdo each other with lavish gifts to the newlyweds, they bought a brand new but poky house on a small estate but, since then, under their own steam, they had moved three times, ever onwards, outwards and upwards. There were now six Sazzoni prized delicatessens in the Lakes area, some of them with a small coffee and ice-cream shop attached and she and Jack were settled in the house of her dreams, a house in a prime location beside the lake. Jack split his time between the shops, keeping a close eye on the buying and choosing of the provisions they stocked. Quality uppermost was his motto.

Jack had that keen look about him, ever since she first set eyes on him in the summer of '61 and, although he was caught up at the time with another girl, a short busty brunette, she just knew that he was the one for her. It was just a question of waiting for the right moment and, as soon as the other thing fizzled out as she had guessed it would, she made sure she was there.

It niggled for a while that she was required only in her capacity as a 'good listener' but she was patient and eventually that was rewarded. She had never been entirely certain that Jack wouldn't have dropped her like a ton of bricks if the other girl had changed her mind about ending their relationship, but by then it was too late for she was utterly won over by his charm. They found they had much in common – a love of the same kind of music, books, rather a serious outlook on life and when he proposed, she accepted without a moment's hesitation. Things were made easier because her parents liked Jack and also the verve and enterprise of the Sazzoni family, so they had been terribly gracious about it all and genuinely thrilled when Alice was born.

Sometimes she wondered if Jack proposing to her had been a throwaway 'see if I care' gesture to that girl of his, the girl that she remembered still. She was not one of their set, so she scarcely knew her and they all thought that Jack was slumming it a little with that girl from Riverside but he wouldn't listen. He had been besotted. Seeing them together had made her heart ache, the way he looked at her mirrored the way she looked at him. Valerie had wondered if they were sleeping together but, surprising maybe to today's youth, things like that were considered private and were rarely talked about, at least not in her set. Maybe the boys discussed it amongst themselves but not in mixed company, and she certainly never discussed that side of things with her girlfriends. All she knew was that, old-fashioned or not, she kept Jack at arm's length until they were married and he maintained later that he had loved her all the more for that.

Valerie was nearly home, that final bend, and she remembered how the house had looked when they first saw it on that fine spring day. Wordsworth had clasped it in a nutshell when he talked of the splendour of a host of golden daffodils for that frankly had swung it for her. The condition of the house itself was a disappointment but that could be remedied. She was a frustrated gardener and the garden, packed with spring flowers, was a joy, its location by the lake an added bonus. She quickly pooh-poohed the idea that the house was too big. What were a few extra rooms? Jack was persuaded.

Jack could always be persuaded.

Valerie turned into the drive at last and the security lights came on showing up the softly descending silent snow as she clicked open the automatic doors of the garage and drove in. The empty space beside her car signified that Jack was still out at the charity auction, but she did not mind because it would give her the chance to unwind after the unexpected dash to the supermarket.

The unmistakeable scent of pine invaded the hall for she had placed the larger of the Christmas trees there, simply decorated because she could not bear – Christmas or not – to have too much froth and fuss. There were so many cards, personal and business, and she had chosen just a few of the special ones to put out, the remainder were in a box out of sight. That Bing Crosby song was lodged in her head and she found herself humming it as she made herself a cup of coffee, opening one of the boxes of chocolate that had been brought from the shop for Christmas – well, it was very nearly Christmas and she hadn't had a chocolate for ages. It was such a bore trying to keep to the same weight she had been in her twenties, but she did, if only because she liked to look good in clothes and was proud of her model height and long, long legs. She was the same height as Jack without heels but he did not mind, liked her to wear heels anyway, which she did. She kept her shoulder-length bobbed hair the same colour it had always been and spent a fortune on discreet make-up and clothes – ah, the clothes. She had any number of elegant dresses and tops in silk and linen, her shape showing them off to their full advantage. She and Jack went to quite a lot of functions and she was confident that she always looked good.

'How do you do it, Valerie?' one of her women friends asked. 'You have such style.'

'Perhaps it's because I'm married to a man who has Italian connections,' she would say with a smile. This was true although the Italian blood was by now greatly diluted, each of the male line marrying an Englishwoman as they had, each of the male line becoming ever more English as a result of his mother's influence. However, that little speck of Mediterranean root remained, showing up in odd ways. 'Jack takes an interest in what I wear.'

The truth was she worked at it, taking particular care with accessories, that's how she did it, and it certainly was not in the genes if her mother was anything to go by. She had two new outfits for Christmas but this evening she was wearing old favourites, a long burgundy skirt with a soft ivory angora sweater and because the whole effect would be spoilt by the addition of slippers, she was wearing low-heeled comfortable boots.

Jack would expect nothing less of her. She had once made the mistake of going for comfort instead of prettiness in bed and he had – with a smile on his face – accused her of dressing like a bag lady. My goodness, she had taken that to heart. Jack would very likely buy her something silky to wear in bed for Christmas, for she had dropped a few hints, but he was just as likely to surprise her.

Mrs Parkinson had helped her put up the tasteful Christmas decorations and Valerie smiled as she set a match to the ready prepared fire. It was beautifully warm anyway for they had an efficient gas-fired heating system, but the real fire was a nice touch and reminded her of her childhood when she would sit and gaze at the flames and see shapes in them. Within minutes, the flames had caught and she crossed quickly to the wide bay window, drawing the curtains, shutting out the snow and wondering what on earth it would look like tomorrow morning.

She had long since given up trying to do an *Italian* Christmas, knowing that there was no way she could do it properly. Jack's mother had been indisputably English and as Jack often ruefully observed, the rot had set in by then. To do an Italian Christmas, you need first and foremost an Italian Mama. It might well be *la vigilia di Natale* over there but here it was Christmas Eve. It might well have a truly religious meaning over there but here it was largely an excuse for a few days' holiday and, if Jack regretted the almost complete loss of his roots, he only occasionally let it show.

She was preparing a special dinner for the two of them this evening and, after a hectic pre-Christmas social calendar, she was looking forward to a quiet evening in. The television programmes this Christmas Eve were all too predictable, frantically festive, so they would put on some soothing music and relax, go to bed around midnight. Once upon a time, she would dutifully have accompanied Jack and his father to midnight mass but no longer. When Lorenzo died, there was no need for Jack to pretend any more and, with his father laid to rest in the family plot, he dropped religion with a haste that smacked of insensitivity. No consultation. No arguments. No recriminations. Alice, picking up on it, had lapsed too.

Thinking of her daughter reminded Valerie that this would be the very first time she would be away from home at Christmas and it hurt to know that she was pulling away from her. It was only right and proper that she should and she must wait in judgement on this boyfriend. She had spoken to him, just the once, on the telephone and he had sounded nice. He had a pleasant voice with a light northern accent to remind you of his roots, but the thought of Riverside, Felston, would not go away. She had to get a hold on herself and stop being so snobby. Jack hated it and so did she but she couldn't always help it. The way you had been brought up took some shifting and her mother had always been horribly dismissive of people she thought of as lower class.

She listened to the radio, frowning at the update on the weather conditions, which were worsening by the minute. A white Christmas – wonderful of course and didn't everybody secretly long for one – but not until everybody was safely where they were supposed to be, not in the middle of getting there.

Ah, there was Jack at last. She heard the car, the garage door opening and a few minutes later, he was coming in the back door, stamping feet on the mat, telling her what she already knew – that it was snowing heavily and looked set for the night.

The meal was in hand, the champagne chilling, and she warmed her hands a moment over the coals, turning as Jack came through, a bouquet of flowers in his arms.

'For you, sweetheart,' he said, kissing the top of her head. 'Sorry about leaving you on your own this evening. It was a poor turn-out. There wasn't a lot a lot of support so we'll all have to dig deep and make it look decent as it's for the children's hospice.'

'These are lovely . . . thank you, darling.' She admired the flowers, put them aside a minute as she poured them both a drink. 'Have you heard from Mrs Parkinson? I thought she might have rung. Shouldn't she be there by now?'

'She should unless there was a delay. I hope she's OK. She's getting a bit long in the tooth for flying off on her own across the Atlantic. And this thing at Lockerbie will have unnerved her. Just think, it could have been her.'

'But it wasn't,' she said briskly, glancing at him and hoping that he wasn't going to go all emotional on her again. Of course it was a tragedy, a tragedy of dreadful proportion, but they couldn't let it affect them. There was no point in brooding. 'She'll be fine. It won't happen again. Not so soon.'

'Try telling that to a nervous traveller,' he said. 'It's her getting on the connecting plane that worries me most. I wrote it all down for her, step by step.'

'I know you did and she was so grateful. What more could you have done? We could hardly go with her and hold her hand. She'll be fine,' Valerie said. 'I shall miss her.'

She told him later about the plans she was hatching for a little party on New Year's Eve. She had sounded out a few of their friends and, although she intended to keep it fairly low key with at the most twelve guests, she wanted to make it special for Alice and Matthew.

'He's a carpet fitter of all things,' she said, as they lingered over coffee in the dining room. It was at the back of the house, furnished in a light modern style because she disliked both dark wood and antique clutter.

'Who is?' Jack asked, reaching for a chocolate mint.

'Matthew's father. He's a carpet fitter and his mother works for the treasurer's department. Something to do with accounts, although I don't think she's a qualified accountant.'

'So? There's no problem with that, is there?' Jack had a twinkle in his eye but she sensed a warning there nonetheless. 'Don't go jumping the gun. They're not even engaged. Alice hasn't said anything, has she?'

'Not yet. I just have a feeling. Suppose they announce their engagement over Christmas?'

'That will be great. It's about time and I think she's ready for it I'm looking forward to having grandchildren.'

Ah, the *bambini* . . . it never went away. Valerie sighed at the look on his face but she wasn't going to bring it all up again, the lost babies that they seldom talked about. She often thought about them herself, thinking of them as the young men they now would be and sometimes, oddly, she could almost feel them beside her. She always shook that feeling off quickly, believing it to be faintly unhealthy to be thinking that way, unwilling to prompt another bout of depression and she certainly never ever mentioned it to Jack.

'I'm a great believer in marrying young before you start having second thoughts,' he said with a smile that faded as he caught her expression. 'You're not worried, are you?'

'It's too soon,' she said. 'And we haven't met him yet. Suppose we don't like him? How will we tell her that?'

'We won't tell her that. What *we* think, my sweet—' Jack said, crushing the chocolate wrapper before dropping it on his saucer. 'What we think is neither here nor there. We stand back from this one. She's a grown-up. It's her decision. Parents have to learn to stand back.'

She gave a little huff of disbelief, knowing that he was a typical dad and no man would ever be quite good enough for his beloved Alice. The two of them were so close she felt excluded sometimes and it had been like that from the beginning, them against her.

Now, she was being paranoid but she saw that Jack's mood had changed and she was uncomfortable to have reminded him of the circumstances of their getting together. They never spoke of it. What was the point? The girl, that pretty dark-haired girl, who was surely the love of his life, had lived in Riverside, too, all those years ago. The reasons for ending the relationship had never been spelt out to Valerie but she suspected it was to do with religion – hence Jack's dismissal of it – and the girl's parents disapproving of him, maybe because he was part Italian. The girl had married somebody else not long after she finished with Jack, very likely on the rebound or perhaps to prove a point. It had nearly broken Jack and for a long time it hurt that she was only second best.

She was still jealous. After all these years, she was still jealous as hell. And she had never rid herself of the thought that, if that girl reappeared on the scene, Jack would be off without a backward glance.

For a moment, as Valerie loaded the dishwasher, she wondered where Josie was now.

CHAPTER EIGHT

The previous summer, on one of the hottest days of the year, Alice Sazzoni moved into Brambles Cottage. It was just as well it was a bright sunny day because she had no time for second thoughts, and buying a house seemed such a grown-up thing to be doing.

The sunshine helped to make the little cottage look at its best, linking arms as it did with an identical one on the one side and a slightly larger, double-fronted one on the other. The stone here was a warm grey, tinged surprisingly with pink. Her cottage did not have roses round the door but instead a ravishing crimson clematis and, growing round the window and joining up with it, a white jasmine. Open the window on a summer's evening, the previous owner had told her, and the scent drifts in. She'd had to take his word for it because it had been early February but she saw now that it was true.

Perfect then. But perfection comes at a price and the bend at the end of Brambles Lane was so tight that the removal van driver had been forced to do a seven- or eight-point turn, coming perilously close to demolishing a great chunk of her neighbour's garden wall until the van was facing backwards and they could unload, blocking the lane and marooning the other residents for the duration of the move. Thank heavens she'd had the foresight to explain beforehand so that they could all move their cars; the last thing she wanted was to antagonize them from the outset. There were only five cottages in all and she wanted to be on the best terms possible with *all* her neighbours.

It was a complete hotchpotch of people, a widow in her eighties, a young couple, two guys, and, in the bigger house next door to her, a middle-aged couple with two teenage boys. As soon as she was settled, she would invite them all round for a house-warming but she would not tell her mother about that or it would turn out to be cringingly formal when all she wanted was a free-for-all with drinks and a few nibbles thrown in. With such an eclectic group, it promised to be interesting if nothing else.

Trying to save on cost, Alice had imagined at first, ridiculously, that she could do the removal job herself with the help of a couple of hefty girlfriends but, having inherited some splendid solid pieces of furniture from her maternal grandmother, antique pieces that had been waiting patiently in store for some time, she knew she could not risk amateur enthusiasm. Her grandmother would never forgive her if the furniture was damaged. She had loved her granny, heaven knows, but been a bit scared of her at the same time.

Feeling useless, not wanting to get in the way as the men struggled with her large terracotta-coloured sofa, she did the one thing she could do, put the kettle on, digging out some sweet biscuits, a bag of sugar, a teaspoon, a carton of slightly off milk, four mugs but no plate. It was just as well her mother wasn't here. Her mother would be better organized and have had a tray handy with several plates and napkins, a sugar bowl and pretty cups and saucers rather than mugs from the market, but then that was her mother. No matter what, standards never slipped. She had never seen her mother looking the worse for wear. Even when she was ill, she would be carefully made-up with her nails done, her hair in its perfect bob. She even managed to do gardening, potentially a very scruffy job, and remain clean and unruffled.

'Where exactly do you want this, love?'

'Oh . . . I'm not sure,' she dithered, squeezing into the sitting-room behind them and thinking about arrangement of furniture, trying to do it quickly as they stood there, poised and expectant. She had to get it right because it would be hell on earth to move again on her own. 'Under the window, please,' she said, aware it would block off the window seat but it seemed the most sensible place to put it. She hadn't even been able to see the window seat when she viewed the house because of the previous person's clutter.

Thank heavens they had got professional cleaners in before they disappeared; everything was pleasantly sparkling. There was a busy-patterned wallpaper but that couldn't be helped. It wasn't such a bad colour and went with the curtains and carpet they had left for her. Spicy shades of rich bronze and burnt orange which, whilst they were not the colours she would have chosen, were easy enough on the eye and would make a good background for her dark wood furniture.

'Under the window it is,' said the foreman, standing back and wiping his brow. He was wearing an olive-green vest with 'I'm the Boss' on the front and 'The buck stops here' on the back. It had damp marks now under the arms and there were beads of sweat on his face. Overweight as he was, she wondered at the wisdom of him doing a job like this, feeling rather concerned on his behalf. She did not want him keeling over from heat exhaustion. Apart from anything else, with the lane blocked, there was no way an emergency vehicle could get anywhere near at the moment.

Gently, they lowered the sofa down and then, with the precision of a fussy housewife, rearranged the large cushions that had slipped. A bee, disentangling itself from the jasmine, buzzed in through the open window, circling them and the room before making an exit through the same window. Sunlight flooded in and it all felt so warm and inviting. When she first viewed it on a cold crisp day, there had been a log fire in the hearth and, looking back, that had clinched it for her. Like her mother, she made quick decisions when it came to where she wanted to live.

'Ready for a cuppa?' Alice smiled at them all and, with sighs of relief all round, they followed her into the little kitchen. It was a neat fit for the four of them but they wrestled round each other in an easy enough fashion and the biscuits quickly disappeared.

'Nice place you've got here,' the one called Eric said, spooning three generous spoonfuls of sugar into his mug. 'Cosy.'

You could say that. Three's a crowd but four of them in the kitchen was close to disaster. Not fancying ending up in an accidental embrace with any of them, Alice carefully retreated with her mug and left them to it, taking a seat on her newly positioned sofa. She supposed they must wonder how she could afford a place like this in this prized spot, a young woman on her own, and the truth was she couldn't or, at least, would never have managed it without a little help from her dad.

'Don't tell your mother,' he had said as he handed over the sizeable cheque that not only secured the deposit but also reduced the mortgage payments to a sensible size.

Dad had been saying much the same thing all her life. They had secrets from mum and it made their relationship special. If, heaven forbid, she had to choose between the two of them, there was no choice. It was her dad's presence she remembered most when she thought about her childhood, which was odd because mother was always at home.

Uncharitably maybe, Alice sometimes wondered what on earth her mother had found to do with all that spare time, for there had been help in the form of a nanny when she was little. Her mother was not very robust and spent a lot of time being 'not very well' and recuperating from various things. Mum was always one step removed or so it seemed to Alice. She was not a hugger, never actually pulling away from an embrace with her daughter but never encouraging it either.

She supposed she had reacted to her mother's aloof elegance by becoming a scruff, never quite recovering from the jeans and baggy tops of her teen years, feeling uncomfortable when dressed up and always being pulled apart by her mother for her clothes sense, or rather her lack of it.

'You're just like your granny,' her mother would say, shaking her head in frustration. 'Look at you. My mother was always a mess. Far too academic for her own good. She never cared what she looked like.'

'Do you want your bed putting up, miss?'

Alice turned round, looked into the kindly eyes of the foreman. 'Yes please,' she said, neglecting to remind him that it was actually on the contract she had signed that they would do that.

'Will do,' he said with a funny half salute. 'I always ask. Thought there might be a Mr Sazzoni coming by later. Sometimes the gents want to do that job themselves.'

'No, I'm on my own,' she said, instantly sorry to have admitted that, but he looked a nice man and she didn't think he would be returning at dead of night to break in and molest her.

A few hours later, the van was empty and the interior of Brambles Cottage was looking like home. The sitting room had all its furniture. The oak bookcase in the alcove was waiting to receive its books, the lovely old desk had just squeezed into the other alcove, the sofa was looking settled as if it had been there for ever and the new rug was in place. Next door her granny's dining-table and chairs added some grace and class to the dining-room and with the bed, her lovely big bed, safely installed upstairs, she could begin to relax.

Everything else could wait. At least, she was in and everything was in one piece. The men had even unpacked fragile items, as per the contract, and nothing was broken.

'That's your lot then, love.' The foreman handed over the paper-work, which she signed with a flourish. 'We'll be off. Give us a ring when you've unpacked the rest of the boxes and we'll pick them up.' He gave a little cough as his colleagues waved at her and made their way back to the van. 'We hope you'll be very happy in your new home, miss.'

'Thank you,' she said, feeling herself flushing with embarrassment about the tip she suddenly realized they were expecting. How ridiculous not to have thought about that. She gave her hairdresser a tip for goodness' sake and these three had been at it in this heat for hours and hours. 'Hang on a minute,' she said, disappearing in search of her purse. Agonizing over what to give them, she wondered later if she had been generous enough and, worse, if she had distributed it fairly. The foreman had done the lion's share but the driver had managed somehow to get the van up the lane and out again.

Too late. Closing the door on them, ignoring the packing cases that were stacked in the utility room, she could at last take stock. It felt good, if a little daunting, to be here. There had been a problem a few weeks ago with the seller's solicitor and it had seemed at one time that it might all fall through. It was only then, when she thought it might slip through her fingers, that she realized just how much she wanted to live here. It had felt like home from the first moment she stepped through the door. She had seen beyond the mess that the previous owners lived in. Just a bit of tarting up, that's all it needed, and she wasn't frightened of getting her hands dirty.

The garden, 'a delightful cottage garden' according to the agent's details, was overgrown but everything was in place and all it would take, she told herself confidently, was a couple of days weeding and sorting. As it was the height of summer, everything was out, weeds and flowers mixed together in a happy profusion of colour and texture. Her mother with her vivid green fingers was aching to get her hands on it but Alice was discouraging that. She didn't want her mother seeing it in this state and, just to annoy her mum, she might insist on hanging on to some of the prettier weeds. What was a weed after all? She would invite her mum and dad round shortly but not until she was completely unpacked, for she didn't want her mother helping with the sorting.

Making up the bed for later was the first essential. The quilt was a moving-in gift from her parents and it was utterly gorgeous. In soft lilacs and pinks it would be the inspiration of the colour scheme. Thoroughly hot and bothered by now, Alice slipped off her shoes and lay, fully clothed, on top of the bed seeing the lightweight curtains moving softly in a now welcome breeze. There were sounds outside of summer and the country, and she sighed deeply, knowing she had done the right thing coming here.

It was the best of all worlds. Remote enough for her to feel completely cut off but that was just an illusion because the bustle of the village was just at the end of the lane and neighbours within banging-on-the-wall distance. Smack bang in the middle of the area where she did her teaching, it could not have been better placed. Providing her dance and drama contract with the education department was renewed next year, then all would be wonderful. If it wasn't renewed, she would be hard pressed to make ends meet with the money she made from the little private dance group for under-sevens she had set up in the nearby market town. Eventually opening her own dance studio was the aim, giving all sorts of dance tutoring from ballet to tap to ballroom and, with people keen to keep fit, she saw dancing really taking off as a new leisure activity. If it all went wrong and she had to do something else then she could always admit defeat and step into the family business. The trouble was her plans had all gone wrong once before, when she reluctantly but realistically gave up on any hopes of becoming a professional dancer, so she was already on the second option.

New home and a new start, and maybe it was time she took a fresh look at herself and where she was going. Although she had hesitated about moving out of the house she had shared with some girlfriends, the set-up had begun to stifle her and she yearned for her own space.

It had been tempting to do a house-share with Felicity, the one girl she got on with best of all, but in the end it was not a sensible option and, having negotiated the best possible deal on this place, she could just about afford the mortgage on her current meagre salary. It would be tight but she would do her best to survive on her own, convinced that she had accepted the very last so-called gift from her dad. She was twenty-three and it was time she stood on her own two feet, although admittedly it was comforting to know that, if it came to it, her parents would be there to bail her out. Knowing her dad, there would be no questions asked.

Reluctantly, she swung her legs off the bed and went downstairs and, shuddering at the sheer volume of packing cases standing accusingly by, she picked up her car keys, closed the windows and locked the door before going off to buy something to eat. A gold star hamper would no doubt be already on its way from the mail-order section of Sazzoni & Son and although she wouldn't say no to that, the fact was, and this was something she would never admit, she wasn't really into much of the specialized food they stocked, never mind that each item had been lovingly selected by her dad, hand picked or whatever. Even though it made her feel like a traitor, she certainly did not turn her nose up at a simple supermarket, factory-prepared pizza, the very idea of which would have her dad turning cartwheels.

It was a twenty minute drive to a decent supermarket on the edge of the nearest town and she shopped quickly and efficiently, ending up with yet more things to unpack when she reached home. After the hectic day, the heat was beginning to get to her and she wanted most of all to step into a shower to wash away all the day's grime. To her relief, the shower worked, the hot and cold a bit variable but OK and, as she dried herself, she dreamed of what this bathroom would look like when it was done up, when she could afford to have it done up that is.

Hers. All hers.

Wearing just a towelling robe over her knickers, she wandered into the little back garden. It was, as the estate agent had pointed out, so private that, should she wish it, she could sunbathe there naked. He had been an odd man, given her the shivers, and, although she had made no comment, she thought the remark offensive.

He was right though. It was secluded, hemmed in by tall hedging on both sides, which in fact made her feel a touch claustrophobic. Still, she had time to think about it and, enjoying the last of the evening heat, she examined the plants closely, most of them a complete mystery. She must look them up in one of her gardening books before her mother arrived and took charge. She had seen her mum attack what she called an untidy bed in the garden and it was frightening. She hadn't issued an official invitation but she had no doubt they would invite themselves anyway within the next couple of days.

So, tomorrow, she had to dig in and make a start.

She rang her parents' number but there was no reply – out at one of their dos no doubt – so she left a message saying that she was finally in and all was well and thanks for the 'Welcome to your New Home' card.

It took a while to get to sleep. Her bed was the same but the room was different, the window was at the wrong side and there was no Felicity in the next room. An owl hooted and there were strange rustlings outside during the night that woke her. Heart hammering, she sat up in bed until she calmed down, although Felicity's suggestion of having a cricket bat handy came to mind. There were a few sounds from next door though they were indistinct, the walls being incredibly thick, but it was comforting to know people were there if she needed them.

This was home and she had better get used to it.

But, lying alone in the big bed, she wished there was somebody, a warm loving man, to share it with her.

CHAPTER NINE

The Little Gem Theatre was only ten miles or so as the crow flies from Alice's new home but so difficult to find that it would seem twice the distance. Matthew Bailey liked its remoteness, although it could be a problem for actors and public alike. The number of times he'd had a frantic phone call 'Where the hell are you?' was running well into double figures.

It was worth the effort, worth all the diving and ducking down the narrow lanes and over the little stone bridges, through a ford at one point, and, just when you were about to give up the ghost, what a sense of achievement when there it was in the glade. A perfect little theatre snuggling there, the hills soaring beyond it, a rushing stream somewhere nearby, and, for the public, the three things that came high on the list of must-haves: a decent car park, a coffee shop and good clean loos.

Matthew, although he loved living here in the Lake District, did not intend to stay for ever. This was a stopgap, the opportunity to prove himself. It would look good in a few years on his CV and maybe help him get a job down in London. Here, as assistant stage manager, he was a relatively big cog in a small wheel, part of a solid team of five with some part-timers helping out in front of house. Helen, the general manager, ran the show, a competent fifty-year-old who was grooming him, so she said, for her job when she retired. He was grateful for the confidence she showed in him but kept it under his hat that it was most unlikely that he would still be around in ten years. He dreamed of London or New York, the big time and why not? He was young, fiercely keen and, ever since his mother had taken him to see his first pantomime back home in Felston, he had been hooked on the theatre.

At first he had imagined performing, as an actor, but the inner workings of the theatre, the getting it all together, the behind-the-scenes hullabaloo, had started to appeal more. He loved the excite-ment, the variety and even the blazing rows and tantrums that resulted from working with such talented and volatile people. He often wondered how his mum, bright and vibrant as she was, could have lumbered herself with a job in such a safe and boring environ-ment as local government where, from what she said, doing very little and achieving even less seemed to be the name of the game. 'Don't quote me,' she had said with a laugh when she said that, 'or I'll be out on my heels.'

'Matthew?' Helen breezed in, fair hair frizzing all round her face, wearing her trademark black leggings and large loose grey smock. 'Have you done last night's show report, darling?'

He handed it over. 'Good audience,' he said. 'And Brett was in fine form. I think he's got over his rocky patch. There were three curtain calls.'

'Thank Christ for that. The last thing we need is the leading man going through a crisis.' She scanned the report. 'Has Claire dressed the set for this evening?'

He nodded, not bothering to add that, to save time, he had swept the stage himself first thing as Claire was having one of her worse than useless days. He had fondly imagined he was finished with his stint as props boy but Claire needed somebody to hold her hand and she couldn't handle anything extraordinary. He could not trust her, that was the top and bottom of it and, unless he checked things meticulously, she was quite capable of forgetting to put a vital prop on stage, leaving the poor actor or actress to turn their talents to improvization. To their credit, they often did that and so smoothly that the audience never realized the problem. Troopers, the lot of them, and he admired them, admired their sheer nerve, for setting foot on that stage was not for the faint-hearted. It gave him goose bumps just standing there as he sometimes did on his own, looking out at the empty seats. It took a special person to confront an audience, to seduce them, to win them over, so maybe it should come as no surprise that so many of the actors he came across were ever so slightly unhinged.

Helen leaned on his desk, knocking over a pile of box office leaflets as she did so, cursing loudly as he rushed round to pick them up. His office was a converted dressing room, dingy, windowless and stuffy. The sickly mustard-coloured carpet had seen better days, trodden by the feet of some well-known names no less, but, even with the help of the wealthy and influential members of Friends of the Little Gem and one or two theatre 'names' who acted as patrons, they couldn't run to new carpets in the back rooms. As for air conditioning that was out of the question and the heat of the last week was building up, turning this box of a room into a little sauna. There was an electric fan but it was so noisy that it was like working with helicopter blades on full power, scattering papers in its slipstream.

Helen tugged at the neck of her smock, loosening it a little. 'Things to do this week. We'll need to fix up a rehearsal room for the murder mystery play,' she told him, consulting her diary as he picked up his. 'There's only six characters in all so they can manage with something small. And we'll need to pull in some children for that *Oliver* production. Can you organize that? The director will be up' – she riffled through the pages – 'the week beginning the twentieth. So we'll need to have the auditions for the babes arranged by then. OK? Can I leave that with you, sweetie?'

Like clothes buyers, they were always thinking a season ahead. For summer read autumn and even winter. And, as Matthew was quickly finding out, things could go badly wrong so there had to be a Plan B and sometimes even a Plan C.

The worst possible scenario was when a name signed up to front a play and then cancelled at the last minute. Shit flew then. People brought back their tickets, wanted their money back, grumbled like hell and you could bet your bottom dollar there would be a mention in the local rag. Funny that, when things were running smoothly as they so often did, not a word would appear, not even when Simon, their marketing guy, sent in the copy himself. Simon reckoned that, even if he strode into the editor's office naked, it would make no difference to her indifference. She would still lose the bloody copy or decide in her infinite wisdom that it wasn't newsworthy enough. It didn't happen often because they didn't often get a big name, not here, not in the back of beyond and more, but Helen kept on trying, appealing to the actor's charitable instincts if nothing else.

Matthew loosened his tie and undid the top button of his pale blue shirt. He had to tread a fine line between too formal and too casual and liked to think he had struck the right balance. The tie could be discarded as and when, but could be quickly added if somebody turned up unexpectedly. Helen might dress like a cleaner herself but she expected the rest of the staff to look reasonably smart, keen on projecting the right image. The colour scheme for the front of house crew was royal blue and yellow, very Swedish flag, but effective with it.

Matthew spent the rest of the morning making phone calls and, by three o'clock, he had arranged a meeting for the next day with some woman he hoped would be able to help him out with the children for *Oliver*. It promised to be a good production with a company they had worked with before, a northern outfit whose director was on the lookout for local kids for the chorus, children who could sing and dance and maybe – if this wasn't asking for the moon – act too. Matthew was doing the initial spadework, but he wasn't pinning too much hope on the kids this woman would produce. In his view, children who could act were rare as dinosaurs' eggs and, in his view also, having children on stage often ruined a serious production. He liked kids, but not on stage. If he were the director, he would be in favour of insinuating them into a play but never actually seeing or hearing them. Of course, even he had to admit that you couldn't get away with that with *Oliver*.

'*Ciao*, Matt!' Claire sidled in, dressed ridiculously in the holiday gear she would be wearing for real in a week's time. God knows how she'd managed to slip past Helen. The buttock-skimming, silky turquoise dress with enormous padded shoulders was surely a beach outfit, the sort of thing you wore over a tiny matching bikini. Having seen Claire in a bikini, having seen her without one come to think of it, Matthew felt his heart pound, instantly annoyed that she could still get to him.

'Good morning, Claire,' he said crisply. Have you finished? Are we ready to go out there?'

'Yeah. Slight problem.'

'What?'

'You know those cups and saucers? You know when they have tea in the second act?'

'Go on,' he said, fearing the worst.

'I dropped the tray,' she said. 'In the wings. The pieces went everywhere. I've been on my hands and knees. Look.' She held up her hand. 'I cut my finger. Those tiny slivers are lethal. There was blood everywhere and I couldn't find the first-aid kit, and how on earth are you supposed to open those stupid little plasters when you've got blood pouring out? I could have sliced through an artery. I filled in a works accident form. Who do I give it to?'

'Me,' he said quickly, taking a cursory glance at the offending strip of elastoplast. 'Replacements. Have you done that? Replacements for the tea set?' he added, saying the words slowly and clearly as he caught her puzzled expression.

'Do you want me to?'

'Yes, Claire, I do. I do,' he repeated, hearing his voice suddenly, reflecting in a mad moment that it was just as well he was not uttering those words in a church with Claire, a vision in white, at his side. 'Do it now. Get yourself into Kirkley. Four fine china cups and saucers. Matching ones,' he said, rapidly losing patience. 'I've got to check the lighting and sound and the flats on stage. For God's sake, Claire, can't I trust you to do anything right? You're props. You have to keep track. I'm not telepathic.'

'Matt. . . .' She edged nearer, bringing her heady perfume with her. 'Don't talk to me like that. Don't be mean.'

'Mean?' He glanced at her irritably. He didn't have time for the soul-searching she was apt to engage in these days. And he certainly didn't have time for soul searching when they were only three hours and a bit away from a performance.

'I know you're upset, darling,' she said, so close she was very nearly on his lap. She was drenched in the cloying perfume and he knew now what was meant by too much of a good thing. 'But you have to get over it. It's tragic for you but it's not my fault that I fell in love with Paul.'

No. He knew that and he was sorry he had spoken sharply to her but working together was proving to be difficult if not impossible. He had known at the time of their short-lived but boisterous affair that it was insane to mix business with pleasure, but she was very attractive and, for a while, he had genuinely felt a fondness for her, for her sweetness and even for her wide-eyed stupidity. Now her incompetence merely annoyed him. She was useless at the job and it was just as well that she was working her notice before getting shacked up with Paul and moving down south.

'Sorry, Claire,' he said with a slight smile in case she took a huff and walked out right now, leaving them up the stage creek. 'This weather's getting to me. I don't do heatwaves.'

'Don't be miserable,' she said. 'It's gorgeous. We're having a barbecue tonight. Fancy joining us?'

We? Was she referring to the bloody marvellous Paul?

'How can I? I'm working,' he reminded her tartly. He was always working, snatching a few hours off here and there whenever he could, but he had to be on hand for the performance, so that he could do the show report and sort things out if there was an emergency at the last minute.

'All work and no play make a very dull boy,' she said with a smile.

'Do you know a woman called Sazzoni?' he asked, checking in his diary. 'I'm meeting her tomorrow.'

'Sounds foreign.'

'The name does, she doesn't,' he said, remembering the voice. A lovely voice. Middle pitched, easy on the ear. No discernable accent but verging on the posh.

'What does she look like?'

'How would I know? She lives at Penington Bridge. I thought you might know her as it's your neck of the woods? An Alice Sazzoni?'

The name drew no response and he watched, momentarily mesmerized as Claire sashayed out, knowing perfectly well that, if she hadn't left him for Paul, he would have let the whole thing go anyway. So, in a way, she had done him a big favour because he had dreaded being the one to break it off. And now Paul was doing him an even bigger favour by whisking her away.

CHAPTER TEN

The next day was another scorcher and the constant blue skies were becoming a touch boring. Was there to be no let up? Allowing himself plenty of time, mindful of the holiday traffic, which was at its peak just now, Matthew drove out to Penington Bridge. It was a picturesque place, not much more than a big village, full of hanging baskets and big bright tubs of flourishing flowers. He gave up on the one and only car park, which had a blackboard at the entrance chalked FULL, and he had to drive round three times before eventually squeezing his car into a space by the green.

The place was heaving with hot, sweaty bodies, although they were mostly dressed in cool summery clothes. He had his suit on because it was a business meeting and Helen had watched him leave, peering at him over the top of her glasses, giving him the once-over. On the one occasion he had seen her dressed up, he had barely recognized her – a shocking pink ball gown with peculiar sleeves – hair de-frizzed, make-up carefully applied. He preferred the other Helen – Cinders before she met her Prince Charming.

Locking the car and glancing at his watch, he saw he was now ten minutes late. Bugger. It was so unprofessional and he hated that. First impressions. He could hear his mum talking earnestly about how important first impressions were.

They were meeting, at Miss Sazzoni's suggestion, in a tea shop which seemed a bit twee for a business consultation but who was he to argue? He had proposed she come over to the theatre but she had knocked that one on the head, sweetly but firmly. That had not gone down well with him because he was up to here with work and, from past experience, if anything was going to happen, it would sure as hell happen when he wasn't around. He knew Helen would take the brunt if something went seriously wrong but he could not help feeling the weight of his own responsibility as ASM. He had been in competition for his job with older, more experienced candidates and he was aware they had taken a chance with him, that Helen in particular had championed him, so he had something to prove.

Miss Sazzoni? Voice notwithstanding, the name conjured up a certain image. Curly dark hair, rosy cheeks and plumpish, he assumed, and because she worked with children, she would be of the jollying-along variety no doubt. The name was exotic, but she was a dance and drama teacher so maybe it was made up to make her sound like that. The last woman they had on their books as a dance contact had retired, so he hoped that this Sazzoni woman would be her replacement. They needed somebody they could rely on, somebody who knew about schedules and deadlines and somebody who would not panic. Some of the staff, particularly Box Office Shirley, were on the verge of panic the whole time although, looking back on the last year, he saw that it had been very successful and that the Little Gem was more than holding its own amongst similar small theatres.

There were only three streets of any significance in Penington Bridge, but a preponderance of antique shops, climbing gear shops, gift shops and cafés. The Market Tea Room was a double-fronted café with frilly curtains and, opening the door, he saw it was full of the sort of olde worlde charm that for some reason irked him. The sort of place where you had to be on your best behaviour, the sort of place his dad would hate for fear of dropping crumbs, the sort of place old ladies frequented and certainly not the place for a guy like him.

There were little circular tables covered with white cloths, tiny pots of fresh flowers, dark spindle-backed chairs and a highly patterned maroon carpet. There was a striped maroon and cream wallpaper below a wide dado and, above it, a particularly awful shade of pink on the uneven walls. The framed pictures of old Penington Bridge showed how little it had changed. It was gloomy, too, or maybe that was because he had stepped inside out of the bright sunlight.

'Mr Bailey?'

He whirled round and returned the enquiring smile the blonde girl in the corner was giving him. Wrong on all counts then. Not dark-haired, not rosy cheeked and definitely not plumpish. She was sitting down so he couldn't be sure of her height but she had a lean look about her with fine features, but it was the big brown eyes that really did it for him. They were the sort of eyes that could turn a grown man's legs to jelly. Add that to the voice and he was well and truly hooked.

'Have you been waiting long, Miss Sazzoni?' he asked for she had a settled look about her and there was a cup of coffee in front of her. 'Please forgive me. The traffic was bad and I couldn't find a parking space. May I get you another coffee?'

'Thank you.'

He sat down opposite her and they exchanged an awkward smile.

Silence. Say something, Matthew, you clown, he told himself fiercely, even if it's only 'what a lovely day'. The fact was he was a bit taken aback by his reaction and hoped to God he wasn't staring like a lovesick teenager. The last time he had been struck dumb by a girl was when Marilyn Rawley joined their sixth-form group but then she had silenced the other boys too.

'I moved house just the other day,' Miss Sazzoni spoke first, as they waited for the coffee to appear. 'My best clothes are still packed away somewhere,' she added, indicating her casual get-up with a rueful smile. 'Otherwise I would have dressed up.'

'Not at all. You look fine,' he said, still hot under his collar and grateful for the small smile she gave him.

He went on to explain how many children they would require for the production plus the back-ups and she took notes.

Could she handle this?

She could.

Did she know of a hall they might hire?

She did. She would make enquiries and get back to him but she was sure there would be no problem.

'Fine.' He gave her an outline of the proposed future programme, indicating where her help might be needed and she made the appropriate notes. She had lovely hands, long slim fingers, no rings but a narrow silver bracelet nestled comfortably round her slender wrist. Right-handed. No polish on her nails but they were cared for and he liked that. A fresh floral scent was drifting his way, barely discernible but there none the less and he liked that too, wanting to get closer, so that he could lift up her lovely fair hair and plant a tiny kiss by her ear.

'Anything else, Mr Bailey?'

'What?' He caught her amused glance, pulled himself together. This was going well, too well, and after the fiasco with Claire and her rambling incompetence, it was refreshing to be dealing with somebody who looked as if she knew what she was doing. If she needed any help, any more information, he told her to call him at the theatre, handing her his business card.

'Leave it with me,' she said, tucking the card away into a small, cream, envelope-type bag, the sort Princess Diana was fond of. Miss Sazzoni, it would seem, travelled light.

'Good.' He settled back in his chair, glancing across the room as a bunch of American visitors loudly took their seats before requesting pots of English tea and crumpets.

They shared a smile, business concluded.

'Were you an actor?' she asked as they found themselves dallying over the last of the coffee. Matthew wanted to prolong this, wanted to ask her out socially but it was a bit soon and he worried that she might snub him. His chat-up lines were at a minimum and always

68

sounded bloody corny.

'Never,' he said. 'Well, I was in school productions, but I think I knew then it wasn't for me.'

'I wanted to be a dancer,' she said quietly. 'I trained in ballet. I had an audition for the Royal Ballet School, which I was told was an honour in itself but it came to nothing. My sole professional roles were in a couple of musicals in Manchester. I was in the chorus. *Carousel* and *Oklahoma*.'

'They're great musicals,' he said, glancing at her and seeing the disappointment that she was trying her best to hide. 'Didn't it work out then?'

'No. Various reasons. I am rather tall but I think I could have got round that if I had persevered. Perhaps I wasn't hungry enough. Who knows? I did go to an audition for a West End show and I had great hopes for that but. . . .' She shrugged. 'Nothing doing. So I did the next best thing. I did a course in speech and drama and turned to teaching.'

'Lucky for me you did,' he said, anxious to see her smile again. 'Maybe you're best out of it. I've seen what happens behind the scenes. All the bitching. And I'm talking about the men here. All that 'darling' stuff is complete crap . . . sorry, but it is. They're all jealous as hell of each other. Give me admin anytime. It gets the adrenalin going in exactly the same way. There are still deadlines to meet and so on. It's no picnic.'

'I'm sure it's not. Your theatre's got a really good reputation, hasn't it? Not that I've actually been myself.' She grimaced. 'Sorry, I shouldn't say that. I did look at the summer programme but—'

'A bit top heavy,' he conceded, glad she'd pointed out what he had been worrying about. 'We need some comedy to lighten things up. We've got two comedy plays coming up in autumn.'

Walking back to his car, he sensed she wanted to say something but she waited until they were at the car before she said it.

'I know it's very cheeky of me as we've only just met but could I possibly ask a favour?'

'Shoot,' he said cheerfully, thinking that he might well lie down in the middle of the street if she so desired.

'It's the light fitting in my dining-room,' she said. 'I can't work out how to make it stay up. It's one of those things that fit snugly to the ceiling and it's fallen on my head three times already when I've tried. Could you possibly have a look at it? I would ask one of my neighbours but I don't want to start off by looking as if I'm a complete incompetent.' She blushed. 'Sorry. It's OK if you're dashing off but I'm only just round the corner.'

You bet.

'Pity you couldn't ask my dad,' he told her as he finally and not without some considerable effort got the light in place. She could not find her set of steps so he was standing precariously, shoes off, on what was a very nice dining chair. 'He can do this sort of thing standing on his head. He's a marvel round the house. And still my mum complains because he's not much of a gardener.'

'It's the opposite with my parents,' she said. 'Have you time for another cup of coffee?'

He was swimming with coffee, did not even much like coffee, but he grabbed the opportunity to chat a while longer, watching as she rummaged in several cupboards in the kitchen before she found the cups she was looking for. Just for a moment, he thought of telling her about Claire and the sorry episode with the stage china cups but decided not to, as it might look as if he was being critical of a colleague.

'My mum's the gardener in our family and you should see her garden,' Alice went on. 'She does it all herself and it is beautiful. As for my dad – he's not very good at do-it-yourself but mum just calls people in anyway.'

'I like your name,' he said, perching on a high stool at the narrow bench. 'Is it Italian?'

'Oh yes. You know Sazzoni delicatessens?'

'I'm not good with shops,' he admitted. 'But I think I've heard of them.'

'My father owns them,' she said. 'We have Italian connections from way back, but to be honest, I don't feel terribly Italian. My dad does even though he was born in England and had an English mother. We go back from time to time and I speak the language reasonably well, although I wouldn't say I was bilingual. Did you know that it's not as easy as it sounds to make a child bilingual?'

'No I didn't. My parents are both Lancastrians so the question's never arisen,' he said with a grin.

'Last year my parents bought a villa in Italy. It's lovely. It overlooks Lake Como.'

'Very nice,' he muttered, feeling suddenly inadequate.

'So that's him, my dad. That's what he does. What does your father do?' The question hung in the air. It was nothing to do with her what his father did but the moment's irritation passed as he saw that she had not meant to be intrusive but was simply curious to know more about him and his family. He must stop being so sensitive.

'He's a carpet fitter by trade,' he said, looking carefully at her. 'He's very good at it. And he does all sorts of odd jobs too. He's a great bloke.'

She nodded and smiled, and he felt ashamed that he should feel ashamed. It was true. His dad was a great bloke and it was his dad he had to thank for all the encouragement over the years. Given the right opportunities, his dad could have made it to higher things than mere carpet fitting but would he necessarily have wanted that? It seemed to Matthew that, provided you were happy with your lot and didn't start getting dissatisfied with it then it led to a stress-free existence, and his dad was the most laid-back guy he knew.

Alice moved with the grace of a dancer and he just knew as he watched her that he would be doing this – watching her – for a whole lot of years to come. If there was such a thing as love at first sight then that had happened to him when he walked into the Market Tea Room. Maybe he would tell her that someday.

'Must get on,' she said at last, clearing away the cups. 'Sorry to have delayed you and thanks for putting the light up.'

'Give me a call if you're stuck again. I'm not too far away. I have a flat—' He did not want to call it a bedsit. 'A flat in Kirkley.'

'I like Kirkley. It's a good little market town, isn't it? And very convenient for the theatre.'

'Yes, it's convenient,' he said, knowing as he looked round here that he could never take her there. He didn't say it but he wondered quite how she had afforded this. It was a prime location very close to the centre of Penington Bridge, which was one of the most sought after places in this area. It must have cost a bomb. 'I only have a bedsit,' he said, deciding it was best to be up front about it. 'I hope to get a bigger place sometime but it's the cost.'

'House prices are ridiculous,' she agreed. 'I've had a bit of help with this. Dad was keen for me to get my foot on the rung.'

He got the picture. Her family had money and that could be a serious stumbling block. He might very well be out of his depth with her. He had always steered clear of girls whom he considered to be out of his league. Daft really, but something of his dad was stuck inside, this fear of stepping over the threshold and trying to be what you were not. Auntie Margaret was much the same, although it was her shyness that did for her. His mum wasn't like that. She wasn't afraid of what his dad nervously called 'mixing'.

'Will you be at the *Oliver* audition?'

'I can be,' he said, determined that he would find some reason to be there.

'See you there then,' Alice said, opening the door and letting in the sounds and smells of the hot sunny day. 'I won't let you down, Mr Bailey.'

'For goodness sake, call me Matthew,' he said quickly. 'Or Matt. Whichever.'

'I like Matthew better,' she said at once. 'And I'm Alice. Just Alice.'

'Just Alice it is,' he repeated, hearing the word roll off his tongue and loving it.

He just had time to nip back to his flat. He needed a quick shower and a change of clothes for this evening. It was the penultimate performance of a play by a new playwright and it was getting good reviews.

His flat was over a florist's but there was a side entrance he used so he never went through the shop. He spent so little time up there that it showed in the general air of neglect. He did his best but he couldn't keep on top of the cleaning and, looking round, he knew his mum would have a fit if she was to see it now. When he had a minute, he would get the Hoover out and give it a going over.

It was just somewhere to doss down. He never cooked. Somebody, a friend of the woman who ran the florist's, did his laundry as there was no washing machine here and it was worth his while to deliver a bag of dirty washing to her and get it back clean a couple of days later.

His flat was a mess and, after seeing what Alice had achieved in just one day, he frowned as he entered. He had never been tidy and he blamed this mess on the fact that there was precious little storage, so his things had to sit either on the floor or at the bottom of a deep basket.

Looking round with fresh eyes, he realized he could never entertain here. Claire had been here but then she was as bad as he was if her own place was anything to go by. Two messy beings together had no hope and in his childhood home, it was always his mum who tidied up after his dad.

He picked up some fish and chips from the chippy down the road and opened a tin of peaches and a tin of custard for dessert. Gourmet meals he did not do but then neither did his mum. She never could be bothered much with cooking and the meals he most remembered from his youth had been made by his grandma. Guiltily, he wondered how she was for he hadn't been to visit her since she had moved to the nursing home. He would not say that they got on that well but then she was an awkward customer and didn't really get on with anybody. For reasons not obvious to him, she did not consider him to be good grandson material and he knew he had disappointed her. She had once told him in that plain-spoken way of hers that she had always wanted a granddaughter, looking at him accusingly as if it was his fault he was a boy. He had told Auntie Margaret about that, not his mum, and she had laughed and said he hadn't to mind because that was what his grandma was like and she didn't mean it.

'People often say things they don't mean, deep down,' she had said, looking at him with that nice smile of hers but, thank God, stopping short of giving him a cuddle and ruffling his hair as she used to.

When the time came and come it would, he wondered what Alice would make of them all, his grandma, his auntie and his mum and dad.

And, perhaps more importantly, what would they make of Alice?

CHAPTER ELEVEN

Josie's schedule for Christmas Day was in tatters because she had overslept. She had overslept because it had taken her ages to get off last night because her mind had been churning with thoughts of Jack Sazzoni.

It was incredible. She had known even before Matthew had uttered the name. She had known as soon she shook hands with the girl, who was the spit of her mother Valerie. She might well have fainted on the spot but she was made of sterner stuff than that. She was rocked, true, but she did not have the time to ponder on it, not then, because she had so much on her mind, mainly to do with that nerve centre of Christmas: the kitchen. It was just an eating marathon from start to finish. Cooked breakfast to start then the big dinner then the buffet tea and the leftovers would be piling up by then.

'Switch the television off. They've arrived,' she had told Ray the evening before as soon as she heard the car. He had done so, grumbling, but knowing that it stayed off when visitors were in the house. And, although Matthew did not count as a visitor, Alice certainly did. She did not want Alice to think that they spent their days glued to the damned television, even though, when he wasn't laying carpets, that was precisely what Ray did.

After the introduction, numb from the news, she acted thereafter on automatic pilot. Making them feel at home, providing hot drinks, chatting about everything and nothing, working out almost immediately that Matthew thought the world of this girl. Ray did his best, even though he was a bit shy, and she thought that, all in all, she had managed tolerably well to keep the conversation going. Getting a bit desperate at one point, she had even suggested a board game, and was just about to send Ray off into the loft to locate the old sets of this and that but they had declined, tired from the drive. The weather had been horrible, snow when they set off and now this rain, which looked like it was set in for the night.

Christmas Eve. She remembered the excitement of it when she was little. Sometimes, the best times, her dad was on duty over Christmas and they never saw him but, other times, he was around and, although she never remembered him losing his temper over Christmas, it made for a tension that was not there in his absence.

Tonight, this Christmas Eve, she listened for what seemed hours to the rain pattering for all it was worth against the bedroom window. The damned fairy lights outside the window did not help, flickering on and off all night long. Oh heavens, what a thing to happen. She still could not believe it. Lying in bed beside Ray who was off as soon as his head hit the pillow, she thought about the implications. Memories whirled in a heady mix, back and forth, and as always Jack was there.

'Jack Sazzoni's got his eye on you,' Lynn said with a giggle as they waited to be asked to dance. Some people were already on the floor and she and Lynn were doing their best to look as if they couldn't give a bird's feather whether they danced or not. 'I told you he was keen. No, don't look.'

'I'm not looking,' Josie said. She had done the flirting bit already when she had seen him with his friends in the coffee bar they all frequented and she was aware she had caught his attention. Now she had to play it cool for what happened next was entirely up to him. There was a thin dividing line between gently flirting and being thought common.

'These shoes are killing me,' she said, 'My toes are all squashed.'

'So are mine. He's really heavy-footed, that Mick. He kept saying sorry but it's too late then, isn't it? My feet are black and blue.'

'Jack Sazzoni's a good dancer,' she said, for that, in a dance hall full of Felstonian boys like Mick, was something of a rarity. 'I wouldn't mind a dance with him.'

'He's had a few dances already, one with that Penny and one with Valerie whatshername, but he might be saving you for the last waltz,' Lynn said wistfully. Josie gave her a look. Lynn was like this. Full of impossible flights of fancy. She was also having trouble with her hair. Poor Lynn. She had spent all night with rollers in to perfect her 'flick-up' style and it had looked great when they set off but it had drooped by the time they reached the end of Lynn's street and she was not best pleased.

'Will you be going home with Mick if he asks you?'

'Might do. And then you can go home with Jack if he asks you.'

'He's not taking me home,' Josie said. 'He could only take me as far as the football ground. If my dad saw him. . . .'

They had never been alone, the two of them, always seeing each other at a respectful distance in the presence of their friends. They thought they were a touch above, that lot he went round with, but Josie was not having any of that. She thought herself every bit as good as them, even though she wouldn't be keen to broadcast in their company that she lived in Riverside. People were so quick to make generalizations, often didn't give you a chance, labelled you straight off. It got on her wick, that sort of thing.

She tried not to look Jack's way because that was such a give-away, but then, as the band returned for the second half of its performance, starting with some upbeat stuff before they switched to their smoochy late-night mood, she saw him pushing his way through the crowd towards her and there he was, standing there in front of her. He was wearing a snappy suit and she was glad now that she was wearing her favourite dress, a good one to twist in, red with its own net petticoat that showed as you danced. She'd done her eyes on the sly over at Lynn's before they arrived and, as he stood there smiling, she gave him the full benefit of her extra lush, super-long lashes.

'You dancing?' was the normal way to do it in Felston, but he asked her properly, holding out his hand as he did so and she warmed instantly to that, smiling and allowing him to draw her gently on to the floor. She caught Lynn's raised eyebrows but ignored her.

And then, as the music soared, she was pulled into his arms.

And that really was that.

'Why didn't you tell me she was Jack Sazzoni's daughter?' Josie hissed, drawing Matthew into the kitchen, ostensibly to help her bring the coffee through. 'Talk about knocking the wind out of my sails. You could have said her name was Sazzoni. Why all the mystery?'

'There is no mystery. I thought I had mentioned it and you never asked what her surname was. I didn't think it would matter. How was I to know you knew her dad from way back?' he replied with a puzzled smile, not understanding the significance of all this. 'I knew her family came from Felston originally but it never occurred to me that you might have met him. It's a big town. It didn't seem likely.'

'Why not? Why shouldn't I have met him?' she asked aggressively. 'Was I not good enough for him? Is that what you mean?'

'No, mum. But she did tell me where they used to live and I didn't think you would know anybody from that side of town,' he said.

'The posh side,' she said, unable to keep the bitterness from her voice.

He looked squarely at her. 'Let's be honest. It doesn't matter to me but people like grandma – and dad . . .' he added with a grimace. 'You know what they're like. Do you know what inverse snobbery is?'

'Of course I do. It's what those two suffer from. I could knock their heads together. Your dad in particular has this inferiority complex. It gets my goat, I keep telling him he's every bit as good as the next man.'

'Exactly. Better than most. What if Alice comes from money? What does it matter? She can't help it Anyway . . .' he stopped as he saw her face. 'Sorry, but how was I to know you'd had a fling with her dad? It's just a coincidence, that's all.'

'It's an awful coincidence and we didn't have a fling. You ask your Auntie Margaret. She'll tell you. I hate that word, fling,' Josie muttered, placing warm mince pies on a plate and giving them a quick dusting with icing sugar. She poured coffee, the real stuff, from the percolator into a pretty coffee pot that got used about twice a year, and got out the little matching coffee cups that were like doll's china and held about one gulpful.

'What's the matter, Mum?' Matthew's voice was gentle, still not understanding. 'I'm sorry if this has upset you. It's not going to be a problem, is it?'

'It could be. We didn't part on the best of terms if you must know, if it's any of your business,' she went on, furious with him for doing this to her. She was also furious with herself for reacting like this. Talk about making a mountain out of a molehill. Jack Sazzoni would have relegated her to the back of his mind and, by rights, she ought to have done the same. She hadn't a clue why he still lurked there. She had only started to go out with Jack originally because she knew full well her mum would have kittens about it. It was Lynn who had dared her to make a play for him and she *had* done, trying to do it with some degree of subtlety – as subtle as a teenager could be anyway – and it had worked. It had finally worked that night at Bristles. She was like that in her teens, a bit bolshie, maybe she still was. Margaret had tried to warn her off but when did a seventeen-year-old take any notice of her much older sister – twenty years older, in fact – who had never landed a man herself? She knew it wasn't Matthew's fault that Alice was Jack's daughter and it wasn't the girl's fault either, but that didn't make it any easier. This situation, as she saw it, had the potential for one huge blow-out.

'He was my first proper boyfriend,' she said, popping the bag of icing sugar back in the cupboard and avoiding her son's eye.

'Was he?' Matthew smiled but she could tell he was a touch embarrassed.

'Yes, well, we went out together for about six months and then I finished with him. And that's all there is to it.'

'I see. Why did you dump him?'

'We weren't suited and I'd met your dad,' she said. 'And that's all I'm saying. That's all you need to know and that's all you're getting to know.'

'Like me and Claire, I suppose,' he said with a grin. 'She dumped me and then I met Alice so she did me a good turn.'

'Yes. That's how it is.'

'So you've no need to worry about it, Mum. It happens all the time. You'll probably laugh about it when you do meet him.'

'Am I likely to?' she asked sharply. 'Are you two serious?'

He shrugged but smiled anyway and it was as good an answer as any.

'I don't suppose I'll recognize him these days and he won't remember me either.' She fussed with the cups and the little cream jug, a sudden sharp vision of Jack – aged twenty – appearing. 'Does Alice take sugar?'

'No.'

'We're right then. I've sugared your dad's already.' She picked up the tray, put it down again. 'Look, Matthew, the fact is her dad really gets up your dad's nose. God knows what will happen when they get together again. They were at each other's throats. I know you can't imagine it, not your dad, but he used to have a temper once he got going. If something really riled him that is.'

'Temper? You're joking. It's a long time ago,' Matthew said, nicking one of the mince pies. 'I hope you're not going to hold it against Alice,' he added, a dangerous glint in his eye that told her she would get nowhere if she did. It also told her, and this gave her a jolt, that she was no longer the number one lady in his life. Alice had already stepped into that role and that was how it should be.

'I wouldn't dream of it,' she said, trying to tell herself to calm down. It wasn't the end of the world and Matthew was right. It was a long time ago.

CHAPTER TWELVE

Margaret, as she so often did, was fussing round, helping her get ready. She never went out herself, not to dances anyway, and she took pride in helping Josie make the best of herself.

She stood there, big for a girl, dark-haired and solidly built like their dad, taking out Josie's rollers and handing her the hairpins one by one and, not before time, Josie stuck the last of them into the French pleat, very nearly piercing her head in the process and grimacing. A final touch up with the tail of the comb and there she had it, a fantastic beehive. She reached for the extra-hold cheap hair-spray and lavishly applied it.

They had the radio on and, from its place on the window ledge, the only place where they could get decent reception, Chubby Checker's 'Let's Twist Again' blared out, still in the charts after goodness knows how many weeks. It was too fast a song to be listening to when you were doing something as important as putting the finishing touches to your hair.

'You look smashing, love,' Margaret said, squeezing her shoulders and smiling. 'Go easy on the make-up. You know what he's like.'

Through the mirror they exchanged a sisterly look. They both knew what *he* was like. She had no idea what her dad had done when he was in the police force but she wouldn't have liked to be a criminal and have him facing her. He was a brute and Josie knew their mum put up with the occasional, what she called, 'lashing out' for one reason only. She was terrified of being 'shamed'. Being shamed as a family was the very worst thing that could happen. You could be knocked about rotten, as she often was, you could watch him knock your kids about, you could defend him and make excuses for him but you could never ever be shamed in other people's eyes.

They were never to breathe a word outside the house. And they never did. Bruises could always be explained away. For some reason, Margaret bore the brunt of it. 'Our Margaret's accident prone,' her mother would often say with a sad shake of her head. 'She can trip over a pin, that girl.'

Josie felt guilty to be going out enjoying herself, as she would certainly do, and leaving poor Margaret here at home. But Margaret brought it on herself, and sometimes, uncharitably, Josie wondered if she deliberately acted the martyr. There was no need for Margaret to act like she was some sort of Cinderella. She had a job and some money and she could go out and enjoy herself as well, except it wasn't so easy now she was in her thirties and most of her friends were married ladies. She didn't know why Margaret had taken the decision to put a stop to all thoughts of finding a man and getting married and, more importantly, moving out of here. That wasn't an option, Margaret had told her, for she wouldn't leave Josie here on her own with them.

The general public assumption about Margaret was that she had lost a young man in the war, lost in Singapore, and never got over him. Somehow, that was acceptable. That meant you were looked on with sympathy, understanding. Josie suspected there had never been a young man, that he was just a figment of Margaret's romantic imagination, but that was by the by. Margaret had him in her head and, in an odd way, had almost come to believe he had existed. She had once found a photograph in a drawer in Margaret's bedroom, a photograph of a man she did not know.

'Who is it?' she had asked but she never got a proper answer.

'It's him. Put it back,' Margaret would reply and that was the end of it.

Margaret was plain with slightly bulbous eyes, not at all pretty, but that should be no obstacle. She was nice and thoughtful and had a lovely way with kids. The truth was Margaret had just stopped trying. She was thirty-seven now, which seemed elderly to Josie but she was still young enough to have a baby if she got married and she would be such a lovely mum. She was a nurse, not fully trained, but she worked at the psychiatric hospital just out of town, going there every day on the bus. Josie did not enquire what went on there but she could not help thinking that it did Margaret no good to be work-ing with those sorts of people. She had once said as much but, unusually, Margaret had flared up at that and told her they were lovely folks and they couldn't help it if their minds had got a bit out of skelter. Suitably chastened, not often told off by her sister, Josie had never referred to it again.

Margaret was old enough to be her mum and in many ways, Josie thought more of her than she did their mum. Her mum had got set in her ways, used to having just the one daughter and then she had come along unexpectedly when her mum had turned forty. Margaret had apparently been thrilled to bits but she wasn't sure what her mum's reaction had been. But she could guess.

Coming into the bedroom without knocking – well, it was her mother's room after all, the only one with a decent sized dressing table, her mum waddled over to the window and switched off the radio, coughing and waving the offending whiff of hairspray away as she came over to them.

'Powerful stuff that hair lacquer,' she said. 'It can't do your hair any good. It looks better loose if you ask me. It puts a good two years on you like that. Unless that's the intention?' she asked sharply.

It was, but she had no *intention* of telling her mother that. 'Everybody wears their hair up for the dance,' she said. 'It keeps it neat. And it shows off your earrings.'

She only had three pairs of her own, clip-ons because she hadn't had her ears pierced yet and she had chosen the sparkly ones tonight, the ones that looked like diamonds. At the end of the night, they left ridges in her ears and hurt like mad when she unclipped them, but it was worth a bit of discomfort for the effect.

Her mum sniffed. She was good at disapproving sniffs. 'If you've any thoughts, young lady, of getting serious about Jack Sazzoni, you can forget it,' she said. 'Your dad won't have it that's for sure. Tell her, our Margaret.'

Margaret frowned. 'She knows what's what, Mum.'

'I'm not serious,' Josie said, catching Margaret's warning glance in the mirror. 'I'm only seventeen.'

'I was serious about your dad at seventeen, more's the pity,' Hetty said, folding her arms below her ample bosom. 'And girls have babies at seventeen so just you watch it. If you bring shame on us, the Lord help me, I'll swing for you. Take heed of Margaret. She's always been a good girl.'

She saw the look her mother and Margaret exchanged in the mirror. She could never fathom why her mother could take such a nasty turn with Margaret from time to time because Margaret was not far short of a saint.

'Margaret never does anything wrong and it's not right that he takes it out on her,' Josie said, seeing her mum's expression tighten and doing what she knew was best. Shutting up.

The happy moment between the two sisters was lost now and Josie eyed her mother warily through the mirror, watching as she picked up the new shoes she had bought for tonight, pale blue pointy-toed shoes with tiny Louis heels. She turned them over noting the price label but making no comment; Josie had a job now at the town hall and was earning money although, by the time she had given her mum something for her 'keep', she didn't have a lot left. The shoes were lower-heeled than usual but that was for Jack's benefit. He was not a lot taller than she was and she liked him to be able to look down at her as they danced. Margaret had given her something towards them but she would not blab about that. Margaret liked her to look nice and it gave her pleasure to help out.

Josie continued to put on her make-up, her hand shaking a little under her mother's steady gaze. She didn't know what her mum meant about being serious. She liked Jack, goodness knows, and he was good fun and perhaps more importantly all the other girls were after him. It was the Italian connection, of course, that made him interesting. All the other boys, Felstonians to the very core, were so hopeless when it came to compliments, but Jack was wonderful, slipping effortlessly into Italian and murmuring soft words. She hadn't a clue what he was actually saying, but she could hazard a guess by the look in his eyes and the Italian language was so beautiful, so musical. Jack was so gentle, not afraid to be courteous. He treated her well, like china, putting his hand in the small of her back to guide her along, helping her to her feet. . . little things like that, little things that made her feel good, like a lady.

'That's more than enough,' her mother said, putting her hand on Josie's shoulder but, unlike Margaret's, her touch was like a clamp. 'Your eyes don't need make-up. And go easy on that scent Your dad's waiting downstairs to check you before you go out and you know what he's like.'

Josie put the tiny bottle of Coty L'Aimant in her bag. She would do her eyes later, round at her friend's, but she must remember to wipe it all off before she came home. Her dad usually stayed up until she got back and, like the policeman he had once been, he could spot illicitly-applied eye shadow and sooty layers of mascara from the depths of his armchair even without his glasses on. She had no finer feelings for him, how could she? She looked at her friends' dads with wonder, saw how proud some of them were of their daughters and that was hard. What had she done to deserve this? What had Margaret done? Had he wanted sons? Was that it? Somewhere, deep in the back of her mind, there was a memory of a big man calling her name, lifting her off her feet and twirling her round and round and she was all of a giggle. . . . What had happened? What had gone wrong?

'So, are you meeting him tonight then?' her mum asked, handing her the little boxy handbag.

'Meeting who?'

'Who do you think? That Jack Sazzoni and don't try to be clever with me, Josie Pritchard,' her mum said, lowering her voice. 'Because if you are then think on to what I've told you. It won't do. It can't come to anything. If it carries on, it'll only end in tears. Your dad won't have no truck with foreigners. And that's a fact.'

'Jack's not a foreigner,' Margaret flushed but still spoke up for her. 'He's as English as we are. He was born here. His mother was born here.'

'That's as maybe. He's got Italian roots and you can't shake your roots off. I knew his father Lorenzo and he was as Italian as they come. His accent was terrible. When I say I knew him . . .' her mum seemed flustered suddenly, 'I knew *of* him and I did see him the once. It was during the war and they weren't liked, him and his family. They weren't to be trusted. There was a lot of whispers and it all got a bit nasty and then the men in the family ended up being arrested.'

'What for?'

'What do you think for? The Italians were enemy aliens that's why,' her mother said. 'You have no idea what it was like during the war. Has she, Margaret?'

'She wasn't born until it was very nearly over, Mum, how can she know?'

'Where did they go?' Josie asked, slipping one of her earrings in and admiring it, 'when they were arrested.'

'I don't know and I can't say I cared either. Isle of Man I think. After the war, he came back, large as life, no worse for wear, and that business of his blossomed. It didn't seem fair. He had a big opinion of himself, although he ended up big and fat.' She nodded with satisfaction. 'That's what happens to Italian men and women. They start off lovely but they go off. That English girl he married thought she was better than anybody else. She had to turn for him as well. They won't have it any other way, them Catholics. And that's another reason why you're not to get yourself caught up with him.'

She was off. Josie sighed, caught Margaret's sigh, too, but luckily their mum did not. Her mother was an out and out bigot and there was no talking sense into her because she was too far gone and too set in her ways.

'Anyway, you haven't answered me.' Her mother gave her a shrewd glance. 'Are you meeting him?'

'I'm going out to Bristles with Lynn Mason,' Josie said, to shut her up, pleading with Margaret through the mirror not to say anything, even though she knew she would not. Margaret was loyal to the point of insanity. The things Margaret had done to protect her made her feel ashamed. Margaret had taken punishment after punishment from dad to save her skin. If anything went wrong, she always pushed Josie aside and shouldered the blame. It wasn't fair. Margaret wasn't a child any more and she should be standing up to him. They both should.

What she didn't tell her mum was that, after she had called on Lynn, the two of them were meeting up with Jack and a lad whom Lynn was sweet on called Mick. Before they went dancing, they were going out for a quick drink and she and Lynn would probably opt for a Babycham. After that, they would be having a meal in town and, having starved herself all day, she was looking forward to the prawn cocktail and mixed grill she would choose but wished it was just the two of them, her and Jack, because Lynn was very awkward with boys and, as well as that, she had no style and no conversation of interest. She was good with figures, the paper kind, and had a job in an insurance company, but no idea when it came to making the best of her own shape. Very few girls were perfect but you had to play to your good points. Josie knew that. Hadn't she read that sort of thing time and again in her women's magazines? For instance, she had short legs, which did her no favours but an enviable bosom which did.

She sighed again, stepping into the new shoes, taking a last look at her reflection in the long mirror in her mum and dad's bedroom. She had worn the dress before but Jack had never seen it. It was crimplene, straight, sleeveless, blue, a lovely colour that matched her eyes. Jack would notice. He always noticed little things like that and always offered a little compliment. Round here, you practically had to call up the firing squad and have a lad up against the wall before he could manage to utter a compliment. They considered it soft.

'Ray Bailey's mum says as how he's fixed on you,' her mum said, her voice taking on a wheedling note.

'Does she now?'

'She does and don't take that tone. He's a good lad is Ray. He has a good steady job. He'll look after you, will Ray.'

And he'll never hurt you. But she didn't say that.

'He's a big dope,' Josie said, fastening her bracelets. 'He was a big dope at five and he hasn't changed.'

'He has changed.' Her mother's indignation was comical. 'Ask your sister. Margaret likes him well enough.'

'He's a nice enough lad,' Margaret confirmed. 'But he should speak up for himself. That's what I think anyway.'

Hetty's eyes flashed with annoyance. 'You don't know anything, our Margaret. When you're married with a family then I might take some notice of what *you* have to say.'

They both ignored that. Josie was not getting into a conversation about Ray Bailey, big lump that he was. Imagine having to get his mum to speak out for him. Margaret was right. If he hadn't the guts to ask her out himself then he could lump it. Lynn had a fancy for him. Maybe they'd get together?

'Do you like this colour on me?' she asked, seeing her mum's critical eyes on her.

'It's all right,' her mum said abruptly. 'Could be worse.'

And that was as far as the praise went.

It was left to Margaret to give her a little kiss and tell her, her own eyes shining, that she looked very nice.

CHAPTER THIRTEEN

Margaret went back home after the Christmas buffet tea, saying she had to check on Percy, her blue budgerigar. She thought the world of that bird who seemed to rule the roost at that. Percy of Percy Street, it appeared, did not like to be left alone too long and it seemed a shame on Christmas Day. Anyway, she'd bought him a new little toy and she wanted to see how he liked it. And she had her knitting to finish. She was on the last sleeve and then she could get it stitched up.

Josie had glanced at Ray, saw his deadpan expression, and had to stop herself from laughing, but this was her sister and she was deadly serious.

'I'll get your coat then, Margaret,' she said, retrieving it from the peg in the hall. It was her warm winter coat, rust-coloured with a belt, quite nice, but Margaret wore it with clumpy shoes and a pull-on knitted hat that wouldn't have looked out of place on a teapot. At sixty-five, her face was unlined as yet, eyes clear and in some ways she looked better now than she had for a long time. Dad dying and her mother being shipped off to the nursing home, resulting in her being left in peace at last, had worked wonders. She had done her duty by their mother, looked after her for as long as was humanly possible before it became just too much.

'Jack Sazzoni's girl, eh?' Margaret said, as she slipped her coat on. 'Heck, Josie, that could be awkward for you.'

'It will only be awkward if our Matthew's serious about her,' Josie said. 'You know what they're like these days. It could all blow over.'

'I don't think so.' Margaret spoke as if she was an authority on such matters, clamping her hat on her head, covering her greying curls, before pulling on matching wool mittens. She enjoyed her knitting, always had something on the go. 'If I go now, I'll catch that old film I want to watch. And thanks for the dinner, love. It was very nice. That turkey was a treat. Very moist.'

'It wasn't bad, was it?' Josie said, pleased she'd said that because she'd worried herself sick over the blessed bird. How she'd managed to get herself back on track this morning she would never know, but Ray had for once turned up trumps and succeeded in not making too much of a mess of the minor kitchen tasks she set him. She and Margaret gave each other a little hug, saying that they'd see each other tomorrow when they went to see mother. Margaret never wore perfume or make-up, smelt instead of soap and Vosene shampoo.

'Ray, love, she's ready for off,' she called and he came downstairs, his hat from his cracker still on, shrugging into his best overcoat for, after all, it was Christmas. Josie pulled the tissue hat off his head before shoving the pair of them off into the dark night. 'Watch your step,' she called after them, for it was a lot colder and the path was already icing over. Closing the door on them, she could hear Ray starting up a conversation, not that he would get far because Margaret never said much. Somebody had once asked her why she was so quiet and she had remarked, quite tartly for once, that when she had something to say, she would say it.

Ray would walk Margaret home because it was dark and he didn't like her being out on her own in the dark. The damned budgie was just an excuse, Josie knew that, but she didn't argue. Margaret led her own life. She had not made many changes to the little house they had grown up in, although Ray had redecorated it for her from top to bottom and had got her some end of rolls of carpet that he fitted in the back sitting room and the front room that Margaret kept just for show.

'She's a lovely lady, your sister,' Alice said as the door closed on them. 'She was telling me she's retired now but she used to do nursing. I admire people who do that.'

'She's all right, is Margaret,' Josie said, playing it down. If she told her the whole story, Alice would have a blue fit but then you never understood about domestic abuse unless you'd suffered it yourself. She had kept it quiet as her mum wanted. To be honest, she had never been tempted to tell anybody. She did not want people to know. She hadn't even told Ray who would have been astonished because he and dad had always got on quite well together, and he'd looked up to him on account of his getting the medal. The medal sat in a drawer upstairs and she never looked at it. You couldn't get away from the fact that her father had done it, rescued that child from a blazing house with no thoughts of his own safety. It had left him with health problems, for the smoke had got on his chest and that all contributed to his death and so the medal, like it or not, had to stay.

She'd been a bit funny about leaving Matthew with his granddad when he was little but she needn't have worried. Her father was like Jekyll and Hyde. He was kindness itself to the little lad and, because a bond had developed between them, she'd never ever say anything to Matthew about it. Some illusions were best kept intact.

The honest truth was that she had been glad when he died and never felt an ounce of sympathy during his short final illness. He'd never bent to make amends either. If he had, if he'd begged forgiveness at the last, she didn't honestly know what she would have done.

Alice, to her credit, seemed embarrassed to talk about *her* father and the undoubted success he had achieved. The Sazzonis, as Josie was well aware, had gone from strength to strength. There was a branch of their deli in Felston High Street but she never went in, not because she was frightened she might meet Jack because she knew he had moved away long since, but because it was just too pricey and Ray didn't care for fancy stuff, very much a pea and pie man. He liked plain boiled ham, not the fancy Italian cooked meats that Sazzoni & Son stocked, together with so many different kinds of pasta. It would never catch on, that Mediterranean cooking, that olive oil and so on.

Alice had eaten everything put in front of her and that pleased Josie who could not abide faddy eaters. In fact, she was not spoilt in the least and, in any other circumstances, she would have been thrilled that Matthew had picked such a nice uncomplicated girl. She wasn't afraid to muck in with the chores either, which was another point in her favour. One of his previous girlfriends, a girl called Claire whom he had brought home the once, had just sat there and been content to be waited on hand and foot. A real giggler with nothing between her ears and, although Ray had taken to her for obvious reasons, she was glad that it hadn't lasted. There had to be something other than sex in a relationship for it to last, although try telling that to hot-blooded youngsters.

Alice was tall and slender and had the most beautiful corn-coloured hair that wouldn't need any help for a while to come. She got all that, her shape and colouring from her mother. She had her fathers deep brown eyes and his way of talking with her hands. Tie her hands behind her back and she would be silent as the grave. Ray was taken with her, she could tell that, although it would take a long time for him to thaw out, to get over his nervousness at meeting a stranger, a young lady at that, who spoke nicely and had a classy look about her. He tried to cover up his nerves by striking up a conversation about his blasted carpets which was about as boring as you could get, and eventually she had to silence him rather abruptly to put an end to it. Who the hell wanted to know about the merits of different types of carpet? Although Alice had gallantly put on a show of interest.

Margaret had not been a lot of help either, managing about ten words in total, but then she was shy in company and Josie could see, rather to her irritation, that she was overawed by Alice. What was wrong with her family?

When Ray got back, Alice offered to help with the washing-up that was piled any old how on the worktop and, to Josie's surprise, Ray promptly escorted her – there was no other word for it – into the kitchen. At least the kitchen would not disappoint. Ray had just put a new one in, a fitted one, all bought in from IKEA, wood effect and very nice. Ray would be hard pressed to know where the washing-up liquid was but he would find it soon enough.

'Your dad likes her,' she said quietly to Matthew when the door had closed behind them. She had made a brief protest about the washing-up, saying they should leave it, but Alice had quietly insisted. 'Nice girl. Looks like her mother as I remember.'

'What's the story behind it all?' Matthew asked, rummaging for his favourite as she passed him the box of Quality Street. 'Don't say Dad went out with her mum?'

'As if!' Josie managed a laugh. 'Valerie was too good for the likes of your dad. Or thought she was anyway,' she added, feeling a moment's indignation on his behalf.

'Is Dad OK?' Matthew asked, voice casual but a hint of anxiety there nonetheless. 'He doesn't seem himself.'

'Doesn't he? How doesn't he seem himself?'

'He seems preoccupied. His job's secure, isn't it?'

'Oh yes. Safe as houses.'

'Well, something's up.'

Surprised, she stared at him. Ray didn't seem any different to her although, come to think of it, she had caught him out just sitting staring into space once or twice lately. She hoped to God he wasn't ill and keeping it from her. Just you wait, after Christmas, she would tackle him about it. If he thought he could get away with not seeing the doctor then he could think again. She'd drag him there if needs must. They had this new young woman doctor at the practice and he was scared stiff of having to see her.

'Your dad's fine,' she replied with a smile. 'Don't worry about him. I'll sort him out. But, getting back to you—' She checked her voice, looked towards the kitchen where they could hear Alice's cheerful voice amidst the clattering dishes. 'I know it's not something a mum's supposed to ask but just how serious are you about Alice? Come on, you can tell me.'

She had overstepped the mark, she saw at once, saw also from the tight look on his face that she would get nowhere taking the bossy approach. Subtlety had never been her strong point.

'In my day,' she went on, feeling about a hundred years old as she uttered the words. 'Back in the sixties, we generally got engaged at about eighteen, saved up for a deposit for two years then got married. That was the norm round here. It was expected. You had a nice wedding and a honeymoon up in the Lakes or down south. A whole week if you could afford to take that long off. Do you know, Matthew, before we got married, we wanted a house in Long Drive but we couldn't afford it because they wanted £2,300.'

Matthew laughed. 'Time's change,' he said.

'They certainly do.' She smiled with him. 'And then a year on, you had your first child and it was considered nice if you had a boy. A couple of years later, another child and again, it was nice if this time it was a girl. One of each. The ideal family. It was all planned to perfection,' she added with a slight smile. 'Didn't always work out like that of course. Rarely worked out like that. Some had two boys. Or two girls. An extra baby you had not planned. Or just the one sometimes.'

She stopped talking. Josie had known from the moment Matthew had walked in with this girl last night that, for him, this was very much it and, judging from Alice's face, from the way she looked at him, it was the same for her too. There had been no need to ask the question for it was plain for all to see. They were in love. Her boy and his girl. In that case, the only way for her to play it was to be honest. Well, fairly honest.

When she met Jack again and odds were that she would, she would be pleasant and friendly, happy for her son, happy for his daughter. They might mention the past in passing for they could scarcely do otherwise, but plenty of water had passed under the bridge since those far-off days and they were grown-up enough now to deal with it. Ray hadn't realized the significance of the name yet, so smitten by the girl that he had scarcely taken it in. Ray would be fine. He had mellowed a good deal and, after all, he had got his girl, hadn't he?

Valerie would be harder to take. She had not changed. She knew that from one or two things Alice had let slip. She was still the brittle, starched knickers Valerie who, she had heard on the Felston grapevine, had had a tough time with her babies. She was sorry for that, of course, wouldn't wish difficulties like that on her worst enemy. At least, she had managed to produce Alice and that was some achievement.

'You all right, Mum? You look tired.'

'I am tired,' she said. 'It's Christmas and that Lockerbie thing upset me.'

'Yes. It was awful,' Matthew said with feeling. 'But you haven't to let things like that get to you.'

'I know. Your dad says the same but I can't help it.' She smiled at him. She would never say it, not exactly, tell him how much she loved him, how fiercely proud she was of this handsome young man who, once upon a time had been her little boy, but surely he must know it.

She had wanted more babies after him but it hadn't happened and they had never bothered to find out why. Ray would have died of embarrassment in front of the doctor and, to be honest, she wasn't too keen on all the buttering up she would have to do if he had been told he had a low sperm count. It would shatter him, something like that.

So they settled for Matthew.

CHAPTER FOURTEEN

'We'd like to come with you and Auntie Margaret to see Grandma this afternoon,' Matthew said on Boxing Day morning. Josie had done a proper breakfast with all the trimmings and felt now that she couldn't eat another thing for a week. The fridge was still stuffed to capacity and you had to get every damned thing out before you found what you wanted. Eventually, she would have to throw most of it away. But that was the joy of Christmas.

She looked at her son. He had originally said he and Alice would be setting off back to the Lakes directly after breakfast, but it seemed they were hanging on a while. She had not, however, anticipated that they would want to see Hetty. She sighed, trying to hide it, realizing she had been half-expecting this to crop up. Hetty was his grandmother after all and, strange as it might seem, Matthew had some sort of understanding with her, seemed to find something in his grandmother that had slipped by her. Hetty had never been one for the fond grandmother bit, never one for quick cuddles, more on the brusque side with him, so it was hard to credit but there it was.

'I'm not sure that's a good idea, love. She's gone downhill these last six months and she's not looking so well. It will just upset you. It might be best to remember her as she was.'

'No, Mum. I'd like to see her,' Matthew said, adopting his obstinate stance, which told her it was a lost cause. She glanced at Ray hoping for some support but he was engrossed in the *TV Times*, planning his evening's viewing.

'We've bought her a little present,' Alice chipped in. 'It's a lavender gift set. I know it's a bit old-ladyish but I hope she likes it.'

'That's nice of you,' she said, managing a smile. They had bought her a black handbag and a car valeting pack for Ray. Very likely chosen and bought by Alice, so the family tradition would continue. 'She will like that, Alice,' she added, wondering how to put them off when they were so obviously raring to go.

'Good idea,' Ray said, looking up. 'Why don't we all go together. We can make a family trip of it. Get it over with in one go. Mind you, she'll need reminding who you are, Matthew. What have we bought her, Josie?'

'*We* have bought her a nightdress and we have wrapped it in lovely gold paper,' Josie said, giving Ray a withering look which completely passed him by. Turning aside, she exchanged a small smile with Alice. Alice knew what was what.

They had done the Boxing Day visit, ever since her mum had been in the nursing home. Christmas Day was chock-a-block, matron had told them on the first Christmas, and they liked to stagger the visitors. And with so much happening on the day itself, carols, the excitement of the turkey dinner and a few games, the residents were normally very tired, so a visit next day made more sense.

'All right then, but I'll ring first,' Josie said, stalling for time. 'Just to make sure she's well enough to see us. If she's feeling off then it will be a waste of time. We'll just be standing round like spare dinners. I'll see if this afternoon will be all right.'

She went into the hall. The others disappeared into the lounge where *Only Fools and Horses* was on television and she waited a moment until she was sure they would not disturb her before dialling the number. At that moment, she would have welcomed the news that her mother had passed away peacefully during the night, hating herself for thinking such a terrible thing but it would save any embarrassment and she did not fancy one little bit having to sit in that small room at the nursing home, trying to steer the conversation into safe waters. Hetty was like a time bomb, likely to go off at any second.

Her mother was fine, she was assured, although she had enjoyed her Christmas dinner a little too much yesterday, was suffering from indigestion and was a bit grumpy.

So, what was new?

'We were thinking of coming to see her this afternoon if that's all right?' Josie asked, crossing her fingers as she spoke. She knew she could fib her heart out, tell the others that mother was not well enough to see them but that didn't seem right somehow.

'Hold on. I'll have a quick word,' the nurse said. 'It could be a problem, Mrs Bailey.'

Problem?

There was a roar of laughter from the lounge, Ray's guffaw predominant, and she covered the mouthpiece a moment as if it was inappropriate, listening to the silence at the other end of the phone, waiting for the nurse to come back.

'Mrs Pritchard's in a very odd mood,' the nurse's voice at last, breathless with the hint of a giggle in it. 'She says she will see you and your sister but not Mr Bailey or your son. She requests female company only today. I'm sorry. She's very insistent.'

Josie made a decision. Her mother had never mentioned Jack Sazzoni in twenty-odd years so why should she talk about him today? Josie would take Alice along and introduce her as Alice and that would be that. It was all first names only in that place so there would be nothing odd about it. And, if Hetty did show any signs of talking about him, she would divert her and Margaret would help. She was good at that, little diversions. A box of Mum's favourite fruit jellies would do the trick.

It would have to be a flying visit anyway for Matthew was fretting about getting back to Kirkley. Getting time off at Christmas *and* New Year was unknown in his business but Helen, his boss, had insisted on him taking it this once. Everybody else was in and for Christ's sake did he think he was indispensable? It would mean he would never get Christmas off again, she told him, not whilst he was working for her, so he had better make the most of it.

'I haven't told Ray yet that you are Jack's daughter,' Josie said promptly as they set off. Margaret had insisted on making her own way there and she hadn't pressed her. If she wanted to be a martyr to buses, Christmas schedule at that, then so be it. 'It will have to come out though. I'll wait until you've gone. I am right in thinking that Matthew told you about it?'

'Yes.' Alice laughed. 'I couldn't believe it.'

'Neither can I.' Josie sighed. 'It's a big coincidence but there you are. These things happen. It won't matter, not to you and Matthew and I don't suppose we'll be in each other's pockets, not with them living up there and all. We don't get up to the Lakes much. Ray's not one for driving long distances and he hates the motorway. We've only been up to see Matthew once since he's been there and that was because I was beside myself to know what his place was like. Ray made such a fuss. He can't do with packing and holidays. I used to drag him off but he was such a wet week he spoilt my holiday so now we don't bother. What I'm trying to say is that we won't be up to the Lakes much to your mum and dad's. That is. . . .' She paused. 'Sorry, I'm making far too many assumptions here. It's just that you two do look right together. You and Matthew.'

'We get on very well,' Alice said but there was a little caution in her voice and Josie knew she was stepping on thin ice. Stop being so nosey, it was nothing to do with her whichever way it went. It would be more convenient all round for her if it went all ends up and they parted company, but that wasn't fair because she didn't want Matthew to be let down or Alice for that matter. For better or worse, she already liked this girl, was starting to think of her as the daughter she had never had.

'I always feel Boxing Day's a big let-down, don't you?' she said, turning out of Crook Terrace on the way to Upper Felston and the nursing home. 'And it's a complete waste of time planning a proper meal because everybody's too stuffed to enjoy it. Matthew likes his chocolates, doesn't he?'

'He does.' Beside her, Alice laughed. 'He's lucky he doesn't seem to have a weight problem.'

'That creeps up on you. Are you sure you want to do this? I wouldn't have been offended if you'd wanted to stay with Matthew. I hope I haven't dragged you along.'

'No. I didn't want to watch *The Great Escape* and they seem glued to it.'

'You might change your mind by the time you've had a round with my mother,' Josie warned her. 'She might be getting frail but verbally, she's a heavyweight. She can stun you with a word. Speaks her mind. And the annoying thing is I still feel about twelve when I'm with her. Do you feel like that with your mum?'

'Not exactly,' Alice said, relaxing back into her seat. Josie was a good driver, handling the elderly Volvo and the busy traffic with aplomb. 'It's funny you knowing my mum and dad. It's funny, too, that we didn't realize.'

'How would you? Have you told them yet?'

'No. Not over the phone,' she admitted. 'I'll break it gently when I see them at New Year. It seems so strange you and mum knowing each other when you were young. How old was she then?'

'She's a couple of years older than me so that would make her nineteen.' Josie seemed to make a decision as they approached a roundabout, moving quickly into the inner lane and signalling left, with a quick wave of her hand as apology to the driver behind. 'I'll take you round by Bristles,' she said. 'Show you where we used to go dancing. It was where I met your dad. You never lived here, did you? In Felston?'

'No. Mum and Dad moved before I was born. I used to come to visit my grandparents and then. . . .' She fell silent, remembering. 'There was an accident. Granddad had a heart attack at the wheel and crashed the car into a wall and Grandma was injured and died soon afterwards so, after the funerals and everything, we never came back again. There didn't seem any point and I suppose it would have upset my mother.' She wasn't exactly sure about that for her mother had never, as she remembered, shown much emotion when the accident occurred. But then, when *did* her mother show emotion?

'I'm sorry, that was a dreadful thing to happen losing them both at once. I didn't mean to pry. This is it. This is where Bristles was.' Josie pulled up and switched off the engine. 'Over there. It doesn't look much from the outside, does it? Offices now, of course, but believe me, it was a very smart dance hall when we were young. They had a live band and a singer who fancied himself rotten and we loved that. In the interval, they put on records but it wasn't the same.'

'What sort of dancing?' Alice glanced at her, saw the intent expression.

'All kinds. Ballroom and jiving and twisting. That sort of stuff.' Josie shrugged. 'I was never much of a dancer, not like you. I was a bit top-heavy for dancing but your father wasn't bad. A lot better than Ray. He can't dance for toffee. Says it makes him feel a complete twit. But then that's Ray. He blamed his size but that's nothing to do with it. Some big men are very light on their feet. Matthew's quite a bit like him, deep down. Oh I know he's done well for himself and he's ambitious but he's insecure underneath it all.' She stole a glance Alice's way, smiled. 'Sorry. It's not meant as a criticism. And I suppose you've noticed that already?'

'Of course I have. He's very good at his job, you know, but I like it that he's not too full of himself,' Alice told her. 'And it does no harm to be cautious as he is.'

'Will you marry him if he asks you?'

'What?' Alice stared at her. For a moment, it irritated her that Josie – mother of Matthew or not – should ask such a personal question, but then she realized, as she caught something of the anguish in the other woman's face, that she hadn't meant to be rude or nosy.

'Sorry . . . none of my business,' Josie said, flushing with sudden confusion. 'You don't need to answer that.'

'It's OK.' Feeling an unexpected fondness for the older woman, Alice reached over, touched her hand, was relieved when Josie gripped it, surprised when she saw the moist eyes. 'The answer's yes. But I don't know if he will yet. We haven't known each other that long.'

'Huh! That's neither here nor there.'

'I don't think he's looking forward to meeting my mum and dad. Scared that they'll think he's not worthy of me.' She laughed to show that she thought that idea preposterous. 'He's no need to worry. Mum might give him a tough time but Dad will be fine. And frankly, I don't particularly care what my mum thinks.' She withdrew her hand and fiddled a moment with the amber necklace Matthew had bought her for Christmas. It was an expensive gift, one he could not afford, and managed to pale into insignificance the shirt and tie she had bought him.

'Oh, I see.' Josie took a final look at the nondescript building which seemed to hold so many memories and switched on the engine. 'We'd better get ourselves there. It will be afternoon tea and, if we ask nicely, they might bring us a cup of tea and a mince pie.'

'You won't say anything to Matthew, will you?' Alice asked, clicking on her seat belt and seized by sudden doubt. 'I mean, he hasn't proposed and I wouldn't like to think that—'

'Good heavens above, no. It's just between you and me,' Josie said firmly, doing a nifty three-point turn. 'But, just out of curiosity, was it love at first sight?'

Josie was good at listening and by the time they reached the nursing home, stuck for a while in an unexplained traffic jam, Alice had told her pretty much the lot, give or take the details of course. As Alice talked and Josie listened, it occurred to Alice that this woman was much easier to talk to than her own mum. Her mum would have constantly interrupted for one, whilst Josie just let her talk.

The gist of it was that, after their first meeting, followed by the auditions, she had been to the theatre as his guest and then they had managed to grab a few quick lunches and one very special day out together. And before long, they were on kissing terms and then lovers' terms and that was it really. As straightforward as you like. They got on so well, they enjoyed being together and they shared the same interests. In other words, they were friends as well as lovers and that was good because, once the passion evaporated, you needed a friend. And yes, they had talked of living together already, she admitted when Josie gently prompted, but Alice's suggestion of him giving up his bedsit and moving in with her had not been well received. He was proud – Josie laughed at that – holding the view that, like the cavemen of old, he ought to be the one doing the providing of accommodation.

'Stubborn,' Josie commented. 'What did I tell you? He's just like his dad. Or maybe like me. Can I let you into a secret, Alice?'

'Oh yes.' She smiled her way. 'I like secrets.'

'I haven't said anything to Ray because nothing might come of it but I might be up for promotion in the New Year. I don't know what Ray will say if I get it. He won't like it.'

'Why not?'

'Same reason as Matthew wouldn't like it if you were earning more than he was. Daft, isn't it? Marriage is a partnership, love. Or it should be. But Ray doesn't see it that way. I'll have to break it to him gently if I get it. Mind you, chances are I won't.' She pulled sharply into an entrance, driving round the big, old, red-brick house to a small car park at the rear. 'Here we are. Now, before we go in, Alice . . . let me warn you, this will be no picnic.'

'You needn't worry,' Alice told her, feeling nervous now as Josie's nerves transmitted. 'I've had some experience with old people. One of my neighbours, Mrs Osborne, is in her eighties and still going strong. She's a little bit eccentric but we don't know what we'll be like ourselves if we live that long, do we? Anyway, she told me just before Christmas that I should put some weight on. She said

I looked like a bag of bones.'

'Hetty might say a lot more than that,' Josie said, biting her lip. 'The thing is, love. . . .'

Alice held her breath. Whatever it was, it was taking some shifting. Josie was on the verge of telling her, the very verge. After such a brief acquaintance, she liked Josie. She was flamboyant, a little overdressed, and the cerise fingernails, matching lipstick and none too subtle glitter eye shadow would drive her mother mad but *she* liked her. 'Yes. . . ?' she prompted, catching the agony of the indecision on Josie's face.

Too late. The moment had passed. 'It's nothing. We'd best go in,' Josie said, reaching across for her brand new handbag and looking at her nails as she did so. 'Oh hell, I meant to take this polish off. Mother doesn't like it. Now, sometimes she's asleep when you get there and she doesn't wake up the entire time you're there. So, we shall have to talk amongst ourselves.'

Feeling very nervous by now, Alice followed her inside.

CHAPTER FIFTEEN

At the theatre, Claire's replacement was dug in and doing well, so at least that was something positive on the work front. Claire had gone by the end of August, vanished without trace, the cut-off complete. He remembered that, on her last day, he had taken her out for lunch, just the two of them, worried at the wisdom of it but feeling he needed to do it to draw a line under it all. After all, they had had some good times together and, for a while, they had both sizzled under the impression that their relationship was going to run the course.

'Any regrets?' he'd asked her, seeing her fiddling with the cutlery opposite. It was an upmarket venue, recommended by Helen, and Claire was looking pretty in pink, excited and happy at the prospect of a new life with the love of her life. He hoped for her sake that it would not turn out to be a huge disappointment. He could not see what the hell she saw in this Paul but then when did men ever understand women, and might there just be the tiniest bit of jealousy there?

'Regrets about what?' She smiled. 'I have none about the job. None at all. Working in the theatre's not all it's cracked up to be. Frankly, it's bored me to death. I shall look for something completely different. Something in publishing, I think.'

He hid a smile, thinking of the chaos she was more than capable of creating there. He ought to send out advance warnings that she was on her way.

'But I do have regrets about you, Matt.' The smile slipped. 'I am genuinely sorry to be leaving you. I'm very worried about you living all alone in that crappy bedsit. You need somebody to look after you. I'm not sure you can cope on your own. Oh, you can cope at work but privately. . . .'

He didn't want her thinking of him as some sad, lonely guy pining away without her, so it seemed the right moment to set her straight. He told her something of how he felt about Alice, about the impression she had made on him, about the way their relationship was panning out, about how he would like to take it further, make it permanent even.

'Do it then,' she said firmly.

'We haven't known each other long.'

'Oh come on, Matthew. When did that matter? What are you waiting for? You don't need my permission. But be careful. Rebound affairs rarely work out. She's not me.'

He almost laughed aloud at that. Claire had attached more importance to their liaison than he, clearly imagining that he was heartbroken when he was not. But it would be most ungallant to say such a thing.

'I'll be careful,' he promised. But people in love were seldom that; impulsive, jittery, optimistic maybe but seldom careful.

'Wish me luck,' she said as they exited the restaurant.

He felt a stupid lump in his throat. Maybe it hadn't meant the world to him but she had cornered a small space in his heart and he wondered how long she would stay there. 'All the luck in the world, Claire,' he said as he kissed her goodbye.

And with a final '*ciao*, Matt' she was gone.

This year's pantomime *Jack and the Beanstalk* was in full flow, but well-tuned by now and almost running itself. It was a sell out and would get them off to a good start in the New Year. He could take or leave some of the plays but the annual pantomime, whichever one they did, always delighted him and no matter how many times he watched it, he would find himself smiling at the same old terrible jokes, humming the frequently terrible songs.

The stage children were excellent and you could get away with a lot in panto. Alice had done well by him, both with the *Oliver* production and now the pantomime and he marvelled at how she could get these children, some of them very small, to learn the steps of a dance. Christmas being over and having had a couple of days off, he was back to work with a vengeance, putting in extra hours to make up.

'Relax, won't you?' Helen said, coming into his office, carrying two mugs of tea. 'Everything's under control. I like the look of the summer programme, Matthew. I think it's pitched just right. There's only so many serious plays people can take in one go. The Shakespeare season will go down well. And it's a scoop to be doing *A Midsummer Night's Dream* in the middle of June. I wish we could move the whole set outside into the glade – just think how wonderful an open-air production would be?'

'Midges and all.' He pushed his work aside and relaxed with his tea.

'How did your Christmas go, darling?' she asked. 'Did your girlfriend pass the inspection?'

He laughed. 'Hardly that, Helen.'

'Don't you believe it? They can't help it, the old parents. Mine gave me hell I can tell you. In the end, I told them to bugger off the pair of them and John and I sneaked off and just got married. We dragged in two people off the street to act as witnesses. My mother was livid but she couldn't do a thing about it.'

Matthew knew very little about Helen, hadn't even known she was married. She wore no ring and had never, until just now, talked about her husband.

'We're divorced,' she said with a little laugh. 'He turned out to be an absolute pig so perhaps mother was right after all. She never liked him. My point, darling, is that you can't really exist in a vacuum and it is really rather important that you all get along.

So—' She grinned at him. 'How did the inspection go?'

'OK. Or at least . . . it was a shambles to be honest. You'll not believe this, Helen, but it only turns out that my mother and her father had a fling years ago when my mum was seventeen. How weird is that?'

She whistled through her teeth. 'That's very novel. Who dumped whom? That could be crucial.'

'My mum dumped him.'

'Thank Christ for that. That's OK then. No problem. Take it from me, her father will be sweetness on earth when they meet. I take it they are destined to meet?' Her smile reappeared. 'You wear your heart on your sleeve, darling. I'm afraid it's very obvious that you've been on cloud bloody nine ever since you met this girl. It pissed Claire off I can tell you. She wanted you to be heartsick and it peeved her that you weren't.'

'She never said.'

'Well, she wouldn't, would she? You men are hopeless at understanding female logic. So, does he know then? Alice's dad?'

'Not yet.' He pulled a face. 'She's telling them at New Year when we go over. I am still OK for that?'

'Yes. Get yourself off before I change my mind. Are you peeved that things have gone so well in your absence?' she asked cheerily. 'Did you secretly wish that there had been the cock-up of all cock-ups?'

'No,' he said, although maybe he had.

'So, it's your turn now. For the inspection, I mean. Off to meet the prospective in-laws, eh?' Her blue eyes were merry. 'Rather you than me, sweetie.'

He laughed but found the words had hit home.

On New Year's Eve, as they eventually turned into the drive of the Sazzoni's splendid house by the lake, he found, to his great irritation, that he had the most awful stage fright.

CHAPTER SIXTEEN

The food was all ready for the buffet and it would be some time before the guests arrived, so Valerie was taking time out to relax. She needed to conserve some energy for it would be a late night tonight. She was missing Mrs Parkinson because, although she was more than happy attending to the food herself, it had been hard work finding time to get the house up to scratch. Jack had helped in a fashion but she still had to go round checking after him, because men didn't see into corners, round bends, and there was always the chance they would, horror of horrors, forget to put the toilet seat down. It was all very well having three bathrooms but they all needed cleaning and she sniffed her hands anxiously, hoping the disinfectant smell was abating. She had instructed Jack not to use the bathrooms from now on but he had just laughed and told her to stop fussing.

Alice and her young man had arrived earlier in the day and her first impression was very positive. Alice seemed thrilled and Matthew was pleasant and handsome and the wedding photographs – if there was to be a wedding – would look good. She knew she was jumping the gun and there had been no mention of an engagement, but you had to prepare yourself for the eventuality. It would very likely happen someday and it would be nice if they approved of the match. They hadn't had much time for a sit-down and chat but Alice had managed to murmur in passing that she needed to talk about something.

Valerie wished she hadn't said that. From the look on her face, it seemed important, so her maternal mind started working overtime instantly, narrowing it down to three possibilities: Matthew was moving in with her, they were about to announce their engagement or lastly, the most tricky one, she was pregnant and neither of the previous two possibilities were on the cards. Alice had a worried look which might well mean the latter.

The youngsters had gone out for a walk beside the lake. It was cold but fine and she had declined their invitation to join them saying, quite rightly, that she had too much to do. Alice had offered to help but Valerie had said no thanks as, perversely, even though at one point in the afternoon she had wondered if she would ever get the cleaning finished, she was actually rather enjoying the pressure she was putting herself under. She had, she realized guiltily, rather an easy time of it normally. Everything was finished now, on stand-by, and it all looked wonderful.

She had checked all the rooms that the guests were likely to go into. She had refreshed the Christmas decorations, brought in some new greenery from the garden and even found some more holly with berries on it. There was a log fire blazing in the sitting room and she must remember to pop fresh logs on from time to time. The plan was that, over the course of the evening, they would mill about in the adjoining dining room and probably spill over into the conservatory, the long narrow plant-drenched room that overlooked the back garden. The garden was gently lit in the evening, giving it a new dimension but it was unlikely they would go outside although they would no doubt hear the sound of the New Year fireworks, too far away to hear the church bells. The guests were all old friends, members mostly of the various charitable organizations that Jack and she were part of.

Jack was sorting out the drinks and making sure that there was more than enough of the Deli's produce out on show. He never missed a trick and she felt no guilt at taking a few short cuts, knowing that the little salads and mayonnaise were top class.

She had bathed and changed and was taking a few minutes to sit down, even though she felt stiffly formal in the elegant navy dress. She was wearing the lovely sapphire pendant Jack had given her for Christmas. He was wonderful at surprises and rather good at dropping red-herring type hints so that she had guessed – wrongly – that she had been in line for a new handbag.

'What do you think of Matthew, darling?' she asked as Jack came through. 'I think I like him.'

'I'm not sure yet,' Jack said. 'I haven't talked to him properly. Actors aren't really my scene.'

'He's not an actor,' she said quickly. 'He works in theatre admin.'

'What on earth's that?'

'No idea. You shall have to ask him when you get the chance. It sounds interesting.'

'I did hope we might find time for a game of snooker but it's getting too late for that now.'

'Perhaps tomorrow,' she said, knowing that a game of snooker in the room off the conservatory would be an ideal opportunity for Jack and Matthew to get to know each other a little better.

If Alice was pregnant, then Valerie determined to approach it positively. Babies, *bambini*, were only good news as she well knew and she prayed that her daughter would not experience the difficulties she had. It was time they talked about that. She needed to tell her a few things, should have told her before now.

Jack was looking pretty good tonight. He always dressed well, would dress well even if she wasn't there to help him choose clothes, and tonight she thought he had hit the mood on the head. Smart black trousers, highly polished black shoes, a striped shirt, neck unbuttoned with no tie, and one of his beautifully cut jackets. She hadn't seen Matthew yet in anything other than jeans, but she hoped Alice would persuade him to change for the party. Alice was looking well, thin but no thinner than usual, clear skin and shining eyes. Anybody would think she was in love.

*

Matthew could hardly believe the house. He had suspected it would be something special and he was not disappointed. Alice's mum was a keen gardener and it showed even now in winter, when the grounds were still patchy with the last of the snow. Apart from a holly wreath on the front door, there was no other sign of Christmas.

'Where are the outside decorations?' he asked, grinning at her. 'This all looks much too tasteful.'

She laughed. 'I liked your dad's decorations. Don't knock them. He was very proud of them.'

'I know.' Matthew sighed, following her round to the back porch where they slipped off their boots. As they did so, the inner door opened and a woman stood there.

'Alice . . . there you are at last.'

He would have guessed she was her mother and he watched, awkward now, as they smiled at each other, holding hands briefly but not hugging, before Alice turned and introduced him.

'Hello, Matthew, nice to meet you,' Valerie greeted him with a smile. 'Come on through and get warm. Your father's out,' she said to Alice. 'He's expected back in a minute. But we can have a drink and a chat. Or would you like to take your things up to your rooms first?'

They settled on a drink. He had noted the 'rooms' the plural which was fine by him because the arrangement at his house had been embarrassing. It was thoughtful of his mum to put them together, but he knew his dad hadn't liked it, muttering something about the bed settee in the lounge – how they could have pulled that out for him and given Alice the spare room. He and Alice had ended up with the giggles, lying chastely apart in the twin beds, painfully aware of the thin walls.

This lounge, or living room as Valerie called it, was beautiful, simply furnished and his dad would love the creamy expanse of deep pile carpet. And his mum would approve of the furniture for it was just the sort of thing she would like. Everything top quality and effortlessly stylish. As was Alice's mother. He had formed an impression of her from some of the things his mother had said and he was not far wrong. Starchy was a pretty good description.

She was like Alice, facially, and Alice had inherited her tall slimness but that was far as it went. Alice was much warmer. Valerie Sazzoni had unusual grey-green eyes, cooler than Alice's beautiful brown ones, and he suspected that she would be the sort of woman he might never get to know properly, the sort of woman who kept people at some distance. Glacially beautiful then and he could see what Jack must have seen in her but even so . . . the comparison with his own mother was difficult because she and Valerie were so very different. His mum was like a bubbling volcano, seething with merriment and excitement, and over the years she must have mellowed a little, so what must she have been like at seventeen when she had known Alice's father? Firecracker came to mind.

Frankly, he was glad to get out of the house after they had unpacked. It was, on reflection, too tidy, the off-white sofas just too pristine, the bathrooms sparkling to an inch of their lives. It was like being in a high-class country hotel. He and Alice were in rooms at the far end of the house. It would be all right, Alice had whispered, coming into his room as he unpacked his few belongings, if he slipped into her room last thing. They were miles away from her parents' room and nobody would mind, Alice insisted.

He would. He was not into furtive meanderings at dead of night and with the layout of the rooms so confusing, there was always the possibility that, in a sleepy state, he might take a wrong turning at the end of the corridor and end up in Valerie's. He grimaced at the thought. Good start with his prospective mum-in-law. Jack, whom he had met briefly, looked much more approachable.

The cold afternoon air was a shivery contrast to the over-heated interior of the house and, as they walked down the drive, he glanced across at Alice. She looked lovely and he felt his heart give that quick turn that he was beginning to associate with just her. She was bundled up, of course, on account of the weather, but glowing, her softly booted feet making no sound as they crossed the road and took the path down to the lake. The sky was grey, great clumps of cloud, and bits of snow still lay around.

It was quiet today, not a soul in sight, but he liked it at this time of year, could only imagine the bustle of spring and summer.

'Isn't it fabulous here?' she said, jumping ahead of him over the stile so quickly and easily that he had to scramble over it to catch up. Following her, smiling a little at the determined way she was striding out, he debated when to ask the question, the big one, the proposal. They loved each other and he knew that Alice was think-ing of marriage and children eventually, so, in a way, the question was superfluous, but it still ought to be posed. Making assumptions was a dangerous game. He didn't necessarily want to fix an exact date but it had to be there, somewhere, sometime, and in the future. He needed to be able to hang on to that.

'I know it's been a funny sort of Christmas at Mum and Dad's,' he began, anxious to get down to it but starting by skirting round it. 'But you did get on with them, didn't you, and I know they both liked you a lot? And, although it's early days with your mum and dad, things seem to be going all right so far.'

She smiled. 'And?'

'And what?'

'Oh come on, Matthew. I always know when you have something on your mind.'

'OK. I think it's time we got a few things straight. Firmed up on one or two things.The question is this.' He took a breath, grinned at her. 'God, this is hard. Ready?'

'Oh go on,' she urged, eyes shining. 'I think I've guessed anyway. I just knew you'd be really corny and do it now, here by the lake. You're right though, it is a romantic spot. The perfect spot really. If I had to choose the spot then this would be it.'

He smiled. If the answer was no, he was nicely placed to jump in the lake and it would be a quick cold end. 'Here goes then. Alice . . . should I get down on my knees?'

'Don't you dare.'

Her smile had faded though, her eyes had dulled and, even before he uttered the words, she was shaking her head. 'Matthew, I'm sorry to put a dampener on things but all this will have to wait a while,' she said, turning away from him abruptly and very nearly losing her balance on an icy bit of path.

'Hey, don't say that.' He caught her, whipped her round to face him, drawing her close. They were in a dip, out of sight and he traced a cold finger down her cold cheek before holding her close and kissing her. It was too cold to dawdle and they smiled as they drew apart and, he rather thought that tonight, scruples or not, he would end up in her room, in her bed.

'I will marry you, you great fool,' she said. 'I love you, you know that. I want to live with you. We're going to do that anyway, aren't we, but marriage is different. I will only marry you if we can sort this thing out. This thing with the parents. I haven't told my mother yet. Nor Dad. I need to know how they're going to react. After all, if we get married then they'll be in-laws, my lot and your lot. Like it or not, they're going to have to face each other.'

He felt a shiver running from his scalp downwards. She had said no, an iffy no but still no. 'It's me and you, darling,' he said quietly. 'I wasn't including them in the proposal.'

'I know that.' Her smile was awkward. 'But like it or not, we're stuck with them. Let's take it slowly. We have no need to rush things. OK?'

'OK,' he said with a rueful smile.

'Tell me, what was it like growing up in Felston?' she asked changing the subject neatly before putting her hand in his as they slowed their pace. Their breath puffed out into the cold air of this last day of the year, the rutted path under their feet still stiff from the overnight frost, the daytime temperature struggling to get above freezing.

'You never think about it much when you're growing up,' he said, accepting that the proposal, such as it had been, was firmly on hold.

'It was just home. I never felt deprived because I didn't live in the country if that's what you're thinking,' he added. 'And I was happy. Money might have been tight, I suppose, but we laughed a lot. Mum wouldn't have anybody miserable around her.'

'I like your mum,' she said, squeezing his hand. 'But this thing with Dad and her is not going to be easy to resolve. I don't know what we're going to do. Don't you see, it's going to bring it all back to both of them. And don't forget my mother either. What's it going to do to her?'

'I don't understand what all the fuss is about' he said. 'So they knew each other once upon a time? So what? They went their separate ways, don't forget that. And your dad married your mum and my mum married my dad . . . and they all lived happily ever after. More or less.'

'There's more to it,' she said unhappily. 'She's not saying. But she was very agitated when we went to see your grandma. Scared I think of her saying something.'

'About what, for God's sake?' he asked, getting fed up with it all. 'You're making this more important than it is, Alice. I wish you wouldn't.'

Her face closed over in that way of hers. 'I'll tell Mum and Dad when we get back,' she said. 'And perhaps it might be best if you're not there.'

Valerie felt her heart freeze over. Opposite her, Jack laughed. She searched his face, looking for clues, looking for relief or anticipation but seeing neither.

'Matthew's asked me to marry him,' Alice told them brightly. 'And I really want to say yes but I have to make sure that this is not going to be a problem for you.'

'A problem?' Jack echoed. 'What are you talking about? Of course it's not a problem. The only problem is, are you quite sure yourself? You shouldn't be giving a toss about what we think. What we think doesn't matter. Isn't that so, Valerie?'

She nodded, forcing a smile, but her anxiety remained, a solid lump of something approaching fear. She did not want Jack to meet Josie again. She was worried that it might set everything off again, all the old feelings that he had managed to keep buried all these years. Josie, too, for she could never quite believe that she had just gone off him. There had to be another reason.

But, with Alice marrying Matthew, there was no way she was going to be able to prevent a reunion. They were both looking questioningly at her and she had no option, under the circumstances, but to agree wholeheartedly with her husband.

CHAPTER SEVENTEEN

To Josie's relief or irritation – she wasn't sure which – Ray had diffi-culty remembering Jack Sazzoni.

'Bloody hell,' he said at last as it dawned. 'So, he's her dad, is he? Well I'll be blowed. Imagine that. Cocky little devil, if I recall. Snappy dresser. Wouldn't take no for an answer from you, would he? In the end, I had to tell him to leave you alone or he'd have me to deal with.'

'I do remember,' she told him dryly. 'I was there. I didn't know where to put myself, Ray. You carried on something rotten.'

'That I did. My girl, I said,' Ray announced, looking pleased with himself. 'She's my girl and you can bugger off, Sazzo.'

'You didn't say that,' she said. 'You didn't swear so much in those days.'

'Neither did you.'

'I only swear when I'm agitated. Anyway, we'll have to meet them again,' she said, increasingly flustered at the prospect. 'I don't see how we can avoid it. We're going to have to meet them if Matthew gets married to her. I bet she'll want a big wedding. It will look awful if we don't go.'

'Married? Hang on. Where's that come from? Who said anything about them getting married?'

She clicked her tongue. 'Wasn't it obvious? Matthew's a tradi-tionalist. I know he will be thinking of getting married rather than living together. I'm surprised you didn't notice, Ray. He thinks the sun shines out of her and she's as bad the other way. Even Margaret noticed. They're in love, Ray. Remember that?'

He nodded, flushed. 'Like we were?'

She noted the past tense. 'Yes, like we were. That time when you go all goosepimply just thinking about each other.' She sighed, and for a moment was back there. 'That time when your heart turns over when you hear his voice. That time when you'd give your all just to have him smile at you.'

Ray laughed. 'That's a load of bollocks.'

'Maybe.' She came down to earth, gave him one of her looks. 'It happens to youngsters.'

'It happens to oldsters too, Josie love,' he said.

'Does it?' She hid a smile, seeing he was working up to saying something profound. He had that earnest look.

'Bloody hell, I know I don't say it much but I still love you, Josie,' he said and she looked up, surprised and more than a bit pleased, knowing how much it had taken to squeeze that out of him.

'Thank you, kind sir,' she said, dropping a kiss on the top of his head. 'And I love you too. We should say it more often.'

'It doesn't mean as much when you say it too often,' he said.

'That's your excuse,' she said, smiling at him but getting the point.

'I like the scent you're wearing,' he said appreciatively and it seemed there was no stopping him now that he had got going. 'Is that the one I bought you?'

She nodded. It wasn't. It was the one Kenny had bought her but Ray wouldn't know the difference. It made her feel guilty though and she turned away quickly, bringing the conversation round again to Jack.

'It's worrying me sick I don't mind saying. The only hope is that memories will be blurred all round. I said some terrible things at the end to him. I had to,' she added, trying to defend her actions to herself. 'It was the only way to get him to leave me alone.'

121

'Well, I can't remember for sure what he looked like,' Ray said stoutly. 'Nor her. The girl he married. Stuck up piece, wasn't she? Wasn't her dad a doctor?' he asked and she could almost hear his brain ticking over. 'Fair-haired, I think. Tallish. Thin. Oh. . . .' Light dawned. 'She's like her mum, isn't she? Alice?'

'In looks, yes. She's got a nicer nature though. Valerie was always a cold fish. Eyes like pellets. She used to look at me like I was something the cat had dragged in. I could never understand what he saw in her.' She looked at him closely, deciding enough was enough. Time for a change of subject. 'Are you all right in yourself? Matthew said he thought you didn't look well. You're not ill, are you? Because if you are, I'm booking you in at the doctors' after the holiday. They'll be rushed off their feet but I'll get them to squeeze you in. I'll come with you.'

'I'm all right,' he said hastily. 'I don't know where you got that idea from. I'm as fit as a fiddle.'

'Yes, well . . . that carpet fluff must get on your chest after a while. It's time you looked for something else,' she said, fixing him with a warning stare and picking up her handbag, before checking her appearance in the hall mirror. Back to work, first day, and it was always the same after a holiday. You had to drag yourself in and the time would go so slowly, second by second, minute by minute, and by the time it was six o'clock she would be exhausted even though she would probably have done very little actual work.

You had to ease yourself back in gently.

And, after the Christmas she had had. . . .

It was like a museum, her place of work. It was a big stone building. Cold in winter because the heating system was something else. Stifling in summer because you couldn't get the windows open. It had never been designed to be office accommodation but they managed as best they could. At the treasurer's section, there was a public enquiry desk and a little waiting room, and then the big office and the two smaller private ones for Mr Walsh and the office deputy clerk, whose job was the one up for grabs.

The heels of her boots clicked over the tiles in the big entrance hall from where the red-carpeted staircase rose to the first floor level, splitting in two lovely sweeps to left and right. It was a grand staircase, more suited to beautifully dressed ladies in long evening gowns descending slowly and gracefully, rather than unfit office workers puffing up and down.

They shared the building with the clerk's office and the housing department and a basement full of dusty old records, very likely dating back to the Domesday Book. There was a lift, the old-fashioned variety, slow and trundling, but it gave her the creeps because it had a mind of its own and taking the stairs was healthier – after the over-eating and the chocolates, she needed to lose a few pounds quickly.

At least the visit to her mum on Boxing Day had gone fairly well. Hetty had been in a dozy frame of mind and had more or less ignored Alice. Aside from her mother's comfortable armchair, there weren't enough chairs in the room for three visitors but Alice had perched illegally on the bed leaving her and Margaret the two others. It felt suspiciously like a regal audience with Hetty dispensing small ambiguous smiles, quite clearly not sure who they were, in between bouts of drifting off. They had scoffed the mince pies offered during one of her naps, whispering so as not to disturb her.

Margaret, forewarned, had been on hand with the fruit jellies but they were not required for Jack Sazzoni's name was not mentioned. Just as well, Josie thought as they left, that she hadn't blurted it all out to Alice, as she had very nearly done. She had thought a thing like that would be better coming from her rather than Hetty but she had chickened out at the last.

The magnificent town hall tree, greeted initially with such excitement and anticipation was now sitting forlornly at the base of the stairs, its decorations looking tired. This twelfth night thing was a pain. She had given Ray instructions to take the blessed decorations down at home because, so far as she was concerned, it was all over for another year. The Christmas record at the supermarket had been despatched on its merry way until next year, replaced by flat-voiced staff announcements. The Christmas crackers and chocolate selection boxes were half-price and, for the people who had organization off to a fine art, packs of Christmas cards were heavily reduced.

'Josie! What the hell have you done to your hair? I almost didn't recognize you.'

'Hello, Kenny . . . it will grow again,' she said, uncomfortably aware that she had made a mistake with it. Kenny had a nasty habit of sneaking up and taking you by surprise. 'Did you have a nice Christmas?'

'Quiet,' he said, walking up the stairs with her, making no mention of the phone call on Christmas Eve. She wasn't going to remind him about it for it couldn't have been important. 'We had Dorothy's aunt and uncle up from Surrey. They aren't exactly a bundle of laughs. He's nearly ninety, deaf as a post and she has to have every single quiz programme explained to her over and over again and she still doesn't understand the flaming rules.'

Josie smiled, taking a deep breath at the turn in the stairs. One more flight yet. They had to go past the kitchen and little staff rest room first and, as they passed, she felt Kenny's hand on her waist, as he gently guided her in and clicked the door shut behind them.

'What do you want?' she asked. 'It had better be quick.'

'I've got the job,' he said. 'Old Walsh has told me on the quiet. He pulled me back just before I left on Christmas Eve. He said that, after great deliberation, they were giving me the job but I wasn't to tell anybody until it was official. I tried to ring you. I thought you ought to know. You gave me a run for my money, Josie. The others were non-starters.'

They were in the kitchen, safe enough for it was too early for brew-ups, even in the town hall. She looked at him, startled because she had thought they would have to wait a while yet for the announcement. Normally, it took them for ever and a day to make up their minds.

'Congratulations,' she said after a moment, forcing a smile. Damn it, even accounting for the dodgy interview, she had thought she might have a chance; after all Kenny was the new kid on the block. She had been working here absolutely yonks. She could toss the brochure away now, the one about the flat by the docks. Pity because she'd already started to decorate it in her mind. It had been in a really good spot, walking distance from work, in an area they called up and coming.

'I've been bloody miserable over Christmas,' he said. 'And do you know why? Because I can't get you out of my mind, that's why.'

'No, Kenny. Don't talk like that,' she said, as he reached for her and drew her towards him. 'Please don't.'

'How long have we known each other?'

'A couple of years and what's that got to do with it?' she said, moving so that her back was against the door, so that at least if somebody barged in they would have a minute to regroup. 'Look, Kenny, this is just a bit of fun. You know that. I'm married. You're married. And we have to stop it. This is kid's stuff.'

'Oh Josie. . . .' His hands were on her back, moving low and she wriggled free. She had never meant this to become serious in any way but just the fact that she was thinking about it, about him, considering the possibility of secret meetings was enough. It had become sort of serious, but it was not too late to stop it before she ruined everything. She liked Kenny even though he was generally known as a likeable bastard. He had brought a breath of fresh air into the department since his arrival. He had blown the pants off the stuffy set. He was a bit of a clown but he was good company, intelligent and she knew perfectly well that he would do a lot to get his hands on her. She had known for some time that she was slowly succumbing to his winning ways and not liking it, not liking it that she was beginning to find Ray dull and predictable these days. When had Ray last pinned her in a corner and kissed her just for the sake of it?

Throwing caution temporarily to the wind, she let Kenny kiss her then, in the damned kitchen of the town hall. Just one kiss and then she pulled free before it got completely out of hand but the tingle of excitement remained and there was a promise in his eyes that was very likely mirrored in her own.

'They can stuff the job,' he said, gently pushing her away. 'I don't want it. I don't want the job. I've had it with local government. I'm going to take it but I'm giving in my notice in a couple of months when all the paperwork on the villa comes through. Now, this is a secret, Josie, but I'm buying this villa in Spain.'

'Are you? A second home?'

'The only home. Our home.'

She laughed. 'You are joking? I'm not coming with you to Spain. Are you daft?'

'You'll love it, Josie. All that sunshine and views of the sea. The garden slopes down in terraces. We can relax and take a swim in the pool whenever we feel it. Starkers if you like. There's nobody to see.'

'Kenny—' She flashed an agitated glance at him. 'What about Dorothy?'

'It's kaput,' he said. 'As near as. It's run its course. I should never have married her. I think it was rebound stuff on both our parts.'

Josie frowned. It hadn't looked rebound stuff when she had seen Dorothy with him.

'And another thing, I'm fed up with work, with this rotten weather, with England. I need sunshine,' he went on. 'You need it too. I'm learning the lingo so we'll get by, you and me.'

'How can you afford a villa in Spain?' she asked, although she had a very good idea how. Dorothy was propping up the expensive lifestyle he led, a lifestyle a mere local government clerk could only dream of. They all suspected it, although Josie was reluctant to go with the general view that Kenny had married her purely for the money, Dorothy being a very attractive older woman. She was prepared to give him the benefit of the doubt. 'Don't tell me you've come into money?' she teased.

'Got it. I've won on the pools,' he said.

'Really? How much? You kept that pretty quiet,' she said, knowing he was lying.

'Look, I've got the money. Does it matter how I've got it? You don't need to know how.'

'My God—' she looked at him as an awful suspicion gripped her. Surely he wouldn't stoop so low? 'How have you got the money?' she asked. 'You can tell me, Kenny.'

He caught on at once. 'How do you think? Does it matter, darling?'

'Of course it matters and don't call me that,' she gasped, hearing somebody coming past the door. 'I hope you haven't been doing anything underhand, Kenny.'

He laughed. 'I can't believe you. You think I've been fiddling the books?'

'I don't know what the hell you've been doing. It's nothing to do with me.'

'Josie.' He pulled her towards him again suddenly, tilting her chin so that she was forced to look at him. Even features. Devastating smile. He had a nice aftershave and, up close, he felt strong and, even now, despite everything, against all her instincts, she could feel her body betraying her, softening. 'Come with me,' he murmured against her hair. 'Don't you crave a bit of excitement in your life? We were made for each other. That bloke of yours is a dead loss. You've said so yourself.'

'When have I said that?' she said hotly, managing to break free and sorting herself out. 'I'm not coming anywhere with you. You can't leave Dorothy.'

He shrugged. 'She'll be relieved. She'll still have the house here. I'm letting her keep that.'

'Is it your house then?'

'Oh yes. I inherited some money way back, before I married Dorothy.'

'Who from?'

'Family, darling. And that's all I'm saying.'

She did not believe him. The impossible tumbled round in her mind and turned itself into a highly probable.

'Tell me you haven't been . . . doing some imaginative accounting?' she looked round anxiously. 'Oh God, Kenny, you could end up in prison.'

He laughed. 'I bet your old man wouldn't have the nerve to do it.'

'No, he would not,' she said, horrified at the excitement she felt. 'Be careful, won't you?'

'Of course,' he said with confidence. 'Just leave it with me.'

'How?' Against her better judgement, the excitement soared. 'How the hell have you done it? And how do you know I won't go straight to Mr Walsh and tell him?'

'Tell him what? What are you talking about?' He grinned. 'Your word against mine, sweetheart. Oh come on, Josie, you won't shop me. After all, you love me. Don't you?'

The door rattled and the junior walked in, apologizing and walking out again.

'We'd better go,' he said, his hand finding its way once more to her waist and slipping to her bottom, giving it a squeeze. 'Give it some thought, darling. I've done it all for you, you know. You'll have a life of Riley out there. And by God, when I get my hands properly on you, I promise you one thing. You'll wonder why on earth we've waited so long.'

It was horrible twilight of the year weather. Grey and dark and dismal all day long and the town hall was hardly what you would call an airy light place to work in. Even though her in-tray was crammed with papers, she had done nothing all day. Oh, she had fussed round, looked busy, but how could she work with that whirling round in her head?

Kenny Balfour was out of his mind.

Ray was not in when she got back. She flung her bag on the chair and went to get a cup of tea. What she really needed was a stiff drink but she couldn't bring herself to drink alcohol at half past five in the afternoon. She was on flexitime and had left early simply because she couldn't stand the knowing looks Kenny kept shooting at her. She had no idea how he had done it and perhaps that was just as well. He was respected in the office despite his cockiness and she knew that Mr Walsh had been treading water for the last couple of years and was more than happy to palm a lot of work his way. Money flew in and out. Here and there, everywhere. It was like cooking an enormous hotpot, she supposed. You could take out a few onions and carrots and the end result would look much the same. It would take a very good chef to notice or, in the case of accounts, a very astute auditor. The accounts were audited internally and that probably explained it. Somehow or other, he had discovered a way of bucking the system.

My God, what should she do? She could shop him twice over now. Once for sexual harassment and also for being an embezzler. Embezzlement. She let the word roll off her tongue. It didn't feel like stealing, not properly; half of this wretched council didn't really know what the other half was up to and filtering money from a very full pot could be done. The council was always denying it, saying they were barely making ends meet these days, forced to make cuts, puffing the blame squarely on Mrs T., but they had money, quite a lot of it from various sources, and, in her opinion, they wasted it left right and centre, and she wasn't referring to the controversial statues either. They wasted it on damned fool ideas, frittered away thousands on seminars about meetings, on management training and courses when, if folk were left to their own devices, they could manage very well thanks.

Even so. She knew the difference between right and wrong. Hadn't she had that drummed into her as a child?

She was shocked into stillness and sat a while, thinking about it. Kenny was a bit free and easy with his hands and not to be trusted in that department but this was a completely different game.

129

She shivered, switching the fire fully on and warming her hands. Something like this, a shock like this, chilled you to the bone and she wanted to talk about it, tell somebody. She did not have much time. If she did not walk into Mr Walsh's office tomorrow morning at nine prompt and tell him, then it would be too late. Had the junior stood at the door and listened in before he came in? If he had heard anything, he might try to blackmail her and then Kenny might have to silence him. . . .

She laughed. Alone in the house, she laughed, aware that she was in danger of becoming hysterical. The ringing of the phone startled her and she went to answer it, switching on the hall light and pausing a moment with her hand on the receiver before she picked it up.

This might be the junior blackmailing her.

Calm down.

To her relief, it was Margaret ringing from the nursing home. 'Now, you're not to get yourself into a state, Josie,' she said. 'But mum's had a mild stroke. A turn they call it. They sent for me this afternoon and I'm with her now.'

'A stroke?' She felt her heart pound, imagined the worst. 'They're serious, aren't they? Is she going to die?'

'She's all right now, but at her age. . . .' Margaret hesitated. 'It's the next forty-eight hours, love. That's what matters. If she does have another, it could see her off. And that's the truth.'

Josie felt her heart miss a beat, had to sit down abruptly on the chair by the phone table. What with Christmas and Kenny and now this . . . it was all getting to be too much to take in.

'I'm coming over. Do you want me to bring anything? Is she wearing her new nightdress?'

'Don't worry about nighties,' Margaret said. 'Don't you worry about anything, Josie. It will be all right, you'll see.'

Josie was not fooled. Margaret was using her big sister, mothering voice and that could only mean she was very worried herself.

She left a hastily scribbled note for Ray and left the house, not even bothering to apply a fresh coat of lipstick.

CHAPTER EIGHTEEN

The speech was slightly slurred, the face just a little twisted, the eyes strange and empty.

Her mother didn't know what had hit her.

Margaret half-rose and smiled as Josie bustled in. She had come straight here, not even stopping off for some flowers. They had moved Hetty to another room, a simply furnished room nearest the nursing office, where they could keep an eye on her. Josie knew that, once here, the residents rarely made it back to their own rooms. They either ended up in hospital proper, or dead.

'Here's Josie now. Mum was waiting for you to get here. She's going to have a little sleep now that you've arrived,' Margaret said, speaking in a gentle motherly voice, holding their mother's hand, trying to tell Josie with her eyes that she must pull herself together and not look so shocked at what she saw. 'Take your coat off, pull out a chair and sit down,' she instructed, taking over as she was sometimes, rather surprisingly, apt to do.

Without a word, Josie did as she was told and they sat there, either side of the bed, and, just for a moment Josie was surprised at how emotional she felt. She could not, just then, trust herself to speak. She had felt pent-up on the way, feeling a sort of sob building up and it was taking a lot of effort to keep it at bay. The last thing she wanted was to start crying.

She did not want to feel like this about her mother.

131

This woman who had ruined her life.

'I don't know what you see in that Jack,' Lynn said with a sniff. 'He's too short for one.'

'He's not too short for me.' Josie gave her a look. She could take an awkward turn, could Lynn, if the mood was on her. Well, to heck with her. She wouldn't bother drawing her attention to the fact that she'd not smoothed her rouge in properly on one cheek. Lynn was hopeless with make-up. She was tall, always the tallest in the class, and she had tried to compensate by slouching. Now it seemed she could not straighten up, not fully. And she always wore flatties, which did nothing for her legs.

Glancing at her, Josie straightened herself up as tall as *she* could get, sticking out her bosom as she did so. Well you couldn't do one without the other. She noticed a boy on the other side of the arcade glancing her way appreciatively but she turned her back on him, not interested.

They were standing waiting for the boys to arrive and Josie was having kittens hoping to goodness they weren't going to be stood up. The trouble was that this arcade of shops where they had agreed to meet was the favourite spot for meeting – everybody eyeing everybody else up – and she didn't like to wait more than ten minutes at most or it looked bad. It was an elegant glass-roofed arcade with some fancy shops and more than a few jewellers. She kept her eyes on the rings and things. She fancied a diamond solitaire and her nails were ready for such an event; they were perfect tonight, painted a silvery pearl. It did no harm to dream.

'Is your watch fast?' she asked accusingly. It would be just like Lynn to have put them in this embarrassing position.

'Only five minutes and I allowed for that,' Lynn told her. 'Why don't you put your watch on?'

Because it was an old one, her school watch, dead plain with a black leather strap, and she liked to wear a few jangly silver bracelets instead. She had been on the bus the other day, moved her arm and the whole lot had slipped off on to the floor. Somebody had whipped them up, handed them back but she felt hot even now at the memory.

Nobody she knew of her age had a car, not yet, but Jack was having driving lessons and his father had promised to buy him a nearly new Mini if he passed. That brought it home more than anything how different they were. Her dad had bought an old car recently, splashing out over a hundred pounds, but he only used it for special occasions and on Sunday afternoons when he took her mum out for a drive. The buses were good anyway, less than ten minutes into the middle of town and that included all the stopping and starting. She had got away with half-fare until last year but, after she left school and was no longer wearing school uniform, she had to pay full. She wanted to pay full in any case. She didn't like being thought of as a child as much as her mother tried to make her out to be one.

'Five more minutes,' she told Lynn. 'And then we're off. Who do they think we are? Standing here like spare dinners.'

'It'll be Mick's fault,' Lynn said with a smile. 'You know what he's like.'

She did. He might be a mountain of a man, easily tall enough for Lynn, but he did not have a brain to match. Josie sighed. Lynn might be mystified about her interest in Jack but how Lynn and Mick had become almost inseparable was a complete mystery to her. Lynn for all her faults was a very bright girl and would have gone to university but there was a money problem and her parents just couldn't run to it. Lynn's mother needed her to be earning a wage, chipping in like the rest of the family.

Lynn was already muttering about getting engaged and Josie, at nearly eighteen, was getting fed up with it. If Lynn appeared first with a ring on her finger, she would go spare. Jack had made no move in that direction. No mention. And even if he did, she would be hard pressed to say yes because it would give her parents a heart attack. How she had managed to keep it a secret these last few months, she had no idea. Margaret knew and Margaret was getting herself into a state about it. And her mother was always on at her about Ray Bailey and what a good catch he would be.

'Here they are,' Lynn said triumphantly and, smile at the ready, Josie turned to face them, accepting Jack's profuse apologies with a murmured. 'That's OK'. He was here now and that's all that mattered. He kissed her once on each cheek as he always did, but Lynn and Mick just grinned daftly at each other as *they* always did.

West Side Story was showing at the new cinema in town and they took their turn in the queue. They ended up in the stalls, middle of the row, limited therefore to just holding hands instead of having a snog in the back row. Jack squeezed her hand at the important moments in the film, particularly when Tony sang about his Maria. It didn't escape her notice that it was a Romeo and Juliet type thing, lovers from the wrong families and it occurred to her that their story was a bit like that too. At least on the part of *her* family who would go bananas if they knew where she was and who she was with at this very minute.

He chatted about his family, that Sazzoni mob as her dad called them, but she never talked to him about her family because she knew, deep down, that her mother was right.

It would never come to anything.

But she just wanted to hang on to it, this lovely warm feeling, for just a little bit longer.

'I want no ministers coming here to see me.'

They were both startled by the words for they had been sitting quietly, not speaking, smiling gently at each other from time to time across the bed. The counterpane was a very pale orange, a terrible sickly colour, doing no favours for mother's apricot nightdress.

'I want no ministers sitting there, spouting God words. Do you hear, you two?'

How she knew they were there was a mystery because she had only opened her eyes a few times and not seemed to be aware of them. For the last twenty minutes or so, she had been asleep, breathing quite calmly although Josie was watching every breath with some alarm, almost ready for the one that would never come. Hetty had lost weight recently and she was surprised that she hadn't noticed until now.

'No ministers,' Josie repeated, squeezing her mum's hand, suddenly aware of her own bright nail polish. Normally, she took off her nail polish before she visited because her mum just went on and on about it. She reckoned she was safe enough today.

'No ministers. After what happened to your dad, all that suffering, no ministers. I can't be doing with ministers. And no church service when I'm gone. No hymns. No nothing. Just pop me up the crem.'

'Mother, don't talk like that,' Margaret said, shaking her head at Josie.

'I'll talk how I want. If there is anybody up there waiting then I'll just have to explain that, with one thing and another, I've had enough.'

'Ssh,' Josie soothed, feeling their mother/daughter role beginning gently to reverse. She looked across at Margaret, who had tears in her eyes. 'It's all right, Mum.'

'I've never been one for babies,' she said.' I'm not that maternal. And I can understand why you stopped at one, our Josie, after all you went through. One's enough if you ask me.'

Josie didn't bother to explain about Ray and his probable low sperm count. No point.

They watched as, seemingly exhausted by the effort of saying those few words, Hetty closed her eyes again.

After a moment, Margaret spoke, almost in a whisper, carefully watching their mother. 'When she told me she was expecting you, I was so happy.'

'*She* wasn't.'

'No. She'd had a bad time with me and she was frightened. She was right to be because she had another bad time with you. Wasn't that right, Mum?'

With her head against the pillows, Hetty sighed, opening her eyes briefly and then closing them again. Opposite her, Margaret mouthed the word 'careful'. Josie knew what she meant. Hetty was probably listening to all this.

'Dad should have supported her a bit more,' Josie said. 'Getting rid of her like that. It wasn't right'

'Things were different just after the war,' Margaret said. 'Women got on with those things themselves. Men didn't like to be bothered and Dad was worse than most. He wanted nothing more to do with her when he heard. He was more than happy for her to go to Auntie Jenny's until it was all over. He had seen how bad she was when she was expecting me. She was really poorly from beginning to end. It wasn't unusual, Josie.'

'No wonder she was thrilled to bits when she found out she was expecting me.'

Margaret smiled, looking at Hetty who was now breathing quietly and easily. 'She wasn't back to normal for a while so she more or less passed you over to me. It was easier. I bottle fed you. Changed your nappies. All that. And I vowed then that he would never hurt you if I could help it. I'd have killed him, Josie, if he had hurt you when you were little. He didn't. For a while, he seemed all right with you. It was only when you got old enough to answer back that the trouble started.'

'He was a bully,' Josie said, glancing fearfully at their mother, but she was still sleeping. 'Why didn't we do something? Tell somebody?'

'Because she—' She glanced down at their sleeping mother. 'Because she didn't want it. You should never have let him do that, make you finish with Jack,' Margaret said and Josie could tell the words were hurting. 'Telling you that if you didn't finish with him, he'd take it out on me. I mean to say, that was blackmail. And you shouldn't have listened to him.'

'I couldn't risk it,' Josie said, feeling all the old emotions welling up. 'I'd known you all my life and I'd known him a few months. I didn't know for sure I loved him. I still don't know. That was all there was to it. You weren't well at the time and I was scared what would happen to you if he gave you one of his good hidings.'

'It wouldn't have mattered to me. I was used to it. I never felt that strap hitting me after a while. I just used to think of something else, something nice. Take my mind off it.'

Josie smiled. 'That's what you do when you're having a baby. It's called mind over matter. When I was having Matthew, they told me to think of a song, my song, and then sing it through the contractions. I chose "Sweets for my Sweet" by The Searchers. Good song but it didn't work. It still hurt like buggery.'

'Ssh.' Margaret glanced anxiously at their mother but she did not stir, her face relaxed now.

'Do you think they heard next door?' Josie asked. 'They must have heard. Why didn't they say something? Why didn't they report him to the NSPCC?'

'They would never have interfered. And I never made a sound. Making a sound meant he had succeeded in getting to me. I never gave him that satisfaction.'

Josie shivered. 'Bloody hell, Margaret,' she said.

'Ssh. Stop swearing.' Margaret looked warningly at their mother. 'It's over now, Josie.'

'Is it?'

They fell silent. Remembering.

She told Margaret first before, together, they told mum.

'How could you, Josie Pritchard?' her mum's eyes blazed. 'How did it happen? No, don't tell me. I don't want to know.'

Jack had passed his test and got his car and he had taken her for a drive out in the country and, afterwards, they had found a quiet spot in the afternoon sunshine where nobody could see them and they would not be disturbed and . . . that's how it happened. It had been sweet and beautiful, the sun hot, the grass fragrant. They had kept the bulk of their clothes on, she had insisted on that, and Jack had kept whispering how much he loved her, how she was so lovely, and she had thought it would be all right. She knew about this pill that had come out, wondered how you got hold of it, had been too embarrassed to ask the doctor, would not dare to ask Margaret who probably wouldn't know anyway. One of her friends was already on it, taking it every day. She had had a terrible time getting it prescribed with one doctor giving her a lecture and telling her to wait until she was married. In the end, she'd had to traipse all the way over to Blackpool where she had heard there was a sympathetic woman doctor who was dishing them out like nobody's business. Josie, whilst admiring her friend's tenacity and her new-found freedom, could not contemplate doing such a thing herself.

Anyway, it never happened the first time, did it?

But it had.

'Your dad will take it bad,' her mum said, stating the obvious. 'How far are you gone?'

'Only a few weeks,' Margaret said, standing half in front of her, protecting her. 'But she'll have it, Mum. We'll look after it. I'll look after it.'

'Oh no, you won't.' Her voice was icy. 'It'll be got rid off. There's no need to tell him. We'll keep it quiet. Just the three of us.'

'Get rid of it?' Josie peeped out from behind Margaret's broad comforting back. She hadn't thought of it as a baby, not yet, not properly, not a little baby but now . . . talking of getting rid of it, she felt something stirring deep inside. 'I will not,' she said, looking desperately at Margaret who was just standing there, in deep shock. 'It's mine. I won't kill it.'

Her mother dragged her then, away from Margaret, shook her and looked straight at her. 'Be told, madam,' she said in that quiet dangerous voice of hers. 'It's for the best. You'll have an abortion. There's nothing to it if it's done early enough. I know somebody who'll sort it out for you. Somebody who owes me a favour at that. There'll be no questions asked. It'll be all above board.'

'Who do you know?' Margaret was astonished, seemed to have

recovered herself. 'Honestly, Mother, she's not going to go through that. I won't let you do it.'

'Will you shut up, our Margaret,' Hetty turned on her. 'This is nothing to do with you.'

'Yes it is,' Margaret said, eyes flashing. 'It's everything to do with me, Mum.'

'You shut up now or I'll clock you one,' Hetty said, making a threatening movement with her hand.

'Leave her alone,' Margaret said, standing firm. 'Just listen to yourself. There's no need for an abortion. It's not as bad as all that. It's not the dark ages anymore. It's the sixties. Lizzie Adams is expecting in Clarence Street and she's not married.'

'She's flaunting it,' Hetty said. 'Mrs Adams might be putting on a brave face but I shan't. Look at your father – a pillar of the community.'

Nobody knew.

Nobody knew what he was like behind closed doors.

Nobody knew that he, a great strapping man, had punched and kicked out at his own family for years. In between bouts, he was calm and quiet but, when he got mad, he lost control and lashed out. He was looked up to in this street, still walked tall and proud in that military gait of his. And just about everybody knew about the damned medal.

'It's not the end of the world,' Margaret repeated, casting Josie a reassuring glance.

'It would be for him,' Hetty said. 'The end of his world.' Her anger had gone, replaced by desperation and, her guard slipping, she looked at them both helplessly. 'You know what he's like. He'd likely kill her, Margaret.'

'He'd have to kill me first,' Margaret said, putting her arm round Josie. 'She's not having an abortion, Mum. I'm surprised at you for even suggesting it. We can brazen it out if we have to. And you never know, they might get married.'

'At her age?'

'Why not? Girls get married young. Some girls.'

'Has he asked you?' Her mother turned on her, spat out the question.

Josie shook her head. 'Not exactly.'

'Has he asked you or not?'

'No,' she mumbled. 'But he will when he knows.'

Her mother laughed then, a laugh without mirth, without warmth. 'That will be the last thing he'll do. And even if he did, your father wouldn't let you marry a foreigner and a Catholic at that. So you can forget that.'

In the event, Jack never did know about his baby and her dad never knew either. She lost it, naturally, a few days later and perhaps under the circumstances it was better like that. She had a few days off work, her mother phoning up to say she had a virus and would be back as soon as her temperature was down. There was no need to bother the doctor, her mother said, once she was over the worst of it. She would be fine now, so long as she kept her legs closed in future.

From then on, it remained a secret between just the three of them. But she knew one thing. For Margaret's sake, if not her own, she could not put them through another of their father's rages and when the news got back to him that she'd been seen out with Jack, he took her in the back room and gave her the ultimatum. She hardly dared look at his eyes for they were very nearly crazed with his anger. That night, she told Jack it was over and that was that. She did not love him any more and he was to forget her. He was bewildered but she was resolute. She took up with Ray Bailey because it was the easy thing to do, and had to call upon Ray eventually to hammer the point home when Jack was slow to take no for an answer.

They never talked of it these days, she and Margaret, but she knew Margaret was shocked when she broke the news about Alice being Jack's daughter.

'Oh Josie—' she'd said, putting a hand to her mouth. 'Oh heck, Josie.'

The three of them had kept the secret, although lately Hetty's confused mind had threatened to blab, but soon it was to be just the two of them because, when they were both gone from her bedside, alone and without a comforting hand, their mother had another stroke, massive this time, and died next day.

CHAPTER NINETEEN

Ray had a long drive out to one of the villages out in the country, where he was fitting a big bedroom carpet. It was a lovely shag pile that he had worked with before and it would present no problems. He might finish early and, if he did, he might catch Lynn in. It was Wednesday and it was her day off.

He was no good at all with this secret liaison stuff. He'd make a fine James Bond and no mistake. His face was a dead giveaway for a start. He would be a rotten poker player. He hated keeping things from Josie but he wanted to surprise her. Hadn't she accused him of being too damned predictable? Well, he was going to show her this time.

It had been a bit awkward at home since Christmas, what with Hetty going and dying shortly afterwards, and that to-do with Matthew and Alice. She was a nice girl and he'd taken it upon himself, knowing that Josie was iffy about it, to speak to Matthew on the phone to put him straight.

'What's wrong, Dad? Is Mum OK?' Matthew had sounded alarmed. Not surprising because Ray couldn't remember ever ringing him before, not off his own bat. Josie always did that, sometimes passing the phone over to him when she had finished. Whenever she did that, he and Matthew could never think of anything to say, so they resorted to talking about football or cricket, nice safe subjects

142

like that, nothing personal, never anything personal.

'Nothing's wrong,' he said. 'Just thought I'd give you a call. I liked that girl of yours, Matthew. Make sure you look after her.'

Matthew laughed. 'Right. Thanks, Dad.'

'Take no notice of your mother,' he went on, needing to get this over with. 'You just do what you think fit. She'll come round. I'll see to that.'

And then, because there was nothing much else to say, he'd hung up pleading he was busy. He had not mentioned the phone call to Josie but he hoped that it would have cleared up any misgivings Matthew might have.

Hetty was gone now and he couldn't pretend it wasn't a relief, her being so frail and with nothing left to look forward to. He had never got on as well with Hetty – a ratty sort – as he had with old Jimmy. Jimmy had been a nice quiet man, could tell some tales about his time in the police, although he kept very quiet about that bit of bravery he had got the medal for. That's what proper heroes were like. Self-effacing. Ray was bloody proud of that medal but Josie, for some reason, would not display it, keeping it tucked away in a drawer. It was going to go to Matthew one day as Jimmy had stipulated in his will.

Josie and Margaret had taken their mother's death well, supporting each other and, although he was being careful with Josie, he worried that it hadn't sunk in properly yet and she might burst into tears at any given moment. Margaret had insisted on doing the worst bit – sorting out Hetty's things – and the will was going through, although neither of them was going to be left a fortune. Margaret would inherit the house she lived in which was only right and proper and there was just a bit of cash left over, nothing to write home about. Hetty, mindful of her age and condition, had left things in order and that was a relief because he'd heard of some right carry-ons when there was no will. It would get easier as the weeks went by, but he still felt he had to be very careful what he said in case it set Josie off.

As for the other business, he didn't know if Josie had been convinced by his pretending not to remember Jack Sazzoni, because he bloody well did. Right off. He remembered the feeling of wanting to ram his fist down that smug throat and how it had shaken him up having that feeling. He had made him feel inadequate with his fancy talk, breaking off into Italian sometimes. The girls liked that but he didn't. He could be calling him all the names under the sun and he wouldn't be any the wiser. Jack had known Ray was sweet on Josie – everybody knew – and, for a while, as he had watched from the sidelines, seeing the two of them laughing together, seeing the easy way Jack put his arm round her, the way she looked up at him, it had hurt. It had hurt so much that it was a genuine pain in his heart. He wasn't a violent man, never had been, but, when he told Jack to leave her alone, that was the nearest he had ever come to it. He had also felt it to be a hollow victory, because he knew full well where Josie's heart lay and it wasn't with him. His one hope had been that she would fall in love with him eventually, in her own time, and, after Matthew was born he had allowed himself to think that it had happened at last. Together they had produced this little lad, a belter of a little lad at that, and that surely had to count for something?

Would Jack remember that last time they met as he did? When they met again, what the hell would they say? They couldn't take up where they'd left off that was for sure. He decided it would be best to say nothing, not refer to it in any way unless he did. Let bygones be bygones, which had been one of his mum's sayings.

He knew Josie was having problems at work and he could guess it would be something to do with that guy she worked with, that Kenny guy. He was a funny chap, cagey, and he wouldn't trust him with the council's money. He was married to this older fancy piece but he had the look of a man who played away, if he got half a chance. He had very nearly mentioned his concern to Matthew over Christmas, man to man, but he had let the moment pass and maybe it was just as well. He didn't want his son to get

the feeling that he was jealous of this Kenny, worse that he didn't
trust Josie.

He did trust her, but she was still pretty and she had a good figure,
and she dressed in a way he liked and, he suspected, other men
would like too. And she spent a lot of time with this guy at work and
he'd read about things that went on in the work place. Nothing went
on at Felston Carpet Centre because Eileen, the only woman in the
office, was close to retiring age and as miserable as sin. But it might
be a different matter at the town hall.

Stop it.

He pulled up outside the house, checked the number against his
work sheet.

'Oh, you're here,' the woman said, opening the door at once,
beaming. 'Lovely to see you. Everything's ready for you. Cup of tea
before you start?'

Now that was more like it.

It was bizarre. Since the conversation in the kitchen just after
Christmas, Kenny had not talked any more about that little matter.
His appointment was now official and he would take up the job in
due course when the changeover was complete. Sometimes she
thought she must have imagined it or managed somehow to read too
much into it, but Kenny had admitted his misdeeds, hadn't he? He
had not denied them anyway. She could not work out why he had
confessed because it would be so easy for her to shop him.

But she had not.

Their mother's funeral had been held at the crematorium as she
had requested with the minimum of fuss. It was a cold clear
January day and Josie kept it together, just about, tissues at the
ready just in case. Margaret was composure itself, like stone, clear-
eyed, level-voiced. They had both dressed in black because mother
had not specified otherwise and Ray had worn his best grey suit and
a black tie. It was a poor turn-out for eighty-five years of living in
the same street, just a few old neighbours who were only after a

nose around and a bite to eat afterwards. The funeral party – what there was of it – came back to Crook Terrace where Josie had got a caterer in to provide a few sandwiches, because she hadn't felt up to a trip to the supermarket, stocking up on sausage rolls and little pork pies and so on. The truth was it had knocked the stuffing out of her. At eighty-five you had to expect it any time but it was still a shock to see the coffin and realize that Hetty was inside it and yet not inside it, if you could fathom that one out. She was gone to wherever it is you went. For a moment, Josie hoped there was something other than a black hole. She sometimes regretted losing the religion as she had, but her dad had put her off it. People like him had no right to claim religion.

It was when the coffin went through those curtains that she nearly lost it. She felt Ray's big hand in hers at that point, felt the comforting pressure, nodded slightly as she caught his worried glance. And then they were outside, in the cold sunshine, being discreetly hurried along because another funeral party was already on its way. A conveyor belt, solemn or not, that's all it was. Wheeling them in one after the other. The man who had conducted the so-called service hadn't known Hetty from Adam, wouldn't know the next one either.

'I want more than this,' was all she said to Ray, hoping he understood.

The things they said about her mum when they got back to the house. It would have been laughable if it hadn't been so earnest. She had wondered for a minute if some of these folks were at the right funeral, if they weren't talking about some other poor soul. Hetty had been, amongst other wonderful things, kindness itself. She would give a stranger her last bite. A lovely woman, one of life's smilers.

That was a good one. Her mother had smiled as if they were on ration.

Matthew could not attend. But he was distraught and he would spend all day thinking about his grandma, he assured Josie, and as for Alice, well she was just pleased that she had met her the once at Christmas. He and Alice sent a nice wreath and she and Margaret clubbed together for a special one, her favourite white lilies.

'What shall we put on the card?' she asked Margaret.

'To Mum, who turned a blind eye,' Margaret said bitterly.

'Now, Margaret. . . .' Josie smiled a gentle smile, 'we can't put that. We shall have to put the usual stuff. We have to give her a good send-off. It's the least we can do.'

She waited until the funeral guests had departed, taking the opportunity whilst Ray was driving some of them home to tell Margaret, on pain of death, the whole story about Kenny. Margaret, recovering now and thawing out, told her exactly what she had expected her to say. She had to go to the boss and repeat word for word what Kenny had said. Well, not quite word for word.

'What's stopping you?' Margaret said, clearly agitated. 'You should have told him straightaway. Now you're going to have to think of a reason why you didn't do that. Oh Josie, you are daft. He's not worth protecting, that chap. He's a common thief, that's all he is. So don't start thinking you're doing him a favour by saying nothing. He's dug a grave for himself.'

They smiled ruefully at that, hardly an appropriate remark for today. Margaret had a point but Josie still hesitated because something did not seem quite right. Kenny didn't seriously expect her to move to Spain with him, did he? It had always been a bit of fun, a lark, and she regretted now that she had led him on, for that's what had happened. But never ever had anything been said about it being serious. No mention of divorce and she would have jumped a mile if there had been. No mention of her leaving Ray and his leaving Dorothy. No mention even of meeting outside work although, once or twice – and she felt hot and bothered now at the idea – that had crossed *her* mind. She had been cross with Ray at the time and would have done it, if Kenny had asked, simply because she wanted to give Ray a reason to be jealous. She wanted to see him fired up on her behalf again.

She had got herself into such a state that Mr Walsh offered her some time off, thinking she was fretting about her mother but she refused because she didn't want to sit at home and worry about it. She collared Kenny eventually just after work. They were both leaving early and exited together, quite naturally, pausing outside before they went their separate ways.

'Kenny?' She glanced nervously back at the building. 'Have you time for a quick coffee? We need to talk.'

'Stewing over it?' he asked with a grin. 'Thought you would.'

There was a snack bar nearby, a bit rough and ready, but it would suit their purposes. The place was packed, full of smokers, and Josie had to clear a table herself, piling used cups and plates and a mucky ashtray on to the one next to it and wiping it in a fashion with a tissue before Kenny appeared with two cups of brown liquid that passed for coffee.

'So you didn't bother to go scooting off to old Walsh then?' he asked, calm as you like, when he was settled. 'I knew you wouldn't.'

'I haven't been to see him because I can't believe what you told me,' she said. 'I think you were having me on. It was just a joke, wasn't it? You're trying to wind me up, that's all. We're not just colleagues, we're friends, Kenny, you and me.'

'A bit more than that.'

'No. Just friends,' she said firmly. 'I never meant it to be anything else. I'm sorry if you got the wrong end of the stick.'

'Oh come on, Josie—' He glanced round but nobody was listening in to their conversation. 'You know it was no joke. I can always tell when a woman is interested. And you are. Like it or not. You're just confused. Wrestling with your conscience.'

'You have a big opinion of yourself,' she said, annoyed because she half admired that peacock side of his nature. He was the exact opposite of Ray and maybe that was what attracted her to him in the first place. 'You're one of those men who think they are God's gift to women.'

He raised his eyebrows, grinned and, to her everlasting irritation, her heart gave a little excited leap. Damn him, he did have something, that elusive 'it' – whatever it was – that Ray, bless his heart, would never have even if he lived to be a hundred.

'I told you what I told you because I knew you wouldn't blab. And, even if I had misjudged you and you did go scuttling off to Walsh, I would claim complete ignorance. After all, it would be your word against mine, darling, and don't forget you're peeved as hell just now because I've got the promotion that, by rights, you think should be yours.'

'I am *not* peeved,' she said hotly, looking up as a waitress, a bit late in the day, appeared with a cloth. 'I've done it myself, thanks,' she said with a frown, waiting until the girl sloped off. 'All right, I admit I would have taken the job if it had been offered but I didn't honestly expect it. I know I've been there longer than you but that doesn't count for much and I'm only part qualified after all.'

'You *are* peeved and trying to make trouble for me,' he said. 'Right or wrong, you can say that the idea has something going for it. And when I point out that perhaps you've got yourself into a panic and are trying to cover up something that you have done yourself. . . ?'

'But I haven't done anything wrong. You can't pin that on me?'

'Can't I? Oh, Josie, you're such a little innocent and it's one of the things I like about you.'

'You bastard,' she said, an icy rage circling her. If she'd had a ready glass of wine, red wine, she would have thrown it at him, but they didn't do wine in this snack bar and there was nothing else handy, except the hot coffee and she couldn't do that for she might scald him and she wasn't into GBH. 'I don't know how you've the brass nerve. Why should I come with you?'

'Because you find me exciting and dangerous, darling,' he said. 'Because you can't quite work out what makes me tick and want to find out.'

149

'You . . . you—' she tried to calm down because a woman at a nearby table was looking their way.

'You are beautiful when you're mad,' he whispered, moving slightly so that the words were for her alone. 'Eyes shining. Cheeks glowing. I bet Ray's never told you that.'

'How do you imagine for one minute that I—' She looked round, lowered her voice as she felt it rising. 'That I would leave Ray for you. You can't love me, not if you'd drop me in it like that given half the chance.'

'Love?' He laughed in her face. 'Who said anything about love? Love is for kids. It's a teenage thing. It's not for the likes of us. Think about it. Sunshine. A gorgeous house. Plenty of free time. As many new clothes as you like. Pedicures. Manicures. It's not something you should dismiss out of hand.'

'I'm not coming with you to Spain, not even if you offered me a diamond ring the size of a marble,' she said firmly. 'You can go on your own. Or better still with Dorothy.'

'I'm leaving her. I don't need her any more, Josie. It'll be a new start.'

'The answer's no.'

He shrugged, not seeming too worried. 'OK. I had you down for somebody who was looking for excitement,' he said, pushing his cup away. 'Obviously I got it wrong but it's not too late, Josie. If you change your mind, the offer's still on.'

'Hah!'

'Your loss.'

In that moment all that she had felt for him went up in a puff of smoke. What a fool. What a stupid fool. She rooted in her purse for some money, the money for *her* coffee, put it down on the table before standing up. Walking out, she caught a sympathetic glance from the woman at the next table, but did not give Kenny the satisfaction of looking back.

As she stormed out, nearly colliding with somebody coming in, she did not notice Margaret standing on the opposite pavement, trying to attract her attention. Having failed to do so, Margaret was still standing there a minute later when Kenny Balfour followed Josie out.

CHAPTER TWENTY

As February, a listless month, limped to a close, Valerie was spending a few days with Alice and Matthew. Officially, she was there in her capacity as gardener, giving her daughter some advice about planting and clearing. Alice had tried her best to sort out the little garden but had finally admitted she needed help. It was the right time of year for a good blitz and Valerie was relishing the challenge. She rather thought she should try her hand at garden design, had enquired about a course that would give her a diploma.

She had said nothing about it to Jack. For all his easy-going ways, he stood firm on her not working. Coming from a family where her mother had always worked, held an important job in fact, his attitude had been refreshing at first. Whatever her mother had done, she wanted to do the opposite and so she had been content to stay at home. Lorenzo, too, held the old-fashioned view that the woman looked after the home and she had not wanted to cross Lorenzo, a fat jovial man. She had liked him for all his faults, listened to him as he grumbled, in an amiable enough fashion, about what he endured in the war. What she did not like was the hold he had on the family, the iron grip, the way Jack never went against his father's wishes. When Lorenzo said something was right, it was right even if it was wrong. It was not a weakness, as Jack saw it, it was a strength. The solidarity of the family was all and, because it became her family as well, she had not wanted to do anything to upset things.

Lorenzo was gone and she wanted to do something else with her life before it was too late. She strongly suspected that Jack would not retire next year even though he was supposed to be considering it. He might hand over the business reins but he would not give up completely and all this talk of spending half the year in their villa was just talk. He would fret about what was happening back home. Home was not Italy any more, never had been for him.

If she got her diploma in garden design then she could start up a little business of her own. What fun that would be and Jack would fund it, get it going, and then it would be up to her to make a go of it. And she had no doubts that she could do it. She loved working in the garden and she thought she had a good eye, a natural talent for design.

Jack was away a few days on business and, rather than stay home and listen to Mrs Parkinson's distressing tale of her trip to America and her sister's subsequent death, Valerie was taking the opportunity to spend time with Alice. Ostensibly, it was to attend to the garden but she knew there was more to it than that. Matthew was at work most of the time and, whenever they could, when Alice was free of her own job, they would have the opportunity to talk.

Now that Alice was engaged to be married, it was time they talked.

Alice was sporting her lovely engagement ring. For somebody who did not earn a huge salary, Matthew was remarkably generous with gifts, although that was worrying in that it might indicate a carefree attitude to money. She and Jack had always lived comfortably within their means and she wondered if Jack was still slipping Alice money on the sly. Once she married, that would have to stop although, remembering their own parents' generosity, that seemed unlikely. It did no harm. Jack was just a normal loving father in the way her own had not been. Her father had never been guilty of violence, heaven forbid, just indifference, and he and her mother had been wrapped up in each other to such an extent that she always felt an intruder. Coming late into their life as she had, unexpectedly at that, she had been treated almost like an unwanted gift except, in her case, they could not wrap her up and return her. They sometimes looked at her as if they were surprised she was there, scarcely acknowledging her before resuming their conversation. They talked endlessly, often about very serious matters.

Mother had died, not so much from the injuries received in the crash for they were not life threatening, but from a broken heart. The doctors did not say as much, certainly something so romantic and medically inconclusive could not be recorded on the death certificate, but Valerie was convinced it was true. On learning that father had died, she had given up. Smiled a sad smile and said 'That's it then.'

And those, so far as Valerie knew, were her last words.

On her knees in the border, scrabbling about giving it its winter tidy, Valerie felt at her happiest. It played havoc with the nails, of course, but she had finally discovered gardening gloves that were not only effective at keeping her hands clean but also not so bulky that she felt hampered by them. It was a good winter day, cool but not bitingly cold, with no wind and no frost. She recognized most of the plants and had discarded some of them already without asking Alice, but she knew best and she was firming up on ideas for what she might suggest Alice put in their place.

Now that Alice and Matthew were engaged, it was just a matter of time before they had to face the ordeal of meeting Josie and Ray Bailey. Try as she would, she could not bring Ray to mind at all. He must have been fairly nondescript then. There had been no happy family snaps taken at Christmas, but Alice had supplied a good description and it tallied exactly with what she might have supposed herself. Josie had not metamorphosed into an elegant, quietly restrained, well-dressed woman and, somewhat to her dismay, it would seem that Alice had taken to her. She had needed an ally in

Alice and it did not look as if she was going to get it. Alice had hesitated when describing Josie's mode of dress, neatly sidestepping the word 'tarty', calling it colourful instead.

However, and she was forcing herself to be honest here, the more Valerie saw of Matthew, the more she liked him. Whatever she might think of Josie, it would seem she had made a decent job of bringing up her son. She and Alice had been to the theatre to see a comedy, best seats courtesy of Matthew, and they had met his boss, Helen, a charming if eccentric woman who reminded her a little of her own mother. Mother had not possessed a decent frock either and the suits she wore for school were sadly lacking in style. But it had not mattered an iota to her and Valerie wondered if she attached too much importance to appearance. It was such a superficial thing to mind what she looked like, to mind what other people looked like and who was she to judge anyway?

Sometimes she did not like herself very much.

'Mrs Sazzoni . . . are you there?'

Startled, she clambered to her feet and saw Alice's neighbour, Mrs Osborne, peering at her through a thinner portion of hedge.

'Hello.' Valerie smiled. 'I'm just having a potter.'

'You need a break,' the old lady said with authority. 'It's not good for your knees to be on them so long. You've been out there nearly an hour, Mrs Sazzoni. I've been timing you. Come and have a cup of tea and a scone.'

'That's very kind.' Valerie had not noticed the time slipping by and yes, she was ready for a break and how could she refuse such an offer from such a sweet lady? Amused that she had been 'timed', she said she would be around in a moment after she had washed her hands.

The cottage was identical to Alice's but there the resemblance ended. This was an old lady's home, full to bursting with memorabilia. A large ginger cat sat amongst the china ornaments on the window ledge, moving gracefully as they entered the room and, amazingly, not knocking any of them over.

155

Valerie surveyed it warily, trying not to make eye contact. She was not a cat person and sometimes the blessed things knew that and deliberately tormented her. It slipped out of the room and she breathed a sigh of relief, sitting down as directed on the little sofa.

'Excuse my appearance,' she said, noting that Mrs Osborne was dressed in a warm lavender-coloured dress with a scarf draped softly around her neck. Mrs Osborne came in the category of 'old lady, well preserved'. She had keen blue eyes and her hair, gently grey, was long, swept up and pinned back. A surprising number of expensive-looking rings adorned her aged hands and there was an air about her of a woman who had had an interesting life. Perhaps she was about to find out.

'Your husband is a charming man,' Mrs Osborne said. She had not volunteered a Christian name and Valerie had not asked.

'Oh yes, I remember him saying that you and he had had a chat last time we were here,' Valerie said, moving some of the large embroidered cushions from behind her back. 'You are right. He is charming.'

'My husband was charming too,' she said, placing a tray on a circular coffee table. 'We were together forty years.'

'How lovely! We have a long way to go until we get to forty years.'

'But God willing, you shall,' Mrs Osborne said. 'You make a very nice couple if you don't mind me saying?'

'That's kind.' Valerie smiled, accepting a buttered scone, freshly made of course, and placing it on the small willow patterned plate. She did not normally eat between meals – a killer – but she would make an exception so as not to offend.

'I miss Norman.' The words were accompanied with a sigh. 'It's ten years ago now since he passed on but I miss him still. Not a day goes by without me thinking of him,' she added, walking across the room and picking up a framed photograph, which she held against her bosom a moment. 'What is it the Queen Mother says of widowhood? "You don't get over it but you do get better at it." How true. And she should know. Isn't she wonderful? I do so admire her. She's six years my senior. I have a feeling she might make it to one hundred and then she'll get a telegram from her daughter. What a joy.'

Valerie did a rapid count. My goodness, Mrs Osborne *was* wearing well. However, she made no comment as it might seem a trite thing to say.

'There he is,' Mrs Osborne said proudly. 'This is Norman.'

Valerie took the photograph, studied it a moment before declaring him to be a handsome man.

'We were never blessed with children,' Mrs Osborne went on. 'You are so lucky to have Alice. She is a lovely girl. Very like you, Mrs Sazzoni.'

'Yes, she is. And we are lucky. We—' She hesitated. 'We treasure her.'

'And the young man. . . .' There was a pause.

'Matthew is her fiancé,' Valerie said quickly. 'They are to be married in the autumn probably. They haven't fixed a date as yet. He works in the theatre. The Little Gem. Do you know it?'

'Oh yes. I go occasionally,' Mrs Osborne said with a smile. 'It's such a good thing in my opinion. This moving in together before you get married. I'm all for it. Aren't you? After all, how on earth do you know if you are suited to each other if you haven't lived together? Make or break I think they call it. I read it somewhere.' Her smile widened. 'I like to keep abreast of the news and the way the young are conducting themselves. I think it's very important that the old try to understand the young. After all, we were young once. All of us.'

'You've got a very modem outlook, Mrs Osborne,' Valerie said. 'A lot of people would be horrified by the idea of cohabitation. We never did. My husband's father would have put his foot down. He was a lovely man but he had very fixed ideas.'

'Stubborn?'

'You could say that.'

'I'm stubborn too,' Mrs Osborne said. 'I shall stay here until they carry me out. I will never go into a home because all those poor things do is talk about the past. They encourage it. I can't think why.'

'I think we all live in the past a little,' Valerie said thoughtfully. 'After all, your past is what makes you, isn't it? You live with your memories and unless you lose your memory, you're stuck with them. You can't shake them loose, even if you want to.'

'How true.' Mrs Osmond popped a piece of scone into her mouth. 'I often wonder how our brains can keep track? They're so small but they hold on to such a vast amount of information. So many things, so many compartments and have you noticed that if you forget something – somebody's name for instance – your brain carries on thinking about it even when you're not aware of it doing so. Oh dear, it is confusing. And then, when you are least expecting it, the name will pop up, like bread out of a toaster. I'm forever doing it. I wake up in the middle of the night and think, "Good heavens, that's it."'

Valerie laughed. 'That is annoying, isn't it? I'm afraid I do that too.'

'And you're half my age.'

'Just a little over half. . . .'

The chat moved on to Christmas. Mrs Osborne seemed keen to explain that, although she had spent the time mostly alone, she had enjoyed it. Visitors had popped in throughout the day and her home-made Christmas cake had soon disappeared.

Valerie told her about their Christmas, about their house by the lake, their villa in Italy, about Jack and the business. And then. . . .

'The strangest thing has happened. I didn't find out about it until New Year when Alice and Matthew came over to see us. You're not going to believe this but Matthew, Alice's fiancé, is the son of one of our friends from way back. We used to live down in Felston and they still do. We lost track over the years but we shall meet them again soon.' She added, 'Won't that be fascinating?'

'Will it?' Mrs Osborne sniffed, poured another cup of tea for herself as Valerie declined. 'You seem quite agitated about it, if you don't mind me saying?'

'Agitated?' She was about to deny it but, looking across at Mrs Osborne, at the knowing expression, she knew better. Good heavens, she hardly knew this woman yet she felt the waves of sympathy and she needed somebody to talk to about it. It was better to say these things to a stranger and she would do very well.

'The thing is—' She took a deep breath, putting down her cup which rattled in its saucer. 'Josie, Matthew's mother, was Jack's girlfriend in those days. They haven't met in over twenty-five years and I just wonder what they will think when they do. It's making me rather nervous.'

To her relief, Mrs Osborne did not laugh. Instead, she fell silent, twisting one of her rings as if she, too, was agitated.

'I've lived here in Penington Bridge a long time, over ten years,' she said at last. 'But you're thought of as a newcomer unless you were born here. It suits me because nobody knows me properly. I prefer it that way. Once people know they can be difficult, wanting to contact their loved ones who have died, that sort of thing, and I wanted to be rid of it, all that. Yes' – she smiled at Valerie – 'I confess. I do have a gift. I find I can keep it at a distance generally and if I do have any thoughts about people, I keep them very much to myself. All I can say is that I am usually proved right. It's all about auras, you know. Bad and good. I have the gift and it won't go away and sometimes I'm glad of it but not always.'

'Oh, I see . . . I'm sorry but I really don't believe in that sort of thing,' Valerie said, impatient to leave now but not wanting to be rude by rushing out. Perhaps the old lady was losing it a little. 'I'm a Catholic. At least, I was brought up as a Catholic. I have lapsed recently but—'

'People are frightened by it, by my gift,' Mrs Osborne said. 'You must not be. You have nothing to fear. I feel positive vibes coming from you and I felt the same about your husband. You have a very strong marriage and it will survive.'

That was such a comfort. Balderdash it might well be but she chose to take comfort from it. She wanted to tell Mrs Osborne that she had always worried that Jack did not love her as much as she loved him, if there could be scales of love that is. But she could not bring herself to be quite so open on that matter.

The door had been left ajar and the cat strolled in, standing still a moment before leaping on to the arm of Mrs Osborne's chair. She stroked it and it settled down, purring.

'If it's any consolation, I understand your sadness. I know about the babies you lost, my dear.'

'Did my husband tell you?' she asked, puzzled that he had done that, because they did not generally discuss that with other people. It was their private grief and they had long decided that they preferred to keep it that way. Too much sympathy even now, so long after the event, could still bring it unbearably to mind.

'Oh no. He didn't say a word.'

Valerie shivered, even though there was a coal fire in the grate and the little room was cosy. 'Then how do you know?' she asked.

'They are with you,' Mrs Osborne said in a matter of fact tone. 'They came in with you. Four strapping sons.'

Valerie felt the room spin, her heart race. Was this woman completely mad? Alice must have said something to her. That was it. That had to be it. 'Oh really,' she laughed, although Mrs Osborne was conspicuously not amused.

To her relief, she heard a car stopping in the lane, saw Alice getting out, opening the gate, walking up the path. This was the signal to leave. And it was not a moment too soon.

'Thank you very much for the tea, Mrs Osborne,' she said, tightly polite.

'Not at all.' The old lady rose to her feet in a single fluid movement, touching her arm as she passed. 'I'm sorry, my dear. I see I have upset you. I do apologize. I shouldn't have said anything. I try not to say anything these days. It just slipped out. They all looked very well. Three of them very like your husband and the other like you. I thought you ought to know that.'

Shaken, Valerie left her.

CHAPTER TWENTY-ONE

'Between you and me, Mum, she's a little overweight,' Alice was saying, helping her with preparations for their evening meal. 'But she's keen to learn and I'm in favour of her being allowed to do that. Obviously, I'll have to keep an eye on things, but the other children are very sweet and I don't think there will be a problem, not at her age. It's only a problem when they get older. It's a shame though, isn't it? She's a lovely child, gorgeous ginger hair, but fairy elephant springs to mind, although I'm only saying that to you.'

'Oh dear. I see what you mean.'

'I have been asked to provide the babes for another musical production at the theatre,' Alice went on chattily. 'Please don't think Matthew's pulling strings for me. Now that I've established I can be relied on to produce the goods, other directors will follow suit. It saves them time if they can be put in touch with a reliable contact. Each production has its own choreographer but, once the children know the steps, he or she are more than happy to leave me to get them up to speed. We shall need two teams of course, red and blue.'

'Teams?' Valerie was chopping vegetables, her mind not on this.

'To alternate, Mother. They are only allowed to work so many hours at a time. And, if they are doing the matinee and evening performance, I have to find all-day chaperones for the under-sixteens. The mothers are very willing to help out with that.'

'Lovely' Valerie glanced at the clock. 'What time will Matthew be home?'

'He won't. Not until late,' Alice said. 'It's a nuisance not having proper hours. Nine to five would be fantastic. But it's not to be so we have to make the best of it.'

'So there will be just the two of us then?' Valerie slid the vegetables into the dish. 'Alice, could we talk a minute?'

'OK.' She looked surprised but stopped what she was doing. 'Let's go and sit down. If this is about me and Matthew and our getting married then—'

'No. It's not about that. Well, not directly.'

There were too many pieces of her mother's furniture in Alice's little sitting room and, as she had not long ago been discussing with Mrs Osborne, it was enough of a jolt to her memory bank to bring it all back. The desk used to sit in the drawing room of the big house in Felston where it was well used by her mother, who was fond of writing letters and drawing up lists. The bookcase had sat in her father's study, crammed with medical books that were never looked at but just sat there gathering dust. As for the rosewood fire screen, she was surprised to see that here, for she found it fussy and over decorative but she had to admit that it suited the room. Alice had achieved an interesting mix of old and new, and Valerie chose to sit nearest the fire on a comfortable chair. The heavy curtains were drawn across against the winter evening and she wished for a moment she was away from all this, in Italy at the villa, returning only in late spring when the daffodils were in bloom.

'What's the matter, Mum?'

'It's Mrs Osborne next door.' Valerie looked at her, shook her head. 'I must be mad to believe a word she says. Did you know she has a *gift*? A gift she calls it. I think your father might have another word for it.'

Alice laughed. 'Oh yes. Didn't I tell you? She thinks it's a secret but everybody knows. Mrs Winter at number four told me. 'Don't catch her eye, she said. And don't ask, never ask.'

'Ask what?'

'Ask her to tell your fortune.' Alice was still smiling. 'What's she been telling you? Oh mum, she's not got you worried, has she? Just ignore it. Don't let it get to you, whatever she's been saying.'

'It has got to me a bit.'

'You shouldn't let it. How old do you think she is?'

'I know exactly how old she is. She told me. She's eighty-three.'

'Is she? She's quite sprightly then.'

'Yes. Body and mind. If she was a touch dippy, that would make it easier. I could just dismiss it then.'

'Dismiss what?' Alice asked as a pause developed. 'Oh come on, Mum, you can't keep me in suspense now.'

'The thing is . . . after we had you—' Valerie paused, stretching out her legs and realizing to her surprise she had not changed and was still wearing the gardening trousers. 'We hoped for more children but I lost them. Four babies in all.'

'I know.' Alice looked across at her, surprised, wondering what had brought on this unexpected revelation. It was not exactly a secret but just something they never talked about. She could only guess how her mother felt about it, Dad, too, and it had seemed insensitive of her to be curious about it. 'Granny told me about it once but she said I wasn't to mention it because it would only upset you.'

'It would have upset me but I should have talked to you about it as soon as you were old enough to understand,' Valerie said. 'I should have told you how I felt. I don't know why I didn't. I could never talk about it with your father because he was as upset as I was. Not talking seemed the best way to deal with it. After you, we had a baby boy who lived only a few hours. We called him John.'

Alice nodded. Granny had told her that much.

'Then there were three pregnancies which all failed. The last got to five months. That was hard.'

'Why did it happen?'

'There were medical reasons. I have a faulty gene which affects baby boys. You were a girl and so you were fine. You might need to be checked at some point yourself, darling. Just to see you're not carrying the wretched thing.'

There was a silence whilst Alice digested this.

'Now you see what I've done,' Valerie said. 'I've upset *you*.'

'No, you haven't. It's just a bit of a shock, but it's not your fault, Mum.'

'Oh, but it is. It is my fault. I carry the gene. And, if I've passed the problem on to you that makes me a very good mother, doesn't it?'

'Look, that's all for the future,' Alice said firmly. 'Let's leave that. I shall tell Matthew but I don't suppose it's going to matter to him. In fact, if it does matter to him then it's best I find out now.' She smiled, shook her head. 'He's not so shallow. I know that.'

'Do you know what Mrs Osborne said?'

'Do I want to know?'

'She said they were with me, that they came in the room with me. And, the question is, if Dad didn't tell her, if you didn't, then how on earth did she know? It's weird, isn't it? Weird and wonderful at the same time.'

'Oh, Mum.' Alice went over to her, squatted beside her. She looked shattered, hair ruffled, and, although she didn't want to tell her, there was a smudge on her cheek – a speck of garden earth that she had rubbed in. It made her human all of a sudden, that and the moisture in her eyes. She looked suddenly every one of her forty-eight years. And the thought of her mother suffering that, the loss of a baby, the loss of several babies, forced up a torrent of emotion for Alice too. 'Poor you,' she said, knowing it was inadequate, holding her hand a minute, half-expecting her mother to push her away.

But she did not.

'So your father never had his son. If he'd married Josie he would have. Don't you see?'

'No I don't see,' Alice said. 'What are you talking about? I know dad would have liked a boy. All men do. But I think you're wrong.

You're making it out to be more important than it is. You've got me,' she added. 'Or is that why you've always resented me?'

'Resented you?' Valerie sat upright. 'I've never resented you, Alice. What a thing to say.'

'But you—'

'I'm sorry if you've felt that way. I don't find it easy to be demonstrative, that's all. My parents were never that way with me either and it must have rubbed off.' Valerie flushed, gently removing her hand. 'But you mustn't think that I don't love you. I do. And as for your dad . . . well, he thinks the world of you. And you don't need me to tell you that. Goodness me.' She made an effort, smiled. 'This is getting very serious. Now, I've been thinking about inviting Josie and Ray over at Easter. What do you think? I'll keep it informal for them. Just the four of us and you and Matthew, of course, if he can get some time off.'

'I doubt it.' Alice pulled a face. 'No chance at all in fact. He reckons he isn't due any more time off until 1994 at the very least.'

'Never mind. They will come I'm sure. We need to meet up with them before the wedding. It will give us the chance to get some things sorted out. Will I send a formal invitation? Or will you just ask them for me?'

'Why don't you phone them yourself? Speak to Josie. She won't bite your head off.'

'I'd rather not. I don't want to speak to her for the first time on the phone.'

Alice smiled. It was so unlike her mother to be hesitant about something like that. But then she had seen a side of her mother today that she had never really seen before. Why had she bottled this up? Something as important as this? Why, when Alice was old enough to understand, why had they not talked about it? She had known about the lost babies but had never thought about them as people, brothers even, but now, for the first time, she did.

'I'll just ask them, Mum, if that's what you want. Josie rings me now. We chat quite often. I'll mention it next time she calls. I just need to know when and for how long?'

That established, Alice recognized the importance of this meeting between the four of them, was beginning to dread it too. She could not believe it would change things greatly. The idea that her father and Matthew's mother would take up where they had left off was plainly, after all this time, completely mad.

And yet, that was clearly what was uppermost in her mother's mind.

CHAPTER TWENTY-TWO

Josie was summoned to Mr Walsh's office and, waiting for the red 'come on in' light to switch on over his door, it took her back to her schooldays when, on more than enough occasions, she had found herself waiting outside the headmistress's office. She had sailed through her eleven plus and gone on to Felston Girls' Grammar but she did not pay attention, could not concentrate, was sometimes disruptive and – let's face it – a real pain in the neck. She remembered being particularly unimpressed by her headmistress laying down the law, even though it was bound to get back to her dad and that meant one thing only to look forward to.

'I hear you've been cheeky again, our Josie. How many times do I have to tell you that you've got to learn respect for your elders and betters? Get yourself in that back room . . . now!'

Sitting outside Mr Walsh's office, Josie flinched, her father's angry voice coming from nowhere, from somewhere, from everywhere. He'd had a softer voice reserved for other people, for Matthew particularly.

There would be no physical punishment today but that did not help much as she waited, feeling her stomach churning with nerves. If Kenny had been found out, lumbered, then he would be wriggling on the hook like a man possessed and, because he'd only ever thought of her as a good laugh, he would have no qualms about landing her well and truly in the dirt. She could not believe she had got herself into this situation. It was all her own fault. She had nobody else to blame.

The light buzzed and she jumped. Well, this was it and she was as ready as she would ever be.

'Come on in and sit down, Josie,' Mr Walsh said, smiling at her. 'I was sorry to hear about your dear mother. Please accept my condolences.'

'Thank you for the card. She *was* eighty-five,' she murmured as if that made it all right.

'A good innings.' Mr Walsh, a keen cricket fan, leant back in his chair, folding his arms over his ample stomach. He was a waistcoat man; sometimes they matched the suit, sometimes, like now, they were rather snazzy in various shades of silk. 'Life goes on.'

She nodded, letting her hands lie loosely on her lap. Waiting. He was apt to go off at a tangent and this might take some time, particularly if he was working up to reprimanding her or even threatening to sack her for something she did not do. The trouble was how could she deny knowing nothing about it when she did? Oh God, Ray would go nuts. And as for Margaret . . . she wouldn't put it past Margaret to come storming in here and shouting the odds. Normally a mild-mannered woman, when it came to protecting Josie, Margaret was like a tigress with her cubs.

'How long have you been with us, Josie?'

'Twenty-eight years with a year's break,' she said promptly. 'I started as a junior when I was seventeen.'

'I remember you as a junior,' he said with a smile. 'You've done well, haven't you? I can always count on you. I've always regarded you as one of our more reliable members of staff. Loyal. Someone I can trust to get a job done.'

'Thank you.' She was trying to read his mind, to see behind the vague smile. Maybe she was a bit of a favourite with him because, over the years, he had been good to her. She had given her notice in when she was expecting Matthew – it was before the days of all these maternity benefits – and never expected to be welcomed back a year later, almost with open arms. Ray had not wanted her to go back to work even though they needed the money and had only relented because she had arranged for Matthew to be looked after by one of her friends with a child the same age. There had never been any question of the baby being looked after by her mother and Margaret was working so that ruled her out too.

The arrangement with Heather suited them both for Heather was happy to stay home and happy to have some money coming her way from looking after Matthew. Having one more to look after was neither here nor there, according to Heather, whose maternal instincts were coming out her ears. Josie in turn, although she loved the baby, was happier to be working, to be with adults, to be doing a job that, way back then, she found interesting and absorbing.

It had surprised Josie, coming back to work, because nothing had changed. *She* had changed. She was now the mother of a little boy, her priorities in life had drastically shifted but work here was just the same, as if time had stood still in her absence.

'There's got to be some continuity, in my opinion,' Mr Walsh said, ignoring the phone on his desk as it rang and rang. Josie knew very little about him, the man, for he kept his private life private. There was a Mrs Walsh, a quiet background lady, and several Walsh children, grown-up now. 'I see myself as captain of the team and it's important to me that it carries on smoothly when I'm gone,' he continued in the pompous tone they found so amusing. 'We in local government do a tremendous job for the community and the adverse publicity we sometimes get really pains me. We are given no credit for the things we do well but regrettably, we have to suffer in silence.'

Josie, tempted to answer the phone herself, remained silent as the ringing ceased. Let him get this off his chest. She had things to do out in the main office, things piling up and she could do without this. The junior had just brought her a cup of tea and it would be stone cold by the time she got back to it. It might take some considerable time to get to the point of all this, the point that she was dreading.

'I have some surprising news, Josie. Mr Balfour has tendered his resignation,' he said and she straightened up at that. If it had to come to it, she would defend herself and sod the outcome. 'We shall be very sorry to lose him but, sadly, these things happen.'

She nodded, as that seemed the appropriate response. What the hell was Kenny up to? It looked very much as if he had been rumbled and, in order to keep it all under wraps, he had been asked to resign. It struck her as a typical local government reaction, willing to go to any lengths to avoid scandal. Sometimes, she liked the organization she worked for, admired it even and sometimes, like now, she despised it.

'Why has he resigned?' she asked.

'Personal reasons,' he said. 'His dear wife is very ill, I'm sorry to say but keep that under your hat. It's not for general consumption. Suffice to say, we wish him well. He and Dorothy. He will be leaving as of now. Obviously, an official period of notice was required but there are occasions when it can be waived. This is one of them. He needs to be with her.'

Josie said nothing. Best say nothing.

Mr Walsh smiled slightly. 'The point of calling you in, Josie, is that as we have only recently had an interview procedure for this particular position as my deputy clerk, we feel – and I have spoken to everyone involved – that we should simply offer the job to the applicant who came a very close second to Mr Balfour. And that. . . .' He beamed. 'That is you. I am, as they call it, sounding you out. If you do accept the position then we can waive all the usual advertisements and so on. It will save us a lot of trouble and time and I am confident you will be an admirable choice.'

'Oh—' She looked at his face, his trusting face, and a huge mix of emotions tumbled about inside. She could think about the flat once again, properly this time, and wasn't this opportunity what she had been working towards for so long? She could do the job standing on her head, take on the extra responsibility with no problem and it would indeed be something to get her teeth into and she could finally implement some of the changes she felt ought to be made to the department. Why then did she feel less than thrilled?

'Perhaps you need some time to think about it?' Mr Walsh said. 'I suppose I can be accused of springing it on you. There is no great rush because Peter is here for another couple of months but I am looking for a smooth change-over period.'

Kenny was going to get away with it, scot-free. What the hell was this about Dorothy being ill? It was the first she'd heard of it. Could he really be going to Spain, courtesy of his ill-gotten gains, leaving a possibly ailing wife, to enjoy a life in the sun? She wouldn't put it past him. He was just the sort of man who would plough on regardless.

Mr Walsh's words stopped her in her tracks.

She would do as he suggested and take some time to think about it.

Dorothy answered the phone but Josie was prepared for that.

'This is Josie Bailey from work,' she said brightly. 'I've only just heard about Kenny leaving, Mrs Balfour.'

'News travels,' Dorothy said, her voice flat and unemotional. 'Does everybody know?'

'Not yet. Mr Walsh has only told me.'

'I see.'

The silence was hard.

'I just wanted to say,' Josie struggled. What on earth *did* she want to say?

'And I want to say something, too, but I can't talk about this over the phone. Have you time to pop round? It won't take long.'

The house was detached, mock Tudor, set well back from the road. She had been here just once before, shortly after Kenny took up his appointment and they were invited to a house-warming party. The house was not to Josie's taste, not the sort of thing she would go for but each to his own. It occurred to her that Kenny had a damned

172

cheek laughing at Ray's Christmas decorations when he lived in a monstrosity like this. There were two large cars in the drive, importantly side by side. Kenny's BMW and a Jaguar. Somehow she was not surprised that Dorothy drove a Jag. She didn't look the sweet little car type.

Pulling up outside, Josie wondered for the moment what on earth she was doing here. She was asking for trouble. Nobody knew, apart from her and Kenny, what had gone on between them, although in effect nothing had gone on. It was all whispering and giggling and the occasional odd furtive kiss. Very teenage and silly. It had been going nowhere. It was never meant to go anywhere.

She had been a fool. She saw that now. She should have clocked him one the very first time he tried it on and put an end to it. And now, here she was, outside his door, feeling very guilty. And to top it all, the rain which had been at it all day had upped a gear and turned torrential. She would get wet through just getting up the path.

Here goes. She opened the car door and by the time she got her umbrella up, her hair was plastered to her head. It had grown a little and the colour was not quite so vibrant but it would take some considerable time to recover.

'Come in.' Dorothy opened the door and managed a smile. She had a stiff smile, little facial expression and Josie wondered if she'd had a face-lift. Good for her if she had. She wasn't entirely sure she wouldn't do the same thing when she got to Dorothy's age, if she could afford it that is. 'Leave the brolly in the porch and would you mind taking off your shoes? I'm sorry to be fussy but it's the carpet. . . .'

Ah yes. Pale cream, no pattern, a bugger, according to Ray, to keep clean unless you paid extra for special carpet protection and then you could drop red wine on it and it would just mop up. Stopping herself just in time from saying what a lovely carpet it was – she was getting more and more like Ray every day – Josie handed Dorothy her coat. Feeling at a disadvantage, shoeless, she followed Dorothy into the sitting room.

'Kenny won't be joining us,' Dorothy said tightly. 'Do take a seat.'

'Awful weather,' Josie said, for something to say. Dorothy looked blooming – so much for her being ill. Mr Walsh had talked about it as if she was at death's door.

'Let's not beat about the bush, Mrs Bailey.' Dorothy did not offer her tea or coffee but sat opposite on a green striped settee. She was wearing house shoes, backless silver mules and beautifully cut pale green trousers with a toning over-printed sweater with extravagant shoulder pads. 'This is all rather delicate but I have been informed by someone who doesn't wish to be identified that you and Kenny have been carrying on, for want of a better expression.'

'That's not true,' Josie gasped, feeling herself colour up which was a dead giveaway.

Dorothy raised her carefully waxed eyebrows. 'I know what he's like, so don't pretend. If it's not you, it would be somebody else. Well, I've had enough. I've given him an ultimatum. Unless he wants me to walk out on him, unless he wants to give up the car and the lifestyle, then he comes to heel. There is no need for him to work as he has a more than adequate allowance from me.'

'Then why does he?'

'A little bit of independence, I suppose. He doesn't care to be thought of as a kept man. A toy boy perhaps. But I should think the most likely reason he works is to get away from me for a while. We really cannot stand the sight of each other for too long at a time. Kenny is wonderful in small doses but we can't live in each other's pockets. Although that is what we are just about to do.'

Josie, not sure if she was serious, shared a slight smile with her.

'He is totally useless. He wastes a tremendous amount of money gambling and I refuse to fund that so he has to find that from his own sources. Did you know about the gambling?'

'No.'

'Did he ask you to move with him to Spain? To the villa?'

She nodded, knowing it was pointless to pretend otherwise. 'I

174

said no. I'm not leaving my husband.'

'I should hope not. I remember your husband very well. A nice man.'

Josie managed a nervous smile, thinking it odd that Ray should have made an impression on a woman like this, but then she did recall the two of them huddled a while in a corner at that house-warming party. She couldn't imagine what on earth Ray had found to talk about to a sophisticated woman like this, unless he had had a hand in getting her the carpet at a special discount.

'Can I tell you something about this wonderful man of mine?' Dorothy said, taking a cigarette from a packet that lay on the coffee table and offering one to Josie who declined. Dorothy took her time lighting up and seemed to relax a little as she inhaled. 'He lives in a complete fantasy world, Mrs Bailey. For a start, it's my villa not his. I am buying it with my money. And that's where we are heading. He's coming with me to Spain and I intend to keep an eye on him in future. There will be no more straying or I'll be suing for divorce. I told him to say I was desperately ill so that he could cut short the notice. I wanted him out of there as quickly as possible so that we can get on with things. I shall be renting out this property and we shall be flying out in a couple of weeks.'

There was a steely glint in her eyes and Josie knew she meant it. It was difficult to imagine Kenny kowtowing to any woman, let alone his own wife, and it bemused her. This was developing into a girly chat and Josie found herself relaxing a little. It was all out in the open and about time – after all nothing had happened and now, thank God, nothing would happen.

'Where is he?'

They exchanged a womanly look that ultimately acknowledged the daftness of the male species in general and Kenny in particular.

'He's suffering from a severe bout of sulkiness,' Dorothy said with a small smile. 'He's thought about the options available and he now realizes that he's not going to get rid of me as easily as that. I can't believe he asked you to go with him to Spain. It's my villa, in my name, so I could have put a stop to that little scheme very quickly. Did it not occur to him that I would follow him? Did he imagine for one moment I would tolerate a little threesome? And, just to set the record straight, he has not been embezzling funds. I believe he told you that too? As I say, he tells these silly tales and ends up believing them. He craves excitement. He likes to be thought of as the bad boy. The girls always crowd round the bad boy. Hadn't you noticed? He's like a child. It's happened before. I have great trouble keeping him under control.' She laughed. 'How ever a man like that came to be working in local government of all things never ceases to amaze me. He has the qualifications. They're not fakes. And I believe he has the expertise but it's not enough for him.'

'Why don't you leave him?'

'Or rather, why do I stay with him? It does seem extraordinary, doesn't it? But I suppose I enjoy having him around. It's lonely on your own and I'm not somebody who enjoys her own company. I need a man about the house and you have to admit he's dishy. And he is rather good at some things.' She raised her eyebrows. 'My first husband was as miserable as sin. The only good thing he did was die and leave me pots of money. When I met Kenny, I found his outlook so refreshing. He can be very amusing. I don't mind the little flings but when they start to get serious . . . then something has to be done.'

'It was never serious,' Josie said, picking up on that.

'No. Looking at you, I don't suppose it was.'

She never did get the tea or coffee. What she did get was a run-down on their peculiar marriage.

'Just as a matter of interest, who told you?' she asked as she was leaving and slipping her shoes back on.

'I did promise I wouldn't say.'

'It wasn't my husband?' she asked, suddenly horrified that he might somehow have got wind of it.

'No. It was your sister Margaret.'

'Margaret? But I swore her to secrecy,' Josie said, not surprised. She felt a fool now for jumping to that conclusion about embezzlement. Daft idea all round.

Dorothy laughed, seeming to understand. 'Embezzlement eh? Kenny hasn't got the guts to do something like that. I have. I could do it but not Kenny. You were very gullible, Josie, to believe him.' They were on first name terms now.

Gullible. You could say that again. 'I hope things work out for you,' she said, meaning it, standing awkwardly now on the doorstep. The rain had eased and she kept the umbrella down. 'I did like him, Dorothy. I wouldn't have egged him on otherwise. And I'm sorry I did that. It was a very childish thing to do.'

Dorothy smiled. 'He's an arrogant bastard. It's not your fault.'

As she drove home, a weight lifted off her shoulders, she saw that now there was no obstacle to her taking the job. She would see if that flat was still on the market, the one she fancied.

And then she would have to persuade Ray.

CHAPTER TWENTY-THREE

Margaret had a lot to answer for. She had no business doing that. How could she trust her when she did things like that? She stopped off at Percy Street on the way back to have it out with her. As usual, there was nowhere to park and she ended up shoe-horning the car into a space three houses away from Margaret's. By the time she did that, not easy when you had an audience of interested children, her anger had abated a little. But, as she approached the front door, seeing Margaret waving at her from the window, she felt her hackles rising again.

'You had no right, interfering like that,' she said, as she bustled in, almost shoving Margaret out of the way. 'And how did you know Dorothy Balfour anyway?'

'I do have a life of my own,' Margaret said, looking at her reproachfully. 'If you must know, I don't know her that well, she's not my sort, but I have met her and I knew where she lived. And don't you come barging in here laying down the law, getting yourself in a tizzy. I only did it for you.'

'Did you go round to her house?' Josie clicked her tongue. 'Honestly, Margaret, you have a cheek. Why can't you mind your own business?'

'And watch you ruin your life? You forget I've known you for ever, Josie. Sometimes I wonder if you have any sense at all. You might keep landing on your feet but one of these days, mark my words, you'll come a cropper. Poor Ray. I feel sorry for him. He's a good man and here you are going the right way about losing him.'

'It was only a bit of fun.'

'I've heard that before. Sit yourself down.' Margaret picked up her knitting and calmly carried on. 'Has she put you in the picture then?'

'Yes.' Josie sank down in the chair, weary of it all. 'I could murder a cup of tea. She never even offered me a cup of tea.'

'You know where the kettle is. I'll have a cup too.'

Waiting for the kettle to boil, standing at the little window, Josie shivered. Her mum and dad were both gone now but their presence in this house was strong. They were everywhere, in every damned corner. Ray had put fresh wallpaper in the back sitting room but the old one was still there, underneath, the flowery one. She had studied that wallpaper closely. It had been applied the wrong way up so that the flowers were upside down. Her mother had only noticed the mistake when they had done one wall already, so they left it because the general effect had been all right.

Margaret should have moved away. She could have sold up and got another house close by. With a bit of luck, she might have managed to get out, shut the door quick, and leave the memories trapped behind.

'All right then. I forgive you,' she said magnanimously when she returned to the sitting room with the tea and a plate of digestives. 'You meant it for the best and, in the end, it's all worked out. Kenny's left, so I won't have to put up with him any more. I can't believe he'll just let her drag him off like that. He either loves her, deep down, or he really is all about money and his damned car and his nice suits and his gambling. Just as well he's off anyway, I have enough on my plate just now with Matthew getting married in the autumn. She's invited us over at Easter.'

'Who has?'

'Who do you think? Valerie. Starchy knickers. Alice's mother. She wants me and Ray to go for the weekend. Informal, she says. I haven't spoken to her but she asked Alice to ask us. It's a posh house by all accounts, right by the lake. Matthew says it's like a mansion. Ray will have kittens. I don't know if we should bother. You know what Ray's like. He won't know where to put himself, what knives to use and everything.'

'He's not as bad as that.' Margaret tutted and gave her a sharp glance. 'He manages fine these days. You make him out to be worse than he is, Josie. Stop doing it. You'll knock all his confidence.'

'What confidence?' Josie laughed at that.

'Get yourself over there. You never know you might just enjoy it.' Margaret finished the row, switched needles, clicked off again, fingers flying. 'There's no question of you not going and don't you worry about Jack Sazzoni. Forget all that. He never knew about that little matter.'

She didn't spell it out and neither did Josie.

'And you're not likely to tell him.' She paused in mid-stitch, gave Josie a hard stare. 'You've not got any daft thoughts of telling him, have you?'

'No. I have not. Why would I do that? Ray doesn't even know about that. Although I nearly told Alice . . . she's got a nice way with her and I felt she ought to know. Then I thought better of it. I can't think what came over me. It's not fair to lumber her with a secret like that.'

'Talking of secrets, I've got something to tell you,' Margaret said, coming to the end of the row, giving the knitting a satisfied tug and putting it down, needles sticking up. 'We've had an invitation, me and you.'

'To what?'

'Give me a chance.' Margaret rose to her feet, went across to the bureau and rummaged in the drawer. 'Here it is. Read it yourself.'

Josie took the sheet of paper, read it quickly.

'We can't go.' She looked at her sister. 'You weren't thinking of going, were you?'

'My first thought was no, but I think we have to,' Margaret said. 'We can do it, Josie.'

'For him?' Josie spat out the words. 'Why should we do anything for him, Margaret?'

'We're not doing it for him,' Margaret said. 'It's for the girl. Don't you see? Try to put yourself in her position. When somebody saves your life, you would put that person on a pedestal. Wouldn't you? And now that she's grown-up and has a child of her own, she still remembers him. As she says, if it wasn't for him, she wouldn't have had the baby, she wouldn't have been here to have the baby.'

'Fancy naming a baby after him,' Josie said. 'Poor little mite.'

'Don't you see? We can't destroy what she feels about him. So, we're not attending this ceremony for Dad, we're doing it for her. We put on a brave face and just do it. You're coming with me, Josie, you *and* Ray and I shan't take no for an answer. In any case, I've already accepted so it's too late.'

A showdown with Dorothy, a good talking to from Margaret and then, to cap it all, when she rang the estate agents, the flat by the old docks was under offer and off the market.

'Who's buying it?' she asked the girl, knowing she had no claim on the blessed place but feeling hard done by to have missed the opportunity.

'I can't tell you his name,' the girl said. 'All I can say is that he's a doctor and he's paid cash, so there won't be any hitches. We'll keep you informed, Mrs Bailey, if any of the others come back on the market.'

Ray was out when she got back so she rang Alice for a chat, which would help her get over the disappointment. She had taken to doing this, ringing Alice in preference to Matthew. Matthew was not chatty on the phone, just like his dad, and always in a tearing hurry, so she liked to phone Alice who always sounded, rightly or wrongly, as though she had all the time in the world.

'I'm going to be in the local paper,' she told her. 'Margaret and I have been invited to this little do. It's a long story. Did Matthew tell you about his granddad saving this little girl from a fire years ago?'

'Oh yes. That's very impressive, isn't it? He was a policeman, wasn't he? Matthew's told me lots about him. How he used to spend a lot of time reading to him and telling him stories. They got on very well, didn't they?'

'Yes, well . . . that little girl is grown up now and she's had a baby boy and she wants to call the baby after Matthew's granddad. She moved away after the incident and was brought up in Southampton, I think, and now for some reason she wants to come back to Felston and make a little bit of a fuss. She's an artist.'

'Isn't that lovely of her? It's so nice of her to have remembered.'

'It certainly makes a story for the local paper,' Josie said, unable to stop a little sniff. 'Just the sort of thing they like, being a bit soppy and everything. Human interest they call it. So, as Dad's not around any more, they've asked me and Margaret to come along as his representatives. There'll be a photograph and a little report of the incident and so on. It made headline news at the time.'

'You must have been very proud of him?'

'Yes,' Josie said quietly.

'How exciting! What will you wear?' Alice asked, a smile in her voice.

She laughed. 'What do you think I should wear? Is there a dress code for it? I'm more concerned with what Margaret will wear. I don't want her looking too frumpish. She has her black suit and her best coat and that's it.'

'My mother says she's looking forward to meeting you again by the way,' Alice said, acting as go-between as usual between the two of them. 'She's got nothing planned as such. It depends on the weather. You know what Easter's like. So unpredictable.'

'Will you be there?' Josie asked, wanting some support, knowing she would get it from Alice.

'I don't think so. Matthew and I thought it would be best to leave you to it. You can have a nice time together, just the four of you.' She paused. 'Don't worry about it, Josie. You must not feel yourself under any pressure. You mustn't think that you have got to be friends.'

'Just so long as we're not daggers drawn, is that it?' Josie said. 'Your wedding will be fine. Don't *you* worry about that. I wouldn't dream of doing anything to spoil it for you.' She felt a sudden urge to tell Alice that she was starting to think of her as a daughter, the one she had never had, but she felt a bit shy of saying such a thing. Maybe it was too soon. 'Has he said anything about me? Your father?'

'No. When I told them, he laughed. He thought it was funny. Mother wasn't so amused. In fact . . . she's been in a very funny mood recently. She came over for a few days and I don't want to go into it but my next door neighbour upset her. She brought it all back to mum. Did you know she lost four babies after me?'

'I didn't know that. I heard from somebody that things hadn't gone well. But I didn't know it was so many. Four, you say? Poor Valerie.'

'It's still raw,' Alice said. 'Can you believe that? After all this time?'

'Oh yes . . . I can believe it.'

Ray had sworn Lynn to secrecy. He didn't want Josie getting wind of it too soon, not before things were finalized. He kept having cold feet but it was time he took a stand, did something unexpected. She would like that. He had been thinking about doing it for years but he had needed somebody like Lynn to push him a bit, to give him some encouragement. Lynn had changed since Mick had left her. She hadn't folded, as they thought she might, but had got herself over it, over him, and he thought she looked a damned sight better at forty-five than she had at twenty.

They were invited to the Sazzoni residence at Easter. He was not looking forward to that one little bit but, with Matthew and Alice now engaged, it had to be faced. Josie was going mad, buying him new clothes like there was no tomorrow, because, as she said, she didn't want him showing her up in the stuff he had at present.

'I wasn't thinking of taking my work clothes,' he had told her, a bit peeved about it. 'And how do we know what we'll need if we don't know where they'll be taking us?'

'That's why we have to prepare for all eventualities,' Josie told him, attacking one of her lists with a vengeance. 'You never know at Easter. It could be cold, raining, sunny. It's a nightmare knowing what to take. Now, where was I? Oh yes, your list. Underwear—'

'Bloody hell, Josie, nobody's going to see that except you.'

'It doesn't matter. You need new underpants anyway. Are you fussed what I get?'

He shook his head. Underpants were underpants. He had never bought a pair in his life. He left that to the women in his life, first his mum and now Josie.

'They will probably want to take us out to dinner in a fancy restaurant up there and, if the weather's nice—' She chewed thoughtfully on her pen. 'We might have a barbeque in the garden and then they might take us on a boat trip across the lake or we might just be going sightseeing. I don't know what their interests are.'

For crying out loud. . . . 'Matthew says they're into walking, so we'll have to take walking boots,' he told her. 'I've got some but you'll have to get yourself a pair. And some thick socks. And we'll need haversacks.'

'Walking boots?' She looked horrified. 'But I can't walk in flat shoes.'

'We'll definitely need them in case they take us mountaineering. Have you considered that possibility?'

She looked at him, shook her head as she caught his smile. 'Stop fooling around, Ray, I haven't time for this. It's just as well I don't take you seriously. Walking boots indeed.'

He had left her to it. In the end, it would be business as usual. She could fill the suitcases and he would carry them.

In the meantime, they had this little reception in honour of Jimmy to attend and he was only going to that because for some reason Josie wanted him there with her. They were making a fuss because the girl whom Jimmy had rescued all those years ago was now something of a celebrity. He had never heard of her but she was an artist making a name for herself down in London, one of those modern artists, whose work left him bewildered. He hadn't said anything to Josie because it might offend her, but he reckoned that it was all a publicity stunt and that really this girl didn't give a monkey's about Jimmy, but maybe that was him being cynical. He would have to give her the benefit of the doubt.

It was billed as a little reception held at an art gallery in town, cocktails and a buffet at her expense, with some of her paintings on show and then a few speeches. He had no idea who would be speaking and didn't particularly care so long as he wasn't expected to say something. Josie would have a go if she had to but Margaret would be struck dumb.

'You can try out your new suit,' Josie said, laying his clothes out for him on the bed. 'Wear the blue shirt and the blue and pink tie.'

'OK.' He glanced at her. She looked nervous which puzzled him because normally she would love a free do like this. She had already changed twice and he had an idea the dark suit she was wearing at present would not last the course. 'Are we picking Margaret up?'

She nodded and then sat down abruptly on the bed, smack bang on his new suit.

And burst into tears.

CHAPTER TWENTY-FOUR

This living together business was not easy and Matthew's irregular work pattern was a nuisance but there it was. She would have to get used to it and it was worth all the hassle just to have him here with her under the same roof, sharing the same bed.

It just felt right and, even if she sensed the slightest disapproval coming from some quarters, surprisingly her father rather than her mother, she dismissed that. Dad was happy that there was a wedding planned and they were now homing in on several dates with a view to bringing all the arrangements together very soon.

As to her own job, her contract with the education authority had been renewed for a further year, so that was something, and she had started up a Saturday morning dance class in Kirkley for under-tens, which was already oversubscribed.

Alice had said nothing to Matthew about her mother and Mrs Osborne. The thing about the faulty gene was worrying, of course, and she would have to get round to doing something about it at some point.

But not yet.

There was the wedding in autumn to look forward to and they were not intending to have a baby right away. They needed to get themselves sorted out first and Matthew would probably have to move away to get the job he wanted. So, the gene thing could wait.

As to her neighbour, she should have left well alone. Her mother had once suffered from depression and it was therefore irresponsible of the old lady for saying something that might have started it all off again. Putting ideas like that into the head of someone who had gone through a vulnerable period as her mother had was just not on. It was just pure luck that it had seemed to have the opposite effect and done her mother a world of good.

It was March and getting warmer. The daffodils were just out and her little garden was proving to be a constant surprise. Over the hedge, Mrs Osborne had a man in once a week to tidy hers – a neat and rather prim garden with a little pond and fish; not very sensible when she had a cat. The cat sneaked through the hedge into her garden sometimes and she didn't mind that, although she did mind when it caught the little fledgling birds that were starting to appear.

She had been to a show at the theatre last night, a show that had received good reviews, although she found herself disappointed by it for some reason. Matthew had come up with the idea of treating their parents to a Shakespeare play at Easter. He would arrange to get tickets for the four of them, but she was not sure of the wisdom of that. A musical or a comedy would have been fine but somehow, she didn't feel Ray would be exactly enthralled by a Shakespeare production and she did not want him to feel uncomfortable and out of his depth. She liked Ray. He was big and uncomplicated and, in many ways, so like Matthew.

'You've got to give him a chance,' Matthew said when she told him of her concerns. 'He's no fool, my dad.'

'I didn't say he was.'

'You implied it.'

'No I did not.'

'Yes you bloody did.'

'Don't swear at me, Matthew.'

'Is it any wonder? There you are suggesting my dad is only half there when he's as bright as the next man. And he's got a helluva lot more common sense than some.'

'All right. We'll take them to your Shakespeare play,' she said, annoyed because she could not understand why he was being unreasonable. 'I'm only thinking of him. I worry he will feel very awkward and uncomfortable but if that's what you want, then just do it. And, if you're not going to take any notice of my opinion, you needn't bother asking me what I think in future. Just go ahead and do your own thing.'

'For God's sake, there's no need to go all snotty on me, Alice.'

She rushed out at that point, slamming the door rather satisfactorily behind her.

He did not follow. Joy of joys. Their first row.

Matthew had booked the seats that very afternoon before he could change his mind, so that was that. Her mother was thrilled, loved the idea of a Shakespeare play, her dad was more interested in where they would go for dinner the previous evening and when she gave Josie the news, to her surprise Josie asked which play it was.

'*The Merchant of Venice*,' Alice told her. 'It's one of my favourites. It's quite easy to follow. It's about this man called Shylock and—'

'I know what it's about,' Josie said, voice cooling. 'We did it at school. I went to Felston Girls' Grammar, Alice, and we didn't shirk on our Shakespeare.'

'Sorry, I didn't mean—' She stopped, feeling awful.

'No, of course you didn't. It's me. I'm a bit touchy about it. Tell Matthew thanks for that. We'll look forward to it. I'll give Ray a run-down on the plot.'

Alice put down the phone, feeling no better. Had she a touch of her mother in her? How dare she make assumptions about Ray, or Josie for that matter? It was a little warning and she would take note of it.

She and Matthew had quickly made up and he had somehow found the time to buy her some flowers as an apology. Sticking them in a vase, she reflected ruefully that, as a first row, it didn't rate very highly. Certainly nothing had been flung, apart from a few nasty words. It had been rather tame, in fact, and if that was the best they could manage then it would be fine. Mind you, like his mother, he could be a mite touchy about some subjects and, if she was to avoid friction in future, she would do well to remember it.

Josie had accepted the new job but not yet told Ray. She wouldn't be starting it until next month, so there was time enough for that.

A few days before the photo shoot for this medal thing, she had seen Lynn. It was Lynn's birthday, circled in Josie's diary like all the family birthdays, and, daft as it might seem, they still bought each other a little present and a card. She always agonized over what to buy Lynn because, living on her own as she did and earning a good salary, she had pretty much everything she wanted. She had got smarter as she got older, grown into her shape and was more relaxed about her height, even to the extent of wearing high heels. Josie settled on a leather purse because purses wore out and a new one was always appreciated. Then she bought a card, a little girl's pink card with the number 4 on it, a 4 to which she added a 6 to make 46. Silly, but they always did this sort of thing with cards. On her last birthday, Lynn had sent her a card with a badge inside 'I am 5', scratching a 4 in front of it and daring her to wear it for the entire day. She had agreed to do that, even though it was a work day and had spent that day with the badge pinned to her knickers. It had been enough to send the pair of them into a fit of giggles.

They were like two big kids. She couldn't do that sort of thing with anybody else but Lynn. Margaret liked sugary sweet cards with 'To my dearest sister' written on them, big fancy verses, the cornier the better for Margaret. She kept them, too, Josie knew that, kept them in a box in her wardrobe, together with bits and pieces of goodness knows what. A box of secrets and, although she had sneaked a peep from time to time, there wasn't anything in it that interested her.

Lynn lived in Clarence Street, off Clarence Square, in the first-floor apartment of an enormous three-storey town house close to Felston Park. Five minutes walk to her office and the shops, it was in an ideal location and, like Josie, her fingers were not tinged remotely green, so having no garden was a bonus. After Mick had left her, she had got rid of all the furniture the two of them had shared and bought new pieces. Everything was spanking new but it lacked any sense of being a home, more a show place. All photographs of the formerly happy couple had disappeared but, after a shaky start, Lynn seemed to have settled into her new life without him, and had long since told Josie to stop trying to find her a man. She did not want one.

'A purse!' Lynn shrieked, seeming as thrilled as if she had been given a diamond ring. 'Just what I needed. You clever thing.'

Josie beamed. It was always gratifying to be told that, whether or not it was true.

'Sit down. I haven't seen you in ages. We need to catch up,' Lynn said, scrunching up the wrapping paper and placing it in a waste-paper bin. 'Oh Josie, I was sorry to hear about your mum. Just after Christmas at that.'

'Yes. Thanks for your card. She was eighty-five, Lynn. At that age, it's hardly a surprise.'

'Surprise or not, it's still hard.' Lynn said.

'What have you been up to then?' Josie asked, settling back on the sofa. It was a dark blue leather chesterfield – gorgeous – and she could not help but run her hand along the seat beside her, the surface warm and soft to her touch. 'This is new, isn't it?'

'It cost a fortune but I got a bonus,' Lynn told her. 'I've nothing to spend it on except me. Doesn't that sound awful? Really selfish. But I'm darned if I'm going to be the woman who leaves thousands to her godchildren. They never come to see me from one year to the next so they can lump it. I'm booked for a Caribbean cruise in June.'

'Good for you. You never know who you'll meet on a trip like that. Make sure you take some nice bikinis with you.'

'You must be joking,' Lynn said with a sniff. 'Good heavens, Josie, you should stop wearing bikinis when you reach forty. Thirty if I had my way. I've always preferred a swimsuit and I'm taking a few nice ones and some cover-ups.' She reached for a ginger snap, nibbled at it. 'And that's not the reason I'm going. I don't want to meet anybody. I'm happy on my own, thank you very much.'

'I wish I was coming with you,' Josie said. 'Ray wouldn't hear of us going anywhere like that. You know what he's like. Real stay at home.'

'You might be surprised at Ray. He was telling me about your Matthew by the way and that girl of his. I bet that was a shock.'

'When did you see Ray? He never mentioned it.'

'I bumped into him. Can't remember when,' Lynn said, looking shifty.

'You're right. It was a shock. A terrible shock. It spoilt my Christmas I don't mind telling you.'

'What are you going to do?'

'What can I do? Put a brave face on it, that's what. I don't suppose he'll remember me.'

'Do you remember him?'

'Yes.'

'Well then. It stands to reason,' Lynn said triumphantly. 'I wonder what he's thinking about it all?'

'No idea. Look, Lynn, I'm trying not to make too much of it. It's a long time ago. He married Valerie and I married Ray.'

'I've often wondered why you chucked him, Josie. You two seemed so good together. Everybody said that. I know you said it was the religion thing but was it? You could have turned like everybody else does. I mean to say, it wasn't as if you were that bothered, was it? And your mum and dad would have come round. They always do,' she added brightly. 'My mum and dad weren't keen on Mick but they went along with it. Mind you, I could always get round my dad. And so could you have, if you'd tried.'

'No, I couldn't, Lynn,' Josie said flatly. 'You don't know the half of it. I was only eighteen and you do all sorts of daft things at that age. You think you know it all and you know nothing.' She accepted another cup of coffee, watching Lynn closely as she poured it. 'Anyway, why did you finish with that first boy of yours? I can't even remember his name now.'

'Neither can I,' Lynn said with a dash of a smile. 'And that's the whole point, isn't it? I can't for the life of me remember him but you have just admitted you remember Jack. It's not a good situation. You're quite right to be worried. I would be if it was me.'

'Well, thanks for that.' Josie set her cup on the side table. 'What do you think will happen? Do you expect me and Jack to go rushing into each other's arms, just like that? It won't happen, Lynn. And it's not as if we're intending to have much to do with them. Wedding. Christening when it happens, if it happens. Family occasions are the only time we'll have to meet up. It's not as if we'll be in each other's pockets. We have no intention of going with them to their villa in Italy even if they asked, and Matthew seems to think they will.'

'Villa in Italy? Very nice. Just think what you've missed.' She smiled but behind it there was just a hint of satisfaction for the way things had turned out. Sometimes Josie wondered why their friendship had remained solid when sometimes, like just now, Lynn could suddenly turn as sharp as a bitter lemon.

'I've missed nothing,' she said stoutly, tempted to turn the tables on her by mentioning Mick, who was doing very well thank you as a jobbing builder. 'You do yourself no favours by harping back to the past, Lynn.'

'Exactly.' Lynn pounced on that. 'But you're going to be put in that position, like it or not, aren't you?'

Josie ignored that. Time for a swift change of subject. 'You're not to tell Ray yet—' She had not intended to say anything but she was bursting to tell somebody outside the office and she wanted to surprise Lynn, who didn't think much of her accounting abilities. 'I've been offered that promotion. The one I told you about. It will mean a big rise. Ray's not going to like it.'

Lynn did not offer congratulations. 'No, he won't,' she said quietly, almost to herself. 'Oh heavens, Josie, I said I wouldn't say anything but you've put me in an awkward position. He's planning to surprise you, you see.'

'Why? What the hell has he done?'

'He's going into business, business with me,' Lynn said.

'Ray's going into business?' Josie repeated, looking at her in amazement.

Lynn nodded. 'There, I've done it now. I've been looking for something for a while to sink some money into. So, we've joined forces, business partners, and the paperwork is almost through. Ray's bought a little shop, do it yourself leaning towards plumbing.'

'A shop?'

'It's a little gold mine. I've looked through the accounts and it's very impressive, as sound as a bell. It's been family run for years and they have a very solid customer base. Customers like the individual touch. And there's room for expansion so he's not going to be limited. They've never stretched themselves to their full. Ray's very excited about it.'

'I bet he is. Has he given up his carpet job then?' Josie asked, completely bewildered by this. Ray had never done anything unexpected in his life. He was Mr Safe, no two ways about it, and he wouldn't give up a good job like his carpet fitting to take a chance on something else.

'Yes, although they've asked if they can call on him if they get a rush job on. He's highly regarded, Josie.' She looked at her closely. 'Don't you get it? He needs to do this. He needs to show you what he's made of.'

'No, he doesn't,' Josie said. 'I know what he's made of. He doesn't have to impress me. I'm his wife, for God's sake.'

'I know but I don't think you appreciate him fully. You're always doing him down, Josie. It's no wonder he's lacking in confidence.'

'Margaret said the same thing.' Josie moved uncomfortably on the sofa and it squeaked softly. 'You're both doing your best to make me feel guilty. I've not been fair to him, Lynn, and that's the truth. There was this chap at work . . . no, nothing happened. It was all a bit of fun but it nearly got out of hand and it scared me to death. I don't want to lose Ray but. . . .'

'His idea . . . now, listen to this . . . his idea is that you can help him out in the business, save him getting somebody else in and you help him with the paperwork. He wants you to work with him and give up your own job.'

Josie huffed. 'Well, he can stuff that idea for a start. I've just got promoted, Lynn, I'm deputy clerk now. I'd have given my eye teeth for that job when I first started there. I shall have my own office. Ray has a bloody cheek if he thinks I'll give that up for some cock-eyed little shop. I would be a glorified shop assistant.'

'He's got his heart set on it and it's too late to back out now. We're committed,' Lynn told her, eyes hardening. 'Think about it. Oh, and another thing . . . it's got a lovely flat above the shop and you are always complaining about the garden and—'

'Where on earth is it? This shop?'

'Bank Parade.'

'Oh.' She fell silent, digesting that. Bank Parade was quite nice, all right Bank Parade was *very* nice, close to being Mayfair on Felston's monopoly board. A widely curving, tree-lined, cutting through street, the quickest way from Market Street to Pilcher Lane, so there would be lots of customers and now she came to think of it, she knew where the shop was. It would have a nice view out at the back of the top end of the park.

'But what about our house? There's the small matter of selling that first.'

'He's already got a buyer lined up,' Lynn said. 'When he gets an idea, he wastes no time. He's thought of everything. He was laying this carpet and he got to talking with this woman whose son was looking for his first place and he's got his mortgage arranged and everything, and your house is just what he's been looking for.'

'I can't believe it. Why hasn't he said? I can't bear secrets.'

'Can't you? I thought you were good at secrets. You and all your family.'

Josie said nothing. She could never be one hundred per cent sure that Lynn didn't know about that other baby, Jack Sazzoni's baby.

True girlfriends knew about things like that, practically knew when you were having your period before you did. Lynn had come round to visit after she lost it, her mother having rigged up some cock and bull story about a virus.

'What's wrong with your mum?' she had asked, coming into Josie's bedroom after a brief are-you-decent knock. 'She wasn't too keen on me coming up to see you. Are you feeling better?'

'Not much.'

'I've brought you a magazine,' Lynn said, handing her a copy of *Honey*.

'Thanks.' She turned her head away, looked at the wallpaper pattern, the intricate shapes of the pink and blue flowers. Every room in their house had floral wallpaper. Her mother did not go in for real flowers in vases except on very special occasions, but she made up for it with the wallpaper. In answer to Lynn's question, Josie didn't know how she felt to be honest. She felt completely washed out, her mother's favourite expression, and her legs had let her down when she had gone to the bathroom. She felt peculiarly empty, pleased at first when it had happened but not so pleased now. That little slip of a thing had saved the bother of having a forced rejection anyway. . . . She swallowed down a sob, fighting back the tears. If she cried, she might just tell Lynn.

'You look terrible,' Lynn said, eyeing her cheerfully. 'You've no colour. I hope it's not catching. Do you want me to pour you a glass of Lucozade?'

That particular drink was her mother's cure for every damned thing and a new bottle in its orange cellophane wrapper sat beside her on her bedside table. Her mother, thrilled to bits at the way things had turned out, had come over all maternal and caring. Later, there would be chicken soup followed by a milk pudding, which she would have to eat to keep her strength up. Lynn, as bad in some ways as her mother, was already pouring her a glass, screwing the top back on and standing there, poised as Josie awkwardly shuffled up and against the pillow. 'Here.'

No, Lynn, you don't understand. I've just lost my baby. A glass of Lucozade is not going to help. She had felt like saying that but, biting her tongue in order to keep the words in, she said thanks instead and drank the fizzy liquid.

'Don't you dare hurt Ray,' Lynn said, bringing Josie sharply back to the present. 'I know you wanted that promotion, but ask yourself this. Is it worth risking losing your husband? He'll be devastated if you say no. He's so excited about it all. And, don't you forget, he's done it all for you.'

Josie glanced sharply at her.

'I'm not going to hurt him. You make me out to be some sort of monster. You've been underhand though. I'm not happy at you being caught up with us. It ties the three of us together, Lynn, and I'm not sure I want that. Ray should have discussed it with me, something as important as this.'

'You can buy me out eventually if it bothers you that much,' Lynn said with a tight smile. 'You wouldn't be jealous by any chance?'

'Why would I be jealous?'

'I don't know but you needn't be. I'm not after him if that's what you're thinking? Ray wouldn't look at another woman. Surely you know that?'

CHAPTER TWENTY-FIVE

'I don't want to go,' Josie wailed, holding on to him tightly as he sat beside her on the bed, on the suit 'I can't do it, Ray.'

'I know, love,' he said gently, arm round her. 'It's going to upset you coming on top of your mother and everything. But it's got to be done for your dad's sake. I've got the medal out of the drawer. They'll want us to show it in the photo. Now come on, dry your eyes and put your lipstick on and we'll get going. If you'll get off my suit that is.'

'Oh God, it'll be all crushed.' She stood up promptly, fussing, drying her eyes, blowing her nose, fixing her hair. He did not like the new hairstyle but it had grown a bit since Christmas and the colour was fading back to her brown. Why red? She wasn't a redhead. He hadn't fallen in love with a redhead. Each to his own and Prince Andrew's Fergie was a corker but even so . . . not for him.

'You've got to help me through this, Ray,' Josie said as they went out. 'I can't tell you why, but this is going to be dreadful for me and Margaret. I want it to be over and done with as soon as possible. We're not hanging about. We'll be polite, look at her paintings and then we're off.'

'You don't think we'll be expected to buy one, do you?' he asked. He had flipped through a catalogue to get some idea what they were like and he didn't fancy having one of those on his wall, assuming he could afford the price.

'No.' Josie managed a laugh. 'If she has anything about her, she'll be giving us one for free. If she does, look pleased, for heaven's sake. And, remember, I want out of there as soon as possible.'

'Leave it with me,' he said.

The boy who wanted to buy the house was coming to see it again at the weekend so he would have to break the news to Josie before then. He had managed to arrange the first viewing when Josie was out, panicking that she would suddenly turn up and wonder who the hell this strange man was. In the event, it had gone smoothly and it was all going through. The completion of this and the shop and flat would all take place on the same day. And it was looming fast.

He wanted to see her face when he told her. He hoped she would be all right about Lynn's part in it, but he couldn't have done it without her help and it wasn't as if it was charity. It was a good investment and Lynn had a business head on her shoulders. They were on to a winner. Do-it-yourself was booming and he was pretty much an expert himself. He would be able to offer proper sensible advice and he had plans to expand, take over that other room at the back and start selling fancy kitchen gadgets and so on. As to the flat . . . well, it had been rented out for the last few years and was a bit of a mess but nothing that couldn't be sorted out. He was looking forward to getting stuck in up there. Living and working on the premises; he couldn't imagine anything nicer than that.

He drove round to Margaret's and then to the gallery. Now that it was going to happen, he was not sure it was a good idea. He hoped this woman was doing it because she wanted to honour Jimmy's name and not because she thought it would be, what they called, good PR.

She was called Alison Jameson and she rushed over to them directly they were in the room, kissing them on the cheek, an over-familiarity which didn't go down well with Ray and Margaret, although they suffered it well.

Alison was a tiny creature, like a doll, with huge waif-like eyes and far too much gingery hair that made her head look too big. She was wearing a beautifully embroidered silk caftan in a gorgeous turquoise shade and floated about the room as if she were on skates.

Josie did her best. She was annoyed at herself for getting upset before they had even started but it was one damned thing after another and it was getting to her. She had given Ray the chance to say something about the shop but he was keeping it quiet as yet and she needed time to think about it before he supposedly sprang it on her. And still, at the back of her mind, there was this meeting with Jack looming and getting closer as Easter approached. She was terrified she would somehow make a fool of herself, do something stupid, get Jack on his own and come right out with it. Tell him she had loved him back then and she still did.

The press contingent was here already or rather what passed for it. It consisted of one chap in a badly-fitting suit and a bored-looking photographer.

'Here they are,' Alison said, aiming them both at the photographer. 'These are Jimmy Pritchard's daughters. Isn't it just too wonderful of them to come along?'

The reporter, hardly eagle-eyed, came over then and asked if he could have a word. Well, that was the whole point, wasn't it?

'Where do you want us?' Josie asked, taking charge as Margaret seemed struck dumb by the occasion.

'We'll just take a seat over here,' the reporter said, taking them over to a table. On the way, a glass of champagne was pressed into their hands. The room was heaving. Who *were* these people?

'Now, just a few words, ladies.' The reporter took out his notebook. 'I take it you're the older sister?' he asked, looking at Margaret. 'Let me see, you were a young woman at the time of the incident?'

'That's right. Josie, here, was thirteen.'

'And what were your feelings, Margaret, when you heard the

199

news that your father had done this wonderful thing? That he was a hero?'

'No comment. We've nothing to add to what's been said already,' Margaret said firmly. 'We're very proud. Aren't we, Josie?'

'Very proud,' she echoed, looking at Ray who was sitting right beside her giving encouraging little nods.

'We've brought the medal,' he said, taking it out of his pocket. 'It has pride of place at home,' he added, looking pointedly at Josie.

'Right. What we're going to do is run a copy of the original article showing your father holding little Alison and then we'll bring it up to date showing Alison holding her little James.'

'James Jameson,' Margaret pondered, looking at Josie. 'That's a mouthful. Has she thought about that?'

'I think he's going to be called by his middle name, David,' the reporter said. 'Can I ask you ladies a bit about yourselves? What do you do now for example?'

Josie bottled down her irritation. What the hell did that have to do with anything? However, they had to get through this evening and they did. The photographs were taken; Alison in the middle of the two of them holding baby James, Alison alone looking pensive, Alison and baby James, the two sisters – try not to look so stiff, Margaret – a picture of the lot of them with Margaret holding up the medal and lastly, a picture of Josie holding the baby.

They had another glass of champagne and some nibbles and then strolled round the exhibition. They were big bold canvasses for such a little lady and they made agreeable noises, Josie not daring to catch Ray's eye because she knew just what he would think of them. Alison's pictures were mainly of naked men, the nude from a woman's angle, she said with a completely straight face, and they didn't leave a lot to the imagination. On a cringing factor, Josie reckoned they rated a ten but there were a lot of oohs and aahs from those present.

Alison, who had never stopped talking since they had arrived, wanted to say a few words. She deposited baby James with Josie, who had not bargained for that and took the child warily. This navy suit was one of the new ones she had bought for work, suitably expensive for a deputy clerk, and baby James, or David as she preferred to think of him, looked perfectly capable of sabotaging it.

'Ladies and gentlemen . . .' Alison began but they could barely see her, so there was a bit of a kerfuffle whilst somebody searched for and found a box for her to stand on. 'Hello again,' she said, beaming at them. 'May I say how privileged I feel this evening to be hosting this little thank you event and how proud I feel that Jimmy's two wonderful daughters have come along to represent him. It is a deep regret for me that I never had the chance to thank him properly for what he did. I want to tell you what happened that day.' She paused, seemed for a moment to be overcome with emotion. 'At least, what I can remember of it, which is very little because I was only a toddler. The fire started in the living room. I think the paper my mother was using to draw a draught up the chimney caught hold and she dropped it and it set fire to the rug and the chair. Anyway, it was spreading fast and she panicked. She ran into the street screaming and by sheer chance Jimmy was coming by. One of the neighbours set off to call the fire brigade but Jimmy said there was no time to waste. My mother was trying to get back into the house, screaming that her baby – that was me of course – was inside. Jimmy pushed her aside and some neighbours restrained her and then he ran inside and I think I remember him calling my name. It comes back to me sometimes in a sort of nightmare.' She paused and there were a few gasps. 'And then I have this vague memory of strong arms lifting me up, a man saying that it was all right, that it would be all right.'

Josie swallowed the bile that was rising in her throat, found herself clutching the baby to her breast, forgetting about her suit.

'And then he was carrying me out, past the smoke and the flames, holding me, protecting me with his arms and then he passed me over to my mother. By the time the fire brigade arrived, the house was

201

well and truly alight and there was no way I would have been got out alive. He saved my life. Their father,' she pointed dramatically at Josie and Margaret, 'their wonderful father saved my life. And I want to say thank you.'

Margaret was ashen. Ray was standing there with a silly proud grin on his face. Josie wondered what she looked like herself. She passed the baby back to Alison who did seem genuinely moved. Ray had moved over to her, was exchanging a few words with her. Good for Ray. She didn't feel that she could say another word to this woman. The need to tell her the truth, to smash the illusion was intense and, looking at her sister, she knew she felt precisely the same. Catching Margaret's gaze, she saw her shake her head slightly and that was enough.

Illusions.

Strong arms indeed, but in their case, especially in Margaret's case, strong arms used for the wrong purpose.

They were silent on the way home. Alison had wanted to keep in touch, had even asked Margaret to be godmother to the baby but Margaret had, politely but firmly, refused. They had been presented with one of Alison's smaller pen and ink drawings and Josie would find a home for it somewhere, although it would only serve to remind her of her father whenever she looked at the damned thing.

Duty done.

'That went very well,' Ray said when they had deposited Margaret at Percy Street and were on their way. 'I think we should put the medal in a frame or something. Show it off. It's not right, Josie, it being stuck in a drawer like that. It's as if you were ashamed of it.'

'Yes, we'll do that,' she told him, knowing she would not. She would stick it back in the drawer where it belonged. It was fresh in Ray's mind just now but he would soon forget. Perhaps she would give it to Matthew sooner rather than later, let him do with it what he would. Anything to get it off her hands.

She still despised her father. He could do that to a strange child, save her life, hold her and comfort her, but he couldn't do that to his own child. That fleeting memory of being lifted up high and whirled round, giggling, emerged. That was him. That was dad.

Something had happened to change him. And now he was dead, she would never be able to ask him what and why?

CHAPTER TWENTY-SIX

The forecast for the Easter weekend was good and getting better. Hoping to goodness that weather girl had got it right, Josie left her smart mackintosh and some of the heavier-weight clothes behind, still managing to fill two suitcases and a squashy bag.

The itinerary had firmed up to include a quiet at-home dinner, a restaurant meal, the theatre and a lake cruise. Josie had managed to get her hair done and, although it was still shorter than she would like, it was not quite so shorn and the red tone had almost disappeared. For the journey up there, she was wearing a lilac trouser suit, not sure now if the colour suited her. There were two new dresses, one for the restaurant and one for the theatre, some tops and trousers, and most of the shoes in her wardrobe.

She worried all the way up about what she would say when she first saw him. She was remembering the time – *that* time – and the way he had looked at her and, afterwards, the way he had looked when she had told him it was all over. She was remembering her own wedding to Ray and how she had almost expected Jack to come running in to whisk her away just at the critical moment. She would have left Ray standing there at the altar if he had and to heck with the consequences. She would have . . . wouldn't she?

They were on the final leg of the journey, on the lakeside road looking for the house now. The roads had been packed with holidaymakers and caravans which had slowed them up, but now they were as close as they could be and Josie, peering ahead, looking for

the cream-coloured house with the big weeping willow by the gate
told Ray to start signalling because they were here.

Ray pulled into the drive and immediately the front door opened
and Valerie stepped out, smiling at them, directing them into a space
like a traffic warden, her clothes bearing some resemblance in that
her dress was black with gold piping but there the similarity ended.
Never had there been a traffic warden so elegant and good-looking.

'Lovely to see you,' she said as they climbed out. She shook
hands with them both, a firm no-nonsense handshake. 'You must be
exhausted. Come on in and have a cup of tea. Jack's waiting.'

She set off at a fast lick, high heels clicking across a parquet floor,
and they followed. Josie caught Ray's reassuring glance but she was
too far gone by now to acknowledge it and it did not make her feel
any better. She felt so awful, heart pounding, feet dragging, thinking
that she couldn't have felt any worse if she had been heading for the
gallows.

To Valerie's supreme irritation, Josie looked fantastic. Lilac suited
her. Yes, of course she had aged, as she had aged herself, but she had
accomplished it gracefully. She was slimmer than Valerie had imagined but her eyes were the same. Very striking. She was wearing less
make-up than she had expected Valerie and wished she had gone
easy on her own.

Mrs Parkinson had given the house a thorough going over and it
was spotless with lots of fresh spring flowers artfully arranged in
pots and glass vases. Valerie was putting the Baileys in the guest
room at the front, its wide window overlooking the lake, but before
she showed them up, she took them into the sitting-room where they
were to have tea and cake.

Jack had been surprisingly unmoved by all this, acting for all the
world as if Josie and Ray were just any old guests and Valerie kept
trying to catch him out, searching for some sign that he was simply
putting on an act and that in fact, he was as wound up as she was.
She had dreamed last night of finding Josie – as she had been – and

Jack – as *he* had been – locked in a passionate embrace. Waking up this morning, she had reached out for her husband and found him there beside her and, for a moment, thought of telling him about the dream.

'What a lovely room!' Josie said, looking round the sitting-room. 'And such views. You're very lucky, Valerie.'

'Do sit down,' she said, regretting the formality of her voice, trying her best to be as free and easy as Josie seemed to be. 'Well . . . what do you think of our children then? It was quite a surprise, wasn't it?'

'A shock more like,' Ray said looming large by the window as Josie took a seat on a button-backed chair upholstered in pale green silk. 'Josie nearly fainted on the spot when she found out. Didn't you, love?'

'Not quite,' Josie said tightly, giving him a quick glance. 'But then you never know who your children are going to throw at you, do you?'

Valerie found she was looking at Ray, a big solid man, dark and handsome. Why had she not remembered him? He was, she thought, rather striking. Admittedly, he spoke with a pronounced Lancashire accent, more so than Josie and much more so than their son. So, accents diluted too, just like Italian blood.

'It could have been worse,' she said, thinking about the children. 'Is that what you mean, Josie?'

'No, not at all. We're very pleased,' Josie told her, smiling now with determination. 'Alice is a lovely girl. She looks like you.'

'And Matthew is delightful too. We like him very much.'

That was that sorted then.

'I'll get the tea or would you prefer coffee?' Valerie wished Jack would show his face, although in other ways she did not because, looking at Josie who was sitting with her legs crossed, she saw that, from a distance, from the doorway say, she would look very much as she had looked all those years ago, give or take the hairdo.

She heard Jack's footsteps in the hall.

'They've arrived, darling,' she called, waiting for him to come through.

Ray and Jack gave each other a firm handshake, held each other's gaze an instant. He hadn't changed a lot, Ray thought. Jack had put on some weight but that happened round the middle forties and he had lost some hair but it wasn't enough to change his appearance that much. He watched as Jack kissed Josie on both cheeks, saying that she had not changed. She bloody *had* changed. She was his wife now for one and, for two, she was the mother of his son.

Tea was a torture for him. Tiny fine plates. Napkins. Fiddly little pastry forks. And a very squidgy chocolate cake. Result. Crumbs. Why was it that everybody else seemed to accomplish the eating with minimum fuss and kept the crumbs where they belonged. On the plate. His had ended up everywhere, mostly down the side of the sofa which being off-white would not take kindly to chocolate crumbs.

'Ray's setting up in business,' Josie was saying, casting him a wifely glance. It reminded him of the way his mother had used to talk about him to her friends, as if he wasn't there. 'He's bought a shop in Felston.'

Ray smiled to himself. She'd been annoyed at first that he'd kept it from her but she had quickly come round. She liked a challenge, did his Josie, and he had always known that.

They talked round him a moment and he sat there, wanting to join in but feeling uncomfortable about it. All he could do was watch Jack and Josie together. Look at their faces. Try to guess what they were both thinking. Josie was looking fantastic today, eyes sparkling, her whole manner sparkling at that. It was her way, he supposed, of keeping the edginess at bay. A bit of play-acting.

He loved her like this though, the warmth, the vitality, the sheer prettiness and he knew why he had fallen in love with this woman. Catching Jack sitting there, with a carefully neutral expression on his face, he wondered if Jack was thinking the same thing.

If Sazzo tried anything this weekend. . . .

She couldn't believe it. She had, in fact, been hard pressed to recognize him. He was older, fatter, losing his hair and she couldn't take her eyes off him trying, in vain, to bring back the old Jack, the old Jack who seemed to have disappeared.

She had looked him straight in the eye, testing him and seen a quiet amusement there, nothing else. There was no hidden meaning there, no secret signal, and, even though she could not quite believe it, he was acting as if he had indeed forgotten what had happened between them. The talk briefly veered back to the old days, old times, but they did not dwell on it, bringing themselves back to the present day, to reality, to the marriage of her son and his daughter.

Valerie was making preliminary plans. The wedding would be here, of course, and could they pencil a September date in their diaries now? They could and they did although, as Ray didn't have a diary of his own, she did the pencilling in for him. It didn't matter. He always referred to her commitments anyway and she always told him what was what. She wished he would contribute a bit more to the conversation. Sometimes Ray was hard work and particularly in situations like this when they were dealing with strangers, for that was what they were, strangers.

After the tea and cake, Valerie showed them to their room, leading the way up the stairs to a galleried area and then a landing and a heavy cream door. 'You're in here. I hope you'll be comfortable,' she said, opening the door on to a large, rather pink room. 'There's a bathroom,' she said, indicating another door within the room. 'Come back down when you've unpacked and we'll perhaps take a walk down by the lake.'

There was so much space, so much light. There was a pale pink cover on the bed but the room itself was not overly pink, the window framed by curtains the colour of the weak tea they had just had downstairs.

Ray was in the bathroom directly Valerie had gone, on his knees examining the layout and the plumbing fixtures, impressed by the clever way they had managed to get so much into such a small space, wondering how he could adapt the bathroom at the flat in Bank Parade in a similar vein.

Josie refused to be excited by it, unpacking silently, annoyed with him and not quite knowing why. She felt cautiously optimistic about the rest of the weekend. The worst was over. They had met and there had not been any thunderclaps when he had kissed her a welcome. He was the same Jack and yet not the same. She did not know what she had expected, what she had hoped for but, whatever it was, it had not happened.

It was one very big disappointment and yet, at the same time, a very big relief too.

'Try to relax,' she told Ray, once he had completed his assessment of the bathroom and its fittings. 'Don't look so frightened.'

'I'm not,' he said at once. 'I don't have a lot to say. You know me. I'm not frightened of them. Bloody hell, Josie, what do you want me to do?'

'Be a bit more yourself,' she told him. 'Act natural.'

'How?' She caught the exasperated look. 'By being the life and soul of the party? That's not me, Josie my love, and if that's what you want me to be like then the honest truth is I can't. I can't do that. Anyway, I like to listen, take it in. I was interested in what they had to say. I can see Alice in him, can't you? She doesn't look like him but she's got some of his mannerisms.'

That had not passed her by. It had jolted her, in fact, pushing the memory she had of him a step back, as it mixed and mingled with the memory of his daughter.

They changed for the walk but not into walking shoes. Valerie, in charge of the evening meal, did not accompany them and Josie found herself in the middle of the two men as they strolled along, Jack pointing out things of interest on the way. She was not listening. She was too aware of him, of Ray, of both of them. Ray, thank heavens, had loosened up finally, out here in the open air, and was

209

telling Jack about the business and Jack, in turn, was offering up some advice which Ray seemed happy to take.

Could the impossible be happening? Could it be that these two men were actually beginning to get on together? Had they really put the past out of their heads?

By the next evening when they were due at the theatre, the relationship between the four of them had settled into how it would be. It was never going to be over friendly because of the past but they were adult enough to know that and to react accordingly. It would be friendly in a careful way and, so long as they kept to that, then all would be well.

There seemed to be a conspiracy to make sure that she and Jack were never left alone. Josie was not sure who instigated that but it was certainly working. She caught Valerie's glances at her husband, saw the concern there, and knew why and she caught Ray's glances at her, saw the very same thing. As for Jack, he would not look at her, not directly, and nor would she look at him.

And so the weekend passed.

Alice was busy with her dancing class, some sort of special session, but they met up with Matthew at the theatre and he made the time to have a coffee with them before showing them, in usherette fashion, to their seats. Comically, it took a moment for them to organize themselves into who was sitting where. There were, it seemed, an amazing number of combinations of how the four of them might sit in the row of four adjoining seats. Jack, Valerie, Ray, Josie. Jack, Josie, Valerie, Ray. And so on. In the end, forced into making a decision as people jostled impatiently from behind, Josie found herself with Jack on the one side and Ray on the other. Her two men.

'Nightcap anyone?' Valerie asked when they got home. 'And can I tempt you to a light supper? It seems ages since we ate.'

It was tempting to say no, to shoot off to bed before any more conversation could take place and Josie was very tired, the effort she was making finally taking its toll.

'A light supper sounds good.' Ray leapt to his feet, went with Valerie to get whatever it was she was offering and the moment, for good or evil, had arrived.

She and Jack were alone.

CHAPTER TWENTY-SEVEN

'Did you enjoy the play?' he asked from the safety of his seat, the armchair nearest the fire. There was no fire in the hearth this evening and, even though it had been a pleasant day, it felt just a touch chilly now and Josie was glad of her wrap, a cream fringed cotton wrap that she was now allowing to drape loosely round her shoulders. The dress was scarlet with a darker splodgy pattern and with it she was wearing glossy barely-black tights and high heeled black shoes. She had loved it when she bought it, this dress, thought it very glamorous and perfect for theatre going but besides Valerie's gloriously understated pale grey outfit which she had teamed with pearls, it had felt cheap and cheerful.

'Yes I did enjoy it,' she replied, giving him a smile. 'It was a good production. I like the way it was set in Nazi Germany. It was a different slant and I don't expect everybody would approve but I liked it.'

He nodded. 'It wasn't for me. I don't go for modern productions.'

'Ah well—' She shrugged. Ray had liked it. He had been thrilled, too, because he had got the gist of it, despite the complicated language. Of course she had filled him in beforehand on the story but even so, she was dead pleased that he had been pleased.

There was a short silence, awkward when each of them was taking care not to look at the other. Then, as often happened on these occasions, they both began to talk at once.

They stopped. Smiled.

'After you,' she said. 'No, please. . . .'

'All right. I didn't expect to meet you again, Josie. Not ever.'

'No. Look Jack, let's get this clear. Lots of people do what we did when we were young,' she said, anxious to get it over with, to clear the air. 'Meet. Go out together for a while, sleep together even,' she added, looking at him with a wry smile. 'And then it all gets too much, too serious too soon, and they split up. It's just part of growing up. It's not at all unusual but it is unusual to meet up again like this. It's a bit awkward, don't you think, but we've got to make the best of it, Jack. I've put it all to the back of my mind. Have you?'

'Oh yes.' His return smile was reassuring. 'As you say, it's all in the past. You seem very happy with Ray?'

'I am,' she said firmly for there was nothing else to say. 'He's very excited about the business.'

'He has a right to be. It sounds good. He's thought about it, not rushed into it and he has some sound financial backing. It can't go wrong. If ever he wants any advice, just give me a call. I've had a bit of experience in the field.'

Sitting there, wanting to kick off her shoes but refraining because that would make it far too cosy, Josie felt as if the two of them were on the stage at the Little Gem acting their hearts out, as they had just seen the actors do. It was as if this scene had been rehearsed. There was a script from which they must not stray. Lines they had learnt. Certain actions they must do and those they must not do. Sitting here, in this room, they were close but far apart. Just for a fleeting moment, she wondered mischievously what would happen if she were to go across the room, across the stage, and slide herself on to his lap, put her arms round his neck, lower her head to his and kiss him as she had so often kissed him and held him.

She had not heard him speak in Italian since they had arrived but she wondered if he still did. Perhaps he whispered words of love in that language to Valerie as he once had to her?

Did he *still* love her?

That was a question that could never be asked.

Did she still love him?

She knew the answer to that.

'Do you think it's sensible to leave those two alone?' Valerie asked with a smile, bringing out a plate of tiny sandwiches and some other bits and bobs from the fridge. She proceeded to dispense with the cling film, handing him the plates as she did so. 'Goodness knows what they might get up to.'

'It was a surprise all right, our Matthew and your Alice,' Ray said. 'I couldn't believe it at first. But these things happen.'

'Do they? I've never heard of it happening to anybody else. Do you think, Ray, there's still anything left between them? Or has it all fizzled out?'

'All fizzled out,' he told her, telling her what she wanted to know. 'Do you remember me at all from those days?'

She shook her head. 'Sorry. You can't have made much of an impact on me. Oh goodness, that sounds dreadful. I'm sure you must have made some impact a man like you. . . .' She blushed and he found himself warming to her.

'I wasn't on your level, Val,' he said. 'Oh sorry, can I call you Val?'

'Yes.' She laughed. 'Nobody does. But why not? And what on earth are you talking about? On your level? I must have been a terrible snob, Ray.'

'We were young,' he said with a shrug. 'You get these ideas fixed in your head when you're young.'

'I'm afraid I was very selfish. I had my sights set on Jack and I hoped that if I just bided my time. . . . Now, have we got everything?'

They took the things through. If Jack and Josie had been wrapped up in each other's arms, they had moved pretty damned quick, Ray thought with satisfaction, knowing that neither of them had moved a muscle. He caught Jack's glance as he put down the tray. He looked calm, controlled, and yet there was an undercurrent, a

214

sizzling undercurrent, that he alone caught.

Watch it, Sazzo. . . .

Neither of them said a word.

'I want to go home,' Josie said, as they lay in each other's arms in the big bed in the guest room on their last night. They had not drawn the curtains, preferring to watch the night sky and the pale half moon.

'I know.' He moved slightly so that he could stroke her hair, hair that felt wrong, too short, too straight. 'So what's the verdict then?'

'He's not the man I thought he was,' she said quietly. 'It's a big disappointment. I've made him out to be something very special all these years. And he's not. He's just an ordinary man. Like you.'

'I see. So I'm nothing special either.'

'Oh yes, you are, Ray. You are to me.'

He relaxed. For the first time in goodness knows how long, he relaxed. It was going to be OK. And maybe this had been a good thing, all this, because it had finally brought it all to a head. When push came to shove, she was still his girl and always would be.

'Ray, can I tell you something? It's something I should have told you a long time ago. I'm scared of telling you because I don't want you to take it the wrong way. I don't want you leaving me. I couldn't bear it if you left me.'

'Go on,' he said softly, willing her to say it.

'I was pregnant. Before we got married, I was pregnant with Jack's baby. I lost it at just a few weeks. He never knew. And he never will know.'

He continued to stroke her hair. 'Lynn told me that,' he said.

'When did she tell you that?'

'Ages ago. Before we got married anyway. I told her straight it wouldn't make a scrap of difference.'

'You mean you've known all these years and never said a word?'

'I knew you'd get round to telling me one of these days. In your own time that is.'

'Damn her for telling you. She had no right.'

'Let's not talk about her.'

'You seem very close.'

He laughed softly. 'Josie, when will you learn that secrets just aren't worth the trouble? I know all about you and Kenny as well.'

'Nothing happened there either,' she said. 'OK, so it might have at one point but that was when I was really fed up with you.'

He chuckled. He knew his Josie. And he supposed, looking back, he had been a pain in the neck sometimes. He was really going to make an effort, not be so caught up in the things he liked to do that he neglected her.

'Fed up or not, I'm stuck with you,' she said. 'For better or worse was never a truer saying, Ray Bailey.'

They snuggled together comfortably. He would have liked to make love to her tonight but not here, not here in the guest room of Jack's home. He wondered whether to tell her about Margaret, but it wasn't up to him to do it. It would have to come from Margaret herself when she was ready. It amazed him that a family could have so many secrets. His hadn't. It had all been open and above board with his lot.

But Josie's family was something else.

They said their goodbyes, promising to keep in touch. The ladies would consult, nearer the time, about their choice of wedding outfits. After all, they didn't want to clash, did they?

Valerie smiled as Ray and Josie drove off, feeling Jack's arm around her shoulder. He didn't often do that these days, put his arm around her shoulder and, from habit, she leant slightly into him. Why on earth had she worried? There had been no reason to worry because it had gone very well. She was warming to Josie and she really liked Ray. As for Jack . . . well, he had behaved as if they were ordinary family guests and she had never once caught him looking at Josie with anything approaching tenderness. They had mentioned the past in passing but not dwelt on it. They had, she thought, handled it remarkably well in a very civilized fashion. Everything, the meals, the lake cruise, the theatre – everything had gone much better than she had hoped.

She turned to go back indoors. There were things to do. There were always things to do when you'd had guests and she was delighted that she had Mrs Parkinson back with her, helping her. She had been most discreet this weekend, remaining largely in the annexe, for Valerie had not been keen for her to be thought of as a servant.

Standing in the porch, alone, Jack dawdled a moment, waiting until Ray's car had slipped out of the drive into the holiday traffic. With nobody looking, his face crumpled, his emotions rising to the fore at last. It had been hard keeping them in check these last few days. He had been under intense scrutiny, from Valerie, from Ray who had watched him like a hawk, and from Josie herself. She had teased him a little but he had chosen not to respond. She had always known how to tease him.

She was just the same.

His Josie.

It was just as well that Valerie could not see his face at that moment.

It was good to be home, Josie thought, as they passed the Felston boundary. The Lake District was lovely to visit but she wouldn't want to live there. This town for all its faults was home. They were getting the keys to the flat next month but already they were thinking about what they would do to it. She loved it. She loved it from the first moment she saw it. She loved being on the first floor and, from the room that would be their sitting room, they had great views over the town on one side and the park on the other.

The house in Crook Terrace, so long home, was beginning to feel less so as her thoughts shifted to the flat on Bank Parade. The more she saw of the shop, the more she thought they would make a go of it. It was a long thin shop, seemed to go on for ever once you were

217

inside and Ray was giving her free rein, more or less, with choosing the stock for the new part. He was enthusiastic, a changed man because he was doing something he really wanted to do, something that gave him scope, something that would stretch his abilities.

That's all he had ever needed.

The chance.

'Drop me off at Margaret's, love,' she asked Ray. 'She'll want to know what happened this weekend.'

'What *did* happen then?' Ray's voice was full of fun.

'You know full well what happened,' she told him. 'I've got him out of my head, Ray. That's what happened.'

'Thought so,' he said triumphantly. 'Thank God for that. Now we can get on with things, you and me.'

He had to park halfway up Percy Street, nipping smartly into a vacant space. He switched off the engine as Josie fussed around, looking for her handbag. How you could lose a handbag in a car was beyond him but that was Josie?

'Are you coming in then? To see Margaret?' she asked, locating it at last.

'Best not. She might have things to say to you,' he said.

'What sort of things?' Josie paused, handbag on her lap. 'What have you two been up to? You're being very secretive. What's Margaret been saying?' She drew a breath sharply. 'She's never been telling you about Dad, has she?'

He glanced at her. This was a new one.

'What about him?'

'Oh, nothing. Nothing important.'

Before they went to the Lakes, Margaret had come to see him on Saturday afternoon when she knew Josie was out shopping. He was freshening up the spare room because it was scuffed and he didn't want the new owners complaining; he had just started painting the door when he heard Margaret coming up the path.

Bloody hell. What did she want?

'Can I have a word, Ray? It's a bit private,' she said, taking her coat off and hanging it, unasked, on the peg in the hall.

'Course you can, love. Come on in. Make yourself at home while I clean up.'

'Oh sorry, Ray, you're busy.'

'It's OK. It'll keep.'

'It's about Josie,' she said when he was back and she was settled. 'It's all very delicate. There was only me and my mother knew about it. And Auntie Jenny of course.'

He nodded, resisting the urge to look at the clock.

'My boyfriend went off to war, Ray . . . I was only eighteen and he was twenty-five. He had his whole life before him. I said I'd wait for him. Well, that's what everyone said.'

'I know. Hard luck that,' he said. Josie thought the boyfriend was a figment of her imagination but he had never been sure. It wasn't something you asked about.

'He was called Harold,' she said. 'You'll have seen his picture.'

'Nice-looking lad,' he said. 'What happened, Margaret?'

'He died in Singapore,' she said. 'Or thereabouts. We would have been married I think if he had come back. But he didn't and his mum had to tell me that. She was his next of kin, you see, not me.'

'I'm sorry,' he said, worried that she might break down. They got a bit emotional, did the ladies, about things like this.

'And then I met Robert,' she said, folding her hands on her lap. 'It was 1943. You were only a little child at the time. Anyway, we'd gone through a lot during the war but we were starting to hope, to look forward. Robert was older than me, a married man, Ray, and he reminded me of Harold. I know it was wrong of us but he was a lovely man and I felt so alone with Harold gone.' Her face flushed and she didn't look at him. He hoped to God she wasn't going to give him the details. He didn't want them. He could guess what had happened. At least so far as Margaret was concerned. As to the man, a married man, well there must have been a good reason.

He had thought as much. He had always thought that there was more to Margaret than met the eye. 'You don't have to go on,' he told her as she lapsed into silence. 'If it's too much for you. . . .'

'No, no. I have to tell you. Josie's my baby. Robert was her father.'

'What?' That made him sit up. 'What are you saying, Margaret?'

'You heard,' she said sharply.

'But how? I don't get it. How did you keep that secret?'

'It wasn't easy,' she said with a very small smile. 'We had to keep it from dad. At all costs, we had to keep it from him. I didn't know for sure I was expecting until I was very nearly six months. I didn't show or anything.'

Ray shuffled uncomfortably.

'My mum had a bad time with me,' Margaret went on, her face still flushed, although she was looking at him now. 'She was ill for all the pregnancy and she had a terrible labour and she worked out how we would do it. She told dad she was expecting again and said she wanted to go up to be with Auntie Jenny in Carlisle and she wanted me to come with her. Dad didn't mind. In fact, I think he was pleased that he wouldn't have to see her getting bloated. That's what he called it. Getting bloated. He wasn't thrilled about the thought of a new baby and he hated pregnancy, all that stuff, and he wanted to be as far away as possible when it was born. The trouble was he got used to being on his own and it was a shock to his system when we came back, three of us, me, mum and the baby.' Her eyes were bright but there would be no tears. 'I know it's hard to believe and nowadays I don't suppose you would get away with it but nobody ever thought anything of it then. I was so plain. Nobody thought I could be attractive to a man.'

'That's not fair,' he said quickly. 'You should have seen my mum,' he added, trying to make light of it, to make her smile, to ease her pain at the telling.

'I knew your mum,' she reminded him. 'She was a lovely lady.'

'She was,' he said with a smile. 'Not in looks but in every other way.'

'When we came back, the three of us, it was just taken for granted that Josie was mum's baby and my sister. She told everybody she had had a rotten time again and she was glad I was around to help. If anybody guessed, had an inkling, they never said.'

'I'm surprised my mum didn't guess,' Ray said, for she had known everything that happened in the neighbourhood. 'So it was all down to Hetty then. All the conniving.'

'Don't call it that,' Margaret said uneasily. 'It wouldn't have been right for me to have a baby, Ray. Robert was a married man with a family of his own. It wouldn't have been right. And it was unheard of then to have a child out of wedlock.'

He smiled at the old-fashioned expression.

'Well I never,' he said. 'I don't know what to say. Did he ever know? This Robert?'

She nodded. 'He knew. Later. I took a bit of a risk, met him in the park once, took Josie along. She was only little and she didn't know who he was but he was very pleased.' She sniffed back sudden tears. 'He had children of his own and he loved them. And he loved her. He would have loved her. He picked her up and whirled her round and she laughed and laughed.'

'And then what?'

'He had to go back to his wife. There was no question of doing anything else and then, a year on, he went and died of a sudden heart attack and then she moved, went to live with her parents. Took the children with her.'

'Do you want *me* to tell her?'

She shook her head. 'No thanks. I should tell her. I'll pick the moment. I am doing the right thing in telling her, aren't I, Ray?'

'Yes. She should know.'

'I just wanted to be sure. I always knew I would tell her one day when mother was dead. You don't blame me, Ray, do you? It matters to me what you think.'

'Blame you? Oh Margaret.'

He did something then he never thought he would do. He went

over to her, pulled her out of the chair and gave her a hug, holding her close a minute. He could feel her shaking under his touch. Smell the medicated shampoo.

'It's all right, love,' he muttered, stopping short of dropping a kiss on top of her head. 'I'll put the kettle on, shall I?'

'I'll do it,' she said, recovering herself. 'Thanks, Ray.'

'I'll walk back,' Josie said, half out of the car. 'Just take the bags in and leave them in the hall. Don't start rummaging. I know what's what.'

'OK. See you later,' he said.

'Bye, love.'

He watched through the car mirror as she set off, hips swaying in that way of hers, heels clicking. His girl. He was smiling as he moved off.

'It's been a lovely weekend,' Josie said, pushing past Margaret. 'Terrible traffic all the way back. You'll be wanting to know what Jack was like? I've been dying to tell you.' Her eyes twinkled as she glanced at her reflection in Margaret's hall mirror. 'He was short – I'm sure he's shrunk – fat and balding. He talked too much. And we hadn't a thing in common. Tell you what, Margaret, he wasn't a patch on my Ray.'

Margaret smiled.

'I'm going to hand in my resignation,' Josie went on. 'It's my decision. Ray hasn't tried to persuade me one way or the other. So, what if it was deputy clerk, it was just a job and a pretty boring one at that. Ray and me have a business to run together and I want to be sure I'm around. Lynn doesn't fool me. She's always fancied him.'

'You've no need to worry there.'

'I know.' Josie was bubbling. 'You know what Margaret, I feel like a weight's lifted off my shoulders. I can cope now. Ray was great. He calls her Val and she loves it. She's really taken a shine to him. I shall enjoy the wedding and Valerie's all right when you get to know her. I won't be calling her starchy knickers in future. I feel sorry for her, losing all those babies. Only a mother understands such things,' she added gently.

'Have you time for a cup of tea?' Margaret asked.

'It will have to be a quick one,' Josie said. 'I've got the unpacking to do yet.'

'Sit yourself down,' Margaret said, moving her knitting to make room on a chair. 'This may take some time.'

Puzzled by the serious tone, Josie did just that, noticing that the shoebox was out on the coffee table, lid off, full of photos and stuff. She sat down, saw a few of her baby photographs, a tag with Baby Pritchard written on it which must have been round her baby wrist, some baby clothes, a little stuffed rabbit and some letters.

Margaret was taking a long time with the tea.

Josie looked at the photographs of herself, some of which she had never seen. A baby. One year old. A toddler. Three or four maybe. And always, in each photograph, Margaret was beside her. Not her mother but Margaret.

She looked up. Margaret was standing there calmly, smiling slightly.

'You've found the photographs?' she said. 'Well . . . have you worked it out yet?'

'Worked what out?'

'Oh, Josie. Has the penny not dropped? I kept your bits and pieces. Once we were back home, once we came back from Carlisle, as soon as we turned into the street with you, well . . . that was it really. You were Mum's from then on. Not mine. I had to pretend you weren't mine and I've been pretending ever since.'

The penny dropped with an almighty clang.

They stared at each other a minute, a long minute and then Margaret nodded. 'His picture's there,' she said. 'That one on top.'

'This one?' she picked up the photograph of a stranger, not the young man who had gone to war but somebody else. 'Did he ever see me?'

'Yes, that's him and yes, he did see you the once. He said you were a grand little girl. He picked you up and whirled you round and you laughed and laughed,' she said, a slight trembling of her lip giving her away.

'Oh, Margaret. . . .' Josie tried to smile but could not. 'I remember him,' she said. 'I think I remember him.'

'The tea will be brewed by now. Can you pour us a cup? There's extra sugar if you need it. For the shock.'

And then, without a word, she sat down, picked up her knitting and, with a quick check on the pattern, began to click away.

1	7/09	25		49		73	
2		26		50		74	
3		27		51		75	
4		28		52		76	
5	10/12	29		53		77	
6		30		54		78	
7	9/11	31		55		79	
8		32		56		80	
9		33		57		81	
10	.	34		58		82	
11		35		59		83	
12		36		60		84	
13		37		61		85	
14		38		62		86	
15		39		63		87	
16		40		64		88	
17		41		65		89	
18		42		66		90	
19		43		67		91	
20		44		68		92	
21		45		69		COMMUNITY SERVICES	
22		46		70			
23		47		71		NPT/111	
24		48		72		.	